I0788221

RELEASING KEANU

USA TODAY & WSJ BESTSELLING AUTHOR

SIOBHAN DAVIS

This print edition © July 2024

ISBN-13: 978-1-959285-75-5

Edited by Kelly Hartigan www.editing.xterraweb.com
Cover design and logo by Shannon Passmore
www.shanoffdesigns.com
Cover imagery © depositphotos.com and © elements.envato.com
Interior graphics © Robin Harper www.wickedbydesigncovers.com
Formatted by Ciara Turley using Vellum

BOOK DESCRIPTION

Keanu

Selena played me.

Confirming I wasted years loving someone who didn't love me back.

It should be easy to move on, but since she dumped me, I can't shake her from my thoughts, no matter how hard I try.

Dates and random hookups don't help, because no one measures up to the girl I still love with my whole heart.

When she appears at my door, begging me for help, I can't turn her away. My protective instincts kick in, and I grasp this second chance with both hands.

This time, I'm determined to open her eyes.

To help her realize she made a mistake throwing what we had away.

To prove our love is the real deal.

Selena

Keanu has it all wrong.

I let him go because I love him too much to continue holding him back.

And I've paid for it every day since.

I didn't think it was possible to miss someone this much, but my entire being aches for him in a way that isn't healthy.

It's why I continue to keep my distance even though it's killing me inside.

No one understands me the way he does, so, when my ugly past returns, threatening to undo years of progress, he's the first person I run to.

If anyone can keep me safe, it's the love of my life.

Maybe, this time, I'm strong enough to be the woman he deserves.

If my past doesn't take me from him first.

Note From The Author

This is a very different book in the *Kennedy Boys* series. It's an emotional, at times heartbreaking, coming-of-age romance, which focuses heavily on Selena and Keanu, with much lower drama than you are used to from previous books. It is still angsty and suspenseful and romantic and sexy, and you will still get your fix of the other Kennedy brothers (because family is EVERYTHING to this crew), but the vibe is different.

While you do not need to have read the previous books in this series to enjoy **Releasing Keanu**, it is recommended you start at the beginning to have a greater understanding of the *Kennedy Boys* world. However, you can read it as a **stand-alone romance** if you prefer.

Some of the content in this book is dark and disturbing when it references things that happened to Selena as a child. If you have triggers in relation to sexual assault/sexual violence, you might want to skip this installment.

RELEASING KEANU

Prologue
Selena

Age 13

An icy chill creeps up my spine, and I clutch my arms around my shivering semi-naked body, pulling my bent legs more tightly into my chest. The unforgiving cold stone floor numbs my butt, and I wish it had the power to numb the silent screaming in my head.

A sliver of light filters through the iron bars welded to the small overhead window, casting a gloomy spotlight on the dank, depressive space.

I don't know how long I've been locked in here this time, because the moments when I'm lucid are few and far between. I rub at the bruised skin in the crease of my elbow, hating how much I want to feel that needle penetrating my soft flesh. At least when I'm drugged, I can escape to a different world. Exist in a realm where there is only bliss. No pain. No suffering. No longing for death.

Because death would be easier than this existence.

A whimper escapes my swollen, bloodied lips at the sounds of scurrying in the corner, and I scoot sideways, pressing myself up against the wall, clambering to get as far away as possible. The rough stone is coarse against my skin, the flimsy, soiled cotton bra and panties I'm wearing offering little protection, but still I press closer, unwilling to become rodent food.

Piercing screams ring out in the hallway outside as approaching footfalls send my pulse racing.

But not in the good way.

Never in the good way.

I shiver uncontrollably as tears roll down my face. I brace myself for it, but no matter what I do, I'm never prepared.

The creaking of the lock turning induces a full-blown panic attack, but I try to control it, because that will only make things worse.

I count to ten in my head, cautioning myself to calm down as I swipe at the hot tears dampening my cheeks.

Mud-spattered boots come into view, and I struggle to breathe normally as I stare straight ahead, praying he can't see the way my body trembles as potent fear surges through my limbs.

He gets off on fear.

Thrives on the power he has over me.

Delights in knowing how broken and damaged I am because of *him*.

So, I try my best not to be that girl. Even if it's who I am on the inside.

"Get up." His gruff voice is the voice I hear every night when I wake in a cold sweat. It's a voice that will torment me for the rest of my life—no matter how short-lived that turns out to be.

I climb awkwardly to my feet, ignoring the gnawing hunger clawing at my stomach and the weakness in my quivering limbs, holding onto the wall to steady myself. I think this is the longest he's locked me in isolation because I've never felt this frail before. This close to death.

I flinch as he reaches out, tugging on a strand of dirty, mangled black hair. "You stink, and you look like shit." His lips curl up in a sneer. "But we'll fix that." His dark, dark eyes—endlessly swirling with cruelty and sheer evil—appraise me with a calculated lens. "It's time."

Two spoken words have never inflicted such sheer terror before.

"No, please." I drop to my knees, bending my head and kissing his booted feet. "I'll be a good girl. I promise." I hate how much my voice quakes. How feeble I sound. How vulnerable I feel.

He yanks me to my feet by my hair, but I ignore the stinging pain ripping my skull apart, biting back my painful cries as I attempt a smile.

I despise him.

I hate it here.

But the devil you know is better than the devil you don't.

"Don't send me away."

"It could've been different," he says, letting go of my hair and gripping my face in his large, sweaty palms. "We were prepared to make an exception for you, but you never learn. And we've run out of patience."

"I'll try harder," I screech, beseeching him with my eyes. "Don't send me away!"

"It's too late. The deal is done."

I gulp over the lump of anxiety clogging my throat, and my heart starts beating harder and faster. My chest heaves painfully as I struggle to drag enough air into my lungs. Familiar nausea swims up my throat as the blackness swoops in.

"Hudson!" Freddie yells over his shoulder, keeping his eyes pinned on me, a growing look of disgust washing over his harsh features. "Get her out of my sight." He roughly thrusts me at his trusted right-hand man. "You know the drill. One week. Ensure that shit is fixed."

"Please." I make one last attempt to halt my fate.

Searing-hot pain whips across my face and my head jerks back from the force of his slap. "Shut your mouth, bitch."

Hudson grips my upper arm, dragging me from the cell, his

jagged fingernails biting into my exposed flesh, hurting me on purpose, but I say nothing.

I've learned to live with pain.

With punishment.

With the fact that no one cares.

But this is a whole new level of hell.

My mind wanders into scary territory as I map it all out, and by the time Hudson flings me into the room where the doctor and nurse are waiting to tend to my injured, malnourished body, I've checked out.

When they strap me to the bed, I stare at the patchy ceiling, counting the misshapen moldy stains, as they talk in hushed voices around me.

The sharp prick of the needle in my arm is a welcome relief, and when the dark fog sweeps along my body, summoning me to the black void, I race toward it, praying this time I never return.

Chapter One
Selena

Seven Years Later

"I can't believe how much work we have to do already, and it's only week two," Kelly complains as we walk side by side, trekking across the Boston campus.

"Tell me about it," I agree, dropping my eyes to the ground as the group of guys approaching us looks at me with obvious interest. "Sophomore year is *not* going to be a walk in the park."

"It serves us right for choosing to study psychology," Kelly adds, shooting daggers at the group of guys as they walk past.

"I've no clue how I'm going to juggle my modeling assignments around college this year—especially now I landed the Miranda Fanning gig," I admit, my brow puckering in concern.

Jessica—my agent—has already been on my case. During summer break, I worked a lot more than normal, and despite me explaining up front it was only until I returned to Cambridge College, she threw a hissy fit when I emailed her a list of my availability from now until the end of the year.

She blatantly lied to my face, telling me Miranda would rescind her offer, but when I emailed Miranda personally to explain, she sent me a lovely reply, confirming she was aware and happy to work around my schedule. I thought Jessica was going to have a coronary on the spot when she discovered I'd emailed the client directly.

But screw her.

I haven't worked my ass off the last couple of years, trying to get a handle on my PTSD and my associated anxiety, to have her undermine me at every turn.

I might have to consider switching agents when my contract comes up for renewal next year.

Alex Kennedy was the one who recommended Jessica to me, at the time she sold her fashion empire—Kennedy Apparel—to the Accardi Company, and everything changed for me.

Back then, I only modeled for KA. I only did closed shoots, no catwalk shows, and her son was the only other model I ever felt comfortable working with.

While I still can't step foot on a runway, I'm more adaptable when it comes to shoots and working with different models even if it hurts that the guys are never who I want them to be.

A pang of longing hits me square in the chest as thoughts of Keanu invade my mind. It's the same whenever I think of him.

Which is a lot.

Because I can't get the guy out of my head no matter how hard I try. I knew cutting him loose would be difficult, but I'd no idea it would be this hard.

I miss him so much.

All the time.

It's like a lingering sickness in my tissues. One that sometimes recedes a little, but it never fades. It's always there, simmering under the surface. Ready to derail me at the most inopportune times.

It would be so easy to pick up the phone and call him. To beg his forgiveness. Which I know he would readily grant me. Because Keanu is the most selfless, forgiving, caring, loving person I have ever known. I could live for infinity and never be worthy of him. Which makes what I had to do all the more heinous.

Tears prick my eyes, but I force them aside. I can't think about K. I can't keep doing it to myself. I need to have the strength of my convictions and stay the course.

I clutch the strap of my backpack more firmly, stifling an exasperated sigh.

I know Jessica is aware of my situation, and I've always felt like she has my back. But lately, not so much. I understand it's frustrating for her. I'm in high demand, in part because I turn down more work than I accept, and I know she believes I'm not fulfilling my true potential. That she's not reaping the right kind of rewards representing me.

But she's lucky I'm able to model at all.

Especially now I no longer have Keanu's protective force at my side.

And she has no idea how hard the last couple years have been for me since I lied to the love of my life and broke things off between us. How challenging it's been trying to take back control of my life. If she did, she wouldn't harass me like she's been doing.

"Will you need to travel to New York much?" Kelly asks, yanking me back into the present.

I shake my head. "Every couple of months or when there's a new catalogue to shoot."

"Are you worried about bumping into him?" she inquires, her warm brown eyes locking on my face.

I gulp. "Yes, but I can't avoid Keanu forever." Not when we work in the same industry and share the same modeling agency.

Kelly is well aware of my history with Keanu Kennedy. For years, he was the only male model I worked with, and gossip was rife over the status of our relationship. But we never confirmed or denied anything.

Kelly was the only one who recognized me that first day at college last year, but she didn't treat me any differently, and I found myself liking her instantaneously.

Which is most uncharacteristic.

I don't have any other friends besides Kelly and her boyfriend, Todd, because I still have major trust issues and most people who try to befriend me have ended up wanting something from me.

Plus, I want to keep my past in the past.

The last thing I need is anyone in the industry finding out and it blowing up.

I'm not working hard to heal myself—for *me* and so I can be a woman worthy of a man like Keanu—to let it all come tumbling down around me.

So, I'm massively guarded over who I let into my life. And who I trust with the truth.

I only told Kelly about what happened to me over the summer, and I was a basket case for the best part of a week before I plucked up the courage to tell her. But it was one of the tasks my therapist, Denise, had set for me and an important milestone in my recovery.

I felt relieved after I told her. Lighter somehow. And it feels good to have a close friend I trust who knows what happened when I was a kid and who knows my full history with Keanu.

"No, you can't," she agrees, bobbing her head. "It's a miracle you two have managed to avoid each other for two years."

It's not quite two years since we broke up but close enough. "That's only because those in the know have helped that happen."

Jessica knows not to arrange any meetings at the agency if Keanu is scheduled to be there, and she does the same with bookings. Frankie, Keanu's agent, understands the score too, and he works with Jessica to ensure there are no accidental run-ins. I hate that I had to cut him from my life so completely, but this wouldn't have worked otherwise.

Now, I'm at a stage where I need to face up to it. Face him. I only hope I'm strong enough to handle it. To not cave and tell him the truth of why I ended things. Because he wouldn't accept it for one second and there'd be nothing I could do to stop him this time.

And that can't happen. Not yet.

No matter how badly my heart wants it.

Because I'm not ready. It isn't time.

Keanu was there for me when I needed him.

And this is the only way I can repay him, to give him something in return.

I will always love him, because he is my *everything*.

But sometimes loving someone means we must let them go.

"How was your day?" Mom asks when I step into the kitchen an hour later.

"Long, but good." I dump my bag on the floor by the island unit and lean into her, accepting the fleeting kiss on my cheek. "How was yours?"

"About the same," she replies with a smile, turning her back to me to place the tray of chicken into the stainless-steel double oven.

"I read about the case today. It doesn't sound like it'll wrap up anytime soon." I situate myself beside her at the counter and pick up the large, sharp knife. I get started on the vegetables, chopping them uniformly as Mom prepares the sauce.

"It's a complex case and one I'll be involved in for at least another month, if not more." She reaches overhead, pulling a bag of flour out of one of the cream-colored cupboards.

Mom is a well-respected superior court justice, with years of experience, presiding over serious criminal cases that have won her a certain amount of notoriety. She has dedicated her life to the pursuit of justice, and I couldn't be any luckier that she chose to adopt me.

I couldn't ask for anyone kinder and more patient than Sandrine Douglas.

She has devoted herself to her work, the charity she set up three years ago, and to me.

I know if my birth parents are looking down on me that they are grateful she came into my life.

I certainly know I am.

"Mom," I whisper, keeping my gaze focused on the onions and peppers as I cut them up. "I love you."

"Sweetheart." She reaches out, tentatively touching my arm. "Is everything okay? Did something happen?"

I lift my head, smiling at her through eyes brimming with emotion. "Nothing happened. I just want you to know how grateful I am for all you've done for me and how much I love you for taking me in when most everyone else would have let the system swallow me up."

Those early days were not pleasant for anyone involved, least of all my new mom, but she never wavered in her support and her patience, and she pulled me through those first few months when most days I woke up wanting to end it all so the pain would cease.

"Can I hug you?" she asks, similar emotion swimming in the depths of her gray-blue eyes.

I lean into her, wrapping my arms around her, vowing to do this spontaneously more often. It's not right that my mother can't hug me freely. Guilt churns in my gut, but I remind myself of how far I have come and that one day I will be able to openly accept her physical declarations of love.

I shied away from human touch when I first escaped, and it's taken years for me to accept what most take for granted. The only touch I ever felt truly comfortable with was Keanu's, but even that had limitations.

"I'm so proud of you, Selena," Mom whispers as she holds me close. "So proud of the strong, brave, courageous young woman you have become."

"Thanks, Mom." I slip out of her embrace, returning to my prep. "I'm proud of me too." My therapist says I need to acknowledge my progress and praise myself with every new baby step. It goes a long way toward encouraging positive self-belief and self-love, apparently.

"I hope it's okay," Mom says, stirring the sauce in the pan, "but I asked Alex Kennedy to join us for dinner. We have some things to discuss in relation to the charity, and she wanted to see you as she's missed you the last few times she's dropped by."

"That's fine. I like Alex." I have a lot to thank Keanu's mom for, and although it's sometimes painful seeing her—because it invariably reminds me of her son—I genuinely enjoy her company. She's become a good friend to Mom.

After dinner is prepped and in the oven, I take a quick shower and change into my favorite knee-length pink skater-style dress and a white cardigan, slipping my feet into my ballet flats. I don't bother with makeup, and I let my long blonde hair hang loose down my back, letting it dry naturally.

Mom has just uncorked a bottle of red wine when the doorbell chimes. She places it down on the wooden countertop, and we flip our gazes to the row of screens on the far wall of the kitchen, smiling as we watch Alex wiggling her fingers into the camera. "I'll let her in," I supply, my feet already moving toward the kitchen door.

Even though I know it's only Alex standing on the porch of our brownstone, I still glance through the peephole before unchaining the deadbolt on the door.

Old habits die hard.

I swing the door open and smile at the woman I respect and admire. I step aside. "Hi, Alex." I offer her a soft smile. "Come in."

As soon as the door is locked, I turn to face our guest. "It's good to see you."

"You too, honey." She places the bouquet of flowers and bottle of wine down on the hall table before opening her arms. "Would a hug be okay?" I step into her waiting arms, hugging her gently. "How are you?" she asks, when we break our embrace. "How is college?"

"I'm good, and great. Although the course load is heavy this year.

I'm worried about fitting everything in." We walk into the living room, where Mom is waiting.

"Alex. Thank you for coming." They hug and Mom gratefully accepts the flowers and wine. "I already poured you a glass of shiraz," Mom says, gesturing toward the large crystal goblet filled to the halfway point with deep, berry-red wine. "Why don't you two catch up while I plate up?"

"Sounds good." Alex smiles at Mom before sitting down on the couch, reaching for her wine.

I take a sip of my sparkling water before sitting down alongside her. "What's new with you?"

"I'm keeping busy, which you know I love." She waggles her brows. "Our interior design business is booming, so we're expanding. We've just acquired a new building down by the harbor, and we're recruiting a lot of new staff. Faye is helping us manage the process although I'm hoping she might want to come and work with us when she graduates next year. We will need a full-time human resources manager by then."

I only briefly met her daughter-in-law Faye one time, by pure chance, on a busy Boston street. I was having a bit of a meltdown at the time, so it's embarrassing to remember.

Keanu was fifteen when Faye was orphaned and came to live with his family. His dad, James, is her uncle. It was quite the scandal when it was revealed that Faye was dating Keanu's brother, Kyler, even though they are only cousins by way of marriage and there are no blood ties as James isn't Kyler's bio dad. They got married last year, and the media made a big deal out of it again, but that's to be expected. The level of public interest in the Kennedys has always been ridiculous.

"Do you think she'll accept?" I ask.

"I'm not sure. Kyler and Faye have plans to travel for a year, so, if that happens, I will probably have to hire someone else."

"It's good the business is doing so well. Not that I'm surprised." I smooth a hand down over my dress, clasping my hands in my lap.

"And Mom told me about you and James. I'm happy for you." Alex and James Kennedy have been separated for a few years, but they recently reunited.

"Thank you, Selena." Her face glows, radiating happiness. "Life is better than ever right now, and I've a lot to be thankful for." Her eyes penetrate mine. "We are renewing our vows in a small private ceremony in November," she adds. "I would love you to come with your Mom. It's just family and close friends."

I bite down on my lip, swallowing painfully. "I—" My mouth turns dry, and the words flitter away. I hate disappointing her, because she has helped me in so many ways, but I can't be there for her. Not with Keanu there. What if he brings a date? How embarrassing would it be if I had a panic attack in front of his entire family? It's one of the reasons why I never went to his house, never formally met his family, when we were dating. The only members of his family I've met are Alex, Kent, Keaton, Kyler, and Faye, but in the latter three cases, it's only been fleeting.

"It's okay, honey." She reaches her hand out instinctively, withdrawing it to her side almost as fast. "I understand."

"I'm sorry," I whisper. "If it counts, I wish I could be there."

"I know, sweetie." She shoots me a smile loaded with compassion. "This may not be my place to say it, but he still misses you. Still loves you. There hasn't been anyone else."

I know he hasn't been a saint, because I've heard rumors of him hooking up with a couple of models, but I've often wondered if he'd found a new girlfriend.

How can my heart rejoice and feel sad hearing that at the same time?

I don't like to think about Keanu finding another woman to love, but I don't like to think about him alone either, because a guy like Keanu deserves to love and be loved.

"I still miss him too," I truthfully admit. "And there hasn't been anyone else for me either." There never will be, but that's too pathetic to admit out loud.

She nods, sympathy etched all over her face. "I'm still rooting for you two, you know. I never thought James and I would get back together or that I would end up believing the years we spent apart were the best thing to ever happen to us, but the truth is, it was." Hope dances in her eyes. "And I think you and my son needed that too. I understand and respect how much you need to do this for yourself. But I still believe you two belong together, and if it's meant to be, you will find your way back to one another."

My therapist has echoed those same sentiments to me in the past.

And if I'm being honest, it's a truth I hold precious in my heart.

One day, hopefully not too far in the distant future, I pray we can move forward and live the life we both deserve.

It's the only thought that keeps me going on bad days, when I question the decisions I've made in my life and wish things could be different. That belief keeps me strong on days where I long to rush back into the security of his arms, because it keeps me focused on why I did it in the first place and it stops me from undoing all my hard work.

I only hope that, by the time I'm ready to win back his heart, that it isn't too late.

Chapter Two
Keanu

The girl with the purple hair and "fuck me" eyes has finished explaining the setup and confirmed my times, and I finally escape to the safety of the changing area.

I didn't want to be in New York this weekend, but that asshole Frankie booked this show against my wishes. I know it's one of the busiest weeks in the fashion industry and me being here boosts my visibility and strengthens my brand. I know he thinks he's helping, but he's just getting on my every last nerve. Or maybe it's just I'm getting sick of the whole scene.

Perhaps I'll do what Selena does: just focus on photoshoots and refuse the catwalk. It would mean less trips to New York, which would give me more time to focus on my studies. Sophomore year is already kicking my butt, and it's only week three.

Or maybe I'll just retire completely. Honestly, I don't get much of a kick out of modeling anymore. Not when I'm no longer modeling with Sel.

"Sup, man." Travis Kenna raises his fist for a knuckle touch, and I reluctantly oblige even though the guy is a class-A douche. Courting enemies within the industry is a surefire way of invoking drama, which I like to avoid like the plague. So, I usually keep my head down and focus on the work. "Didn't know you were booked for this show."

"Me either," I say, walking in the direction of the petite girl with the clipboard, snapping at some poor sap cowering in the corner. The noise levels in the room are almost deafening, as staff with fixed earpieces rushes around the space barking out orders and models gossip as they rotate between the myriad of stylists lined up to prep us for the show. My nostrils twitch as the overpowering scent of cologne, perfume, and hairspray swirls through the air, aggravating all my senses.

"Kennedy can give you the lowdown," Travis says to Ren Rivera as clipboard girl glares at me while pointing toward a rack of clothes.

"Lowdown on what?" I ask as I head toward the clothing assigned to me.

"Selena Douglas," Ren coolly replies, sniffing audibly.

I slam to a halt mid-step, grinding my teeth to my molars, silently urging myself to calm the fuck down before I turn to face the two douches. "Why do you want to know?" I inquire even though I can guess.

"I want to take her out, but she keeps shooting me down."

That's my girl.

Except she isn't.

Not anymore.

The only place where that still holds court is in the fantasy land in my head.

Rivera rubs at his nostrils, sniffing again, and it's so fucking obvious he's just done a line or two. Asshole still has a spot of white powder under his nose. Not that anyone will care. Cocaine use is rampant within the industry, and it's not unusual for models to abuse it before a runway walk.

I've never touched the stuff, and what happened to Sel is a big part of the reason why. For years, she was forcibly drugged, and she told me it was hell detoxing. But she did it. And she hasn't touched any illegal substances since. That takes iron-strong willpower, and I figured the least I could do was support her by never touching the stuff either. So, even on my darkest days, after we first broke up, when I inhaled JD as if it was oxygen, I was never tempted to turn to drugs.

Travis chuckles, raking a hand through his jet-black hair. "Say what you mean, man." A malicious glint flares to life in his eyes as he looks to Rivera. "You want to fuck her until she can't walk straight." He smirks, and my fists clench into balls at my side.

The rumor mill has plenty to say about my ex, and speculation has been intense over what went down between us, something these fuckwits know.

It's common knowledge that Selena is guarded and private, and I've heard all manner of shit spoken about her. Hearing some sleazeball say he wants to fuck her is nothing new, but Travis Kenna speaking about her like that has blood rushing to my ears and adrenaline spiking in my veins.

He put his hands on her at a Kennedy Apparel party one time, and Selena had a full-blown panic attack. Since then, he's gone out of his way to spread shit about her, and he never loses an opportunity to wind me up.

"Stay away from Selena." I drill a warning look at Rivera. "She doesn't date within the industry." I'd like to think she doesn't date, period, but I still have nightmares about that nerd Todd she was with last year when Kent and I bumped into her at Torment. Seeing her in a nightclub was already a shock to my system, but seeing her with another guy leveled me, and I haven't been the same since.

"She dated you." Rivera is fishing. But I'm giving him jack.

"Leave her alone," I warn before turning my back on him.

"Kennedy's just jealous he never got to sample that virgin pussy. Wasn't for lack of trying," Travis sneers.

My jaw tightens, and every muscle in my body locks up tight. Travis is talking out of his ass, and he has no clue what he's saying. I turn around slowly, putting myself all up in his face. "You still sore over the fact she rejected you years ago? Because that's fucking pathetic. As is your need to badmouth her any chance you get. Get over it already."

Heat flashes behind his retinas. "I always thought she was a stuck-up prissy bitch, but it's more than that. She's a fucking nutjob. She proved it that night."

He smirks, and I've never wanted to punch the fuck out of someone as badly as I want to punch Travis right now. "You know nothing, asshole." My fists clench and unclench at my side, and I'm conscious we're drawing attention from other parts of the room. "And I'm sick of your bullshit. For the last time, leave Selena alone." I put my face right up in his. "If I have to warn you again, I won't be using words to do it."

He pushes me in the chest. "You think you're so fucking hard, but everyone knows you're just a sad little mommy's boy who couldn't even nail the broken bitch he was dating."

Douche is really pressing my buttons today.

I have never used my mother to further my modeling career.

Everything I have achieved has been due to my own determination and hard work. Sure, I could have taken an easier route and got Mom to use her connections, but I've always wanted to do this on my own. "If she's so broken, in your opinion, why are you wasting any time on her?" I challenge.

"Step down." A burly security guard materializes at our side, and I'm guessing clipboard girl called for backup.

Travis leans forward, pressing his mouth close to my ear. "Because fucking the stupid bitch up will bring me satisfaction, and I can't wait to see the look on your face when I take the one thing you wanted but could never have."

Red coats my vision, and I lose it. Grabbing hold of his neck with both hands, I squeeze tight before I slam him up against the wall and pummel my fist in his face. I know he baited me on purpose. To get me kicked off the show. But I don't fucking care. No one gets to talk about Selena like that and get away with it.

"You've got to be shitting me," I mumble to myself as I'm forced to park my X5 at the side of the road. I have an assigned space in the small parking garage underneath the building where we live. But some asshole is in my spot, leaving me with no choice but to park outside.

There are only four condos in this private six-story building. All condos are spread over three levels, so there are two condos occupying the bottom three floors and two on the top. It's a very modern design and not at all usual for this part of town, which is mainly full of student rentals.

We only moved in three months ago, and it's great having a place to call our own.

When we turned eighteen, we received the first lump sum from our trust fund, which gave us the funds to buy our first home. Next year, on our twenty-first birthday, we're due to come into the bulk of the inheritance our grandfather left us.

During freshman year, my brother Kent and I stayed in an apartment belonging to our parents. Our other brother Keaton was supposed to be living with us too, but he ditched Harvard for Berkeley, surprising the hell out of Kent and me.

As triplets, and the youngest in the family, we're close. Closer than I am to any of my other four brothers. Our plan had always been to attend Harvard together. Until Keaton made alternative plans without letting Kent or me in on the secret. We were more than a little pissed, but we've gotten over it.

And sophomore year is off to a good start now we have our own place. I love the independence that comes with home ownership.

I glance up at the impressive gray stone façade, grateful we found something like this so close to campus. My brother Kalvin was the one who discovered it. He's in his last year of his architecture degree program at the University of Florida, and he clearly has his finger on the pulse of the Boston market. I suspect he's planning to move back to Massachusetts when he and his wife Lana graduate next summer. It's just a hunch, but why else would he know enough to recommend this project and an up-and-coming new architectural firm if he hadn't already been scouting the market back home?

Kent and I own and share the top left-hand space of the building.

A space that is currently lit up like a fucking Christmas tree even though it's after two a.m.

I climb out of the car and sigh. Can't say I'm surprised. I'm used to my brother's party boy lifestyle by now. Weary resignation settles over me as the thumping beats of loud music instantly greet my ears. We are lucky we live on a side street in a part of Cambridge notorious for its student population. Otherwise, I'm sure we'd regularly have the cops beating down our door.

I grab my duffel from the trunk, lock the car, and head into the building.

The dark cloud hovering over my head grows thicker and blacker with every step I take. I pause outside the door to our condo, resting my forehead on the door, preparing myself for what I'll find when I cross the threshold.

Kent has a tendency to throw last-minute parties at the drop of a hat, and I'm getting really fucking sick of this shit. Sick of random strangers passed out all over the lower level of our place. Sick of cleaning up puke, filthy cigarette butts, and piss-filled bottles and clearing away evidence of drug use.

For a time, when Sel and I first split up, I lost myself in Kent's world. Drinking myself into oblivion. Fucking nameless, faceless women. And partying like it was my new career. But it's getting old lately, and the stuff we got up to on Nantucket a couple months ago, when we were there for my brother Kalvin's wedding to his childhood sweetheart Lana, put the final nail in the coffin.

I'm so done with that lifestyle.

And Kent needs to learn to compromise better if we are to continue to live together.

Lifting my head, I open the door and step into chaos. The room is teeming with bodies, and a blast of noxious, odor-filled heat hits me in the face. The stench of weed permeates the air as I step over a drunken couple dry-humping right in front of the door. I push through sweaty bodies jumping around the living space, glad to see Kent at least had the foresight to remove the large cream rug from the room and to push the blue velvet couch back against the wall.

I spot my brother leaning against the end of the kitchen counter. His body is pressed between a pair of slim, tan thighs, his face buried in the blonde's barely concealed tits. Her head is thrown back, and she's moaning, wrapping her legs around Kent's waist while she grabs his hair, tugging roughly.

I yank a fistful of Kent's shirt and haul him away from the slut grinding on the place where we eat.

"What the hell?" Kent slurs, raising his fists, ready for battle.

"End this now or I will," I snap, having used up all my patience reserves earlier.

Kent stumbles a little as he turns to face me. "Da fuck happened to your face?" he asks, prodding his finger into my swollen, discolored cheek.

I swat his hand away. "Got into it with a couple assholes at the show. Got kicked out and took the first flight out of JFK."

A pair of small, warm hands curls around my stomach from behind. "Hey, Keanu. I was hoping you'd be here."

I turn around, groaning. Fuck. Will this day from hell ever end? "Casey." I give her a curt nod as I remove her arms from my body.

Undeterred, she steps into me, pushing her oversized fake tits into my chest as her hand lands on my butt. "Fuck me, baby. I'm so wet for you."

I step sideways, shucking her off me as I shake my head, my frustration growing. "It's not happening. That was a onetime thing, and it was months ago. C'mon. You know that." God knows I've told her enough times, but the message is not getting through.

"I'll fuck you," Kent says, reeling her into his body.

"Hey." The blonde on the counter pouts, glaring at Casey.

Kent pulls her down, tucking her into his other side. "Don't worry, baby, I'll fuck you too." He slams his lips against hers while keeping his arm firmly around Casey on the other side. She levels me with a seductive look as she glides her hand over my brother's stomach, slipping it under the band of his jeans. If she thinks I'm jealous, she'll realize quickly that I don't give a flying fuck.

"Get everyone out, Kent, or I'm calling the cops," I warn, and I'm just pissed enough to do it.

"You're no fun anymore, bruh," Kent complains, dragging his mouth away from Blondie.

"You don't need me for fun," I reply, pointedly looking at the two girls draped around him. Casey's hand is pumping hard behind the denim of Kent's jeans, and she's done me a favor because now he's horny as hell and raring to go, so he wastes no time getting everyone out of the place.

The girls titter as they follow Kent up the stairs. Casey shoots me a longing look over her shoulder. "You can join us if you like."

I grit my teeth. "Hard pass," I say, shaking my head. My days of threesomes and foursomes with my reckless brother are a thing of the past.

"Your loss," she says, pouting as she traipses up the stairs after Kent and Blondie.

I survey the mess with tired eyes, deciding it can wait until morning. I grab a fruit bowl from the fridge, along with a bottle of water, and head up to my room.

Although my bedroom is on the second level, along with the guest room, my study, and the guest bathroom, and Kent occupies the master suite on the third level, unfortunately, I can still hear sounds of his rowdy sex session.

Locking my door, I strip out of my clothes and then stand under the pelting hot shower for ten minutes before drying off and getting ready for bed.

I crawl under the covers, popping my earbuds in, and scroll through the music collection on my cell. I quickly pick one of my Selena-inspired selections, because I'm in the mood for some self-inflicted torture tonight. Removing the photo album from my bedside table, I lie on my side, pulling the covers up under my arms as I flick through pictures.

I haven't looked at this in a while because the pain is like a red-hot coal imprinting on my skin every time I take a trip down nostalgia lane.

There are literally thousands of pictures of me and Selena, from our KA modeling days, but this album is the one I'm drawn to time and time again because it depicts our personal journey.

I flip to my favorite photo. It's from Christmas three years ago, and it was taken at the Boston Common Frog Pond. I'd taken Selena ice-skating for the first time. I'd booked out the rink and paid to ensure this area was cordoned off from the public, so we had complete privacy. Sel doesn't do well in crowds so I usually had to be creative.

I run the tip of my finger over the picture, lingering on the wide smile on her face. We were both bundled up in puffy jackets and wool hats. I'm holding her in my arms, her back is to my chest, and we're both smiling at the camera. Our cheeks are red from the biting cold, but I remember I'd never felt warmer.

Because it was the first time I'd ever seen her laugh like that. It was a guttural, belly-deep, unrestrained, joyous laughter that came straight from her soul. Her radiant smile melted my heart, and I knew in that instant that no other girl would ever match up to the girl in my arms. I remember wanting to freeze-frame the moment. Because some innate part of me must've known those precious moments were drawing to a close.

I snap the album shut and close my eyes, fighting the onslaught of tears. A slicing pain makes mincemeat of my heart, and a heavy pressure sits on my chest. I don't know how much longer I can continue pretending everything's okay. Like I'm not utterly destroyed on the inside.

I can't exist without my angel.

And I want to fight for her. For us.

But I don't know how to do that with the demons Selena is still battling.

And I can't do anything to undermine her recovery.

I curl into a ball, hugging a pillow to my chest, wishing it was the woman I love with every part of my being.

Begging someone for some divine intervention.

Only I never expected anyone to listen.

Chapter Three
Selena

"Okay, ladies. See you same time next week," the yoga instructor yells out as she brings the class to a close. I stand, rolling up my mat and heading to the changing area. A couple of the girls smile at me, and I smile back, but I don't engage them in conversation.

I've only been coming to this class for five months. Denise helped me locate it. It's a small class with only ten participants and it's held in a beautiful old building downtown. The room is massive with high vaulted ceilings, and it's light and airy with plenty of space so I don't feel claustrophobic or scared.

Exercise has been very beneficial to my mood, and between yoga and my daily swim in the private pool around the corner from campus, it helps keep my anxiety at bay.

After I've showered and changed, I make the fifteen-minute walk alone to the bijou restaurant where I'm meeting Kelly and Todd.

They are already seated in a booth, snuggled up together looking like the cutest couple in the world, when I arrive.

I smile at two of my favorite people as I slip into the seat across from them. "Hey, lovebirds."

Kelly beams at me. "Todd just informed me that he's taking me to Vermont for the weekend."

"Lucky girl."

"She's worth it," Todd replies, staring dreamily at his girlfriend. "And we need to do something special to celebrate our two-year anniversary."

Sometimes, it's hard to be around Todd because he's a sweetheart and a diehard romantic and he reminds me of my ex so much.

Kelly swoons at her man, and I don't blame her. "Love you, babe," she says, planting her lips firmly on his.

I glance down at my menu even if I already know what I'm having. Vegetarian ravioli. Like I have every time we come here, because it's absolutely delicious. I'm not a vegetarian, but I don't eat a huge amount of meat, preferring fish and vegetarian options with the occasional chicken dish.

Kelly giggles, and I look up, watching her snuggling close to her boyfriend.

I'm happy for my best friend, truly happy she has love in her life, but it only serves to highlight how empty and alone I feel without my one true love.

"Don't worry," Kelly says in an overly cheery voice. "I have time to fit in the open casting call before we leave tomorrow."

"Gee, great," I deadpan, as the waitress approaches our table. We place our orders, and I'm praying Kelly drops the subject.

But no such luck.

"It'll be fun. I bet they offer you a part." She wiggles her brows before puckering her lips around her straw, slurping noisily.

"They are only casting for extras," I say. "And I still don't know how I let you talk me into this."

Kelly had spotted the sign pinned to one of the bulletin boards outside the lecture hall, recruiting extras for a hot new TV show, and somehow coaxed me into putting my name down with hers. Denise was thrilled when I told her, and she has encouraged me to attend the meeting tomorrow.

"It'll be fun." She's practically bouncing in her seat, her dark-blonde hair swaying with the motion. Todd is grinning at her like she hung the moon. "Imagine if we got on that show! It's all everyone is talking about."

I must live under a rock because I'd never heard of it. Apparently, some hotshot director has recently opened a new production studio in Boston, and his company is producing a show which will go toe to toe with The CW's *Riverdale*. That series I *have* heard of, and it's become my secret guilty pleasure. This Boston version is set in college, and they are looking for extras of a similar age.

I can think of nothing worse than being on a production set with people milling about, the director barking orders, and all the hustle and bustle that comes with that world. The craving to ditch the session tomorrow is riding me hard, but I've gotten used to stretching myself out of my comfort zone, and I won't let Kelly down. Unlike me, she actually wants an opportunity to be part of the show. Even if she ends up on the cutting room floor.

So that's how I find myself at The Grand Imperial Hotel the following afternoon, joining a long line of men and women waiting to sign in.

After we've registered, we are shown to a large ballroom which has been fitted out with rows of chairs. I drag Kelly from the top, forcing her to sit in the back row, on the very edge, in case I need to make a dash for it. There are way more people here than I expected. Sweat is already gliding down my spine and sticking my palms to the front of my jeans as I nervously swipe my hands up and down my legs. My foot taps off the floor, and I stare straight ahead as the room fills, avoiding eye contact with anyone.

I'm not aware I'm trembling until Kelly points it out. "We can leave," she blurts, pinning pained eyes on me. "I'm sorry I made you do this."

I shake my head, drawing a deep breath, attempting to ignore the nausea swimming up my throat. "It's okay. I can do this. And you didn't force me."

"You sure?" Her hesitant tone speaks volumes.

"Yesss," I stammer, rubbing a hand across the tightness in my chest. "If it gets to be too much, we can leave, but I want to stay."

"Do your deep breathing," she whispers, looking around to ensure no one is listening. "And I'm right here with you. You say the word and we'll go."

I nod as I inhale and exhale, focusing on feeling the motion deep in my belly, chasing the sensations, and using it to distract me from my growing anxiety.

After a couple of minutes, I've regained my composure.

But it doesn't last long.

A stunning woman with long blonde hair calls for quiet, explaining the setup for today. As there are a lot of us, we don't need to audition, she explains, and a layer of stress lifts off my shoulders. They will perform some background checks as part of the processing procedure, and everyone is asked to upload some recent photos on the casting app. The link is in the paperwork in the A4 envelope they gave everyone at registration. Then she invites the director onto the stage to talk about the show and the opportunities for those selected for the extras pool.

All the blood drains from my face as the director comes into view. My heart slams against my rib cage, and intense pain races through me. I almost choke on the nausea clogging the back of my throat.

His hair is different than I remember, not quite as long, more sleek and professional looking.

But it's the same man.

As long as I live, I will never forget his face. Those piercing navy-blue eyes roam the crowd like a vulture looking for its next feed.

I duck my head as panic lashes me on all sides. I need to get out of here before he spots me. It should be relatively easy to do in a crowd of this size, but I'm fearful if I make a move that I will draw his attention. So, I'm forced to sit here and listen.

"Do you want to leave?" Kelly asks, noticing how I'm shivering, clutching my arms tightly around my middle as if that will hold me together.

I shake my head vigorously, not uttering a word and not lifting my head. I slowly rock back and forth, uncaring how those around me perceive me, willing the asshole to finish talking so I can get the hell out of here.

The crowd laughs at his pathetic carefully planned jokes while bile coats my mouth.

A few catcalls ring out as he unashamedly flirts with the unsuspecting audience, and blood rushes to my ears while I grip the edge of my seat tight, fighting the murderous urges rampaging through me.

It seems like it takes forever for the meeting to draw to a close, but when it does and everyone gets to their feet, giving the pervert a standing ovation, I grasp the opportunity, stumbling out of the room without uttering a word to Kelly.

I dash through the hallways of the five-star hotel, bumping into strangers in my panic to flee. Shouts chase me down the corridor, but I don't hear them over the screaming in my head and the furious pounding of my heart.

I crash through the entrance doors, slumping against the wall, panic sucking all the air from my lungs as I struggle to breathe. The anxiety I was battling inside charges to the surface, and I bend over, expelling the contents of my stomach at the bellhop's feet. My heart is beating so fast I fear I'm having a coronary, and I can't pull enough oxygen into my lungs. I clasp on to Kelly when she appears at my side, shaking as tears cascade down my cheeks.

Flashbacks assault my mind, and I squeeze my eyes shut, crippled in pain, crying out and screaming. "No! No! No!"

Heated conversation carries on around me, but I don't hear it. I can't hear over the panic drowning my system, threatening to pull me under.

Kelly keeps a firm hold of me as she tries to lead me away, but my limbs won't cooperate, and my legs give out. Todd jumps to the rescue and scoops me up into his arms before I slide to the pavement.

My initial instinct is to scream and push him away, but my body is weak, my mind spiraling, and I cling to him instead, needing something solid to help keep me grounded because I'm floundering.

I'm being sucked back into the dark abyss.

My tears and cries dry up as a resigned sort of numbness overtakes me. I'm vaguely aware of being placed in the back seat of a car. Of Kelly talking to me, holding me, crying as I rock back and forth, shivering, barely holding myself together.

She cups my cheeks gently, turning my face to hers. "Selena, you're scaring me. What happened back there? What's going on? I'm so sorry I made you do that. This is all my fault."

It's not your fault. That one clear thought rings out in my mind, but I can't force the words from my mouth. I can't do anything but cling to the person I was becoming even as I'm dragged back to the girl I once was.

"We'll stay," Kelly says, helping me out of the car door. I glance up at the familiar sandstone building I call home. The brown painted double doors look the same. The stone porch with two potted plants residing on either side of the doors is as it was when I left earlier today.

The only thing that has changed since this morning is me.

I shake my head, gripping her arm tight as I experience a second moment of lucidity. I don't want her to stay. She can't help me. I need to process this myself, and I don't want to ruin my best friend's weekend plans. Although it's only Thursday, they are planning on leaving tonight.

Kelly and Todd help me walk up the steps. My bestie takes my house keys from my bag and opens the front door. Todd talks in hushed tones into his cell.

They settle me in my room, but when Kelly takes off her shoes and pulls back the comforter, I attempt to pull myself together. "No," I whisper, shaking my head and holding back tears. "Go. I'll be okay," I lie.

"I'm not leaving you like this," she protests.

"Sandrine is on her way home," Todd announces, hovering in the doorway.

"Take her." I beseech him with my eyes. "I'll be fine until Mom arrives."

"I'm not leaving you," Kelly implores, but she's wavering, thoughts of her romantic getaway no doubt at the back of her mind.

"I ... I need to be alone." I raise my red-rimmed eyes to hers. "Please, Kelly. I just need to be alone." Conflict rages across her face. I slip my hand in hers. "Please go. Enjoy your weekend. I will talk to you on Monday."

"But—"

I shake my head, pinning her with a warning look as I sink deeper into my bed.

Eventually, after persuasion from Todd, they leave.

I remove my cell with shaking hands, tapping out the text, hoping Alex replies quickly.

I'm pulling my tennis shoes on when her response appears in my inbox.

I look at the address, grateful it's not too far away.

I don't remember grabbing my jacket or leaving the house.

I don't remember racing through the busy Boston streets, pushing past people in my haste to get there.

I don't feel the rain dropping on my head, dampening my cheeks, and blurring my eyes.

I don't remember falling and cutting my hands or tearing a hole through one knee of my jeans.

I don't remember the utter panic when I reach the place and no one is home or slumping against the glass-fronted entrance doors, plopping onto my butt, and burying my head in my hands.

I only have one repetitive thought that has been with me from the minute that monster appeared on that stage.

I need Keanu.

Chapter Four
Keanu

Kent is relaying a very graphic account of his threesome from Saturday night as we walk from Harvard toward home after a long day of classes. All week I've shut him down when he's attempted to explain, but I give up. He won't relent until he tells me everything. I zone him out, nodding and smirking every so often so it appears like I'm listening.

But I'm preoccupied. With thoughts of Selena. Not that that's anything unusual, but since that shit went down with Rivera and Travis last weekend, I'm fixated on finding a way to win back her heart. There's got to be something I can do, to make her realize what we had was too good to throw away.

"Who is—Shit!"

Kent's voice breaks through to me, and I flick my eyes to him. "What?"

He scrubs a hand over his prickly jaw. "Look." He jerks his head toward the front door of our building, and I drop my bag, running toward her before I've even realized it.

I scale the steps two at a time, crouching down in front of my ex. My eyes run over her quickly, checking for obvious signs of injury.

Her dirty, torn jean-clad knees are tucked into her chest, and her arms are wrapped around herself. Her head is resting on top of her knees, her white-blonde hair covering her face. But it doesn't matter. I would know my love anywhere. "Selena. Baby," I say in a soft tone. I want to reach out, to touch her, but I don't want to startle her or freak her out.

She doesn't hear me, mumbling to herself as she rocks back and forth. Pain slams into me like a freight train. I'd like to say this is the first time I've seen her like this, but that'd be a lie. It kills me to see her like this again, and I hate to think what has caused her to have such a break.

"What's going on?" Kent asks in a deliberately low tone, looming over me, carrying both our bags on his shoulders, with a frown on his face.

Selena's rocking picks up pace, and her mumbling grows louder. "I need Keanu. I need Keanu. I need Keanu." She's repeating it like a mantra, over and over again.

"Bro. What's wrong with her?" Kent quietly asks.

I glare at my brother. "Nothing is *wrong* with her. She's having a severe anxiety attack." I know Kent didn't mean anything by that, but I hate that's a typical response when people encounter someone with a mental health issue.

There isn't anything *wrong*.

She's *ill*.

Traumatized by her past and for good reason.

"Do you want me to help you lift her inside?" he asks, ignoring my burst of anger.

I shake my head. "I can't touch her."

He looks at me like I've grown two heads, but I don't elaborate. Mom is the only person in our family who knows about Selena's background and her illness.

I know my brothers think I was deliberately secretive about Selena. And, I guess I was. But her story isn't my story to tell, and she's always been so embarrassed over her PTSD and anxiety, and I would never betray her confidence. I haven't told anyone about her. Not even when I've been tempted to speak the truth in her defense anytime Kent spews vitriol about her.

And I get it. My brother thinks he's supporting me. He hates what our breakup has done to me, and he's put all the blame squarely on Sel's shoulders, because he doesn't know any differently. I'm the only one who knows the complexity of our relationship and how nothing is normal with us. Especially not our breakup.

"Selena. Baby. It's me. It's Keanu. I'm here." I speak up this time, and she stops rocking. "Let me help, baby. What can I do?"

Slowly, she raises her head, pushing messy strands of hair out of her swollen, bloodshot eyes. My heart melts, reminding me how crazy in love I am with this woman. Although I hate that she's clearly upset, I can't deny how fucking fantastic it is to see her again.

No measure of time apart will ever erase my feelings for her. Or destroy the connection we share.

"K?" she whispers.

"It's me. I'm here for you." Unbridled emotion smacks into me as her familiar scent of lavender and vanilla swirls around me. Being this close to her is torture. She's obviously in pain, and I just want to make it all go away. I want to hold her so badly, but I won't spook her.

"Hand me my backpack." I stretch my arm out toward my brother. Kent hands me my bag, his face neutral as he watches me remove the small vial of lavender from the side pocket.

It's sad to admit, but I still keep supplies on me wherever I go. Sometimes, I dab it on my wrist, needing the smell to keep the memory of her alive. But mainly, I do it because I spent years making sure I had everything I might need whenever we ventured out of her mom's house, and I kept it up because I'm a sad pathetic prick who can't let the past go.

"Sel." I peer into her beautiful hazel eyes, which look more like brown today. It's always the same when her emotions are heightened, and the brown becomes more prominent than the green and amber specks surrounding her pupils. "I'm going to dab some lavender on your wrist. Would that be okay?"

She nods, painstakingly stretching out her slim arm.

"I'm going to touch you now. Okay?" I look to her for permission, and she nods again, her eyes welling up. Very carefully, I drop a couple drops onto her wrist, massaging the oil in soft, slow circles. Then I lift her wrist to her face, positioning it under her nose. "Breathe in, baby."

She moves her wrist flush against her nose, audibly inhaling.

"That's it," I encourage. "Breathe in and out. Slow and deep. I'll do it with you."

Kent hasn't said a word, and his expression is giving nothing away, but he's got to be wondering what the ever-loving fuck is going on.

But I ignore my brother, focusing on the vulnerable, broken girl in front of me, inhaling and exhaling with her, as she gradually calms down. When she seems a little more settled, I wet my lips and smile softly. "Do you want to come up to our place?"

Her big, beautiful eyes latch onto mine, and she nods. It's like being sucker-punched in the nuts. This girl owns every part of me, and despite the pain, I wouldn't have it any other way. "Can you walk or should I carry you?"

"I can walk," she whispers, clambering awkwardly to her feet.

Kent opens the door, stepping inside and walking toward the elevator. Selena puts one foot in front of the other, swaying unsteadily, her long legs looking like they can't hold her up. She grabs onto my arm, surprising me. "Can you…"

She doesn't need to continue that sentiment because I know what she needs. My heart gallops around my chest, and I struggle to breathe over the massive ball of emotion lodged in my throat as I gently lift her up into my arms. Her arms encircle my neck and she rests her head on my shoulder, her breath puffing out against my skin, eliciting a rake of goose bumps.

Kent is miraculously quiet as we ride the elevator to the top. He shoots me an inquisitive look when we step out on our level, and I know he'll need some answers. He opens our front door, holding it back as I step inside with the love of my life cradled in my arms, exactly where she belongs.

"Can I help?" he asks, as I move toward the couch.

"Could you make her some hot sweet tea? And bring me the first aid kit." She must have taken a fall on her way here, because her hands are scratched and dirty and one knee is bloody and torn with bits of debris embedded in her tender flesh. If anyone was chasing her or anyone forced her to fall, God help them. Because I will fucking hunt them down and make them pay for hurting my girl.

He nods, shutting the front door before making himself scarce in the kitchen.

The main space on this floor is an open-plan living room, dining room, and kitchen. We also have a separate bathroom and game room on this level.

I move to place Selena beside me on the couch, but she clings onto me harder, and my heart swells to bursting point. I can't deny how good it is to feel wanted. Needed. To know she came to me for help. I don't like the fact something bad must have happened to propel her here, but I'm not going to look a gift horse in the mouth even if I'll pay for this later.

I lean back in the couch, closing my eyes and committing the feel of her in my lap, with her face pressed into my neck, into my memory.

Everything about her screams home. From her smell to her soft touch and the feel of her in my arms.

Kent returns with the first aid box and the tea. "What about something to eat?" he asks, setting the tea down on the end table beside us.

"Sel." Gingerly, I reach out, cupping one side of her face. "Do you want something to eat?" She shakes her head, pinning me with those gorgeous eyes. "Kent made you some tea. Let's sit up so you can drink it." At the mention of Kent, she clings to me even harder. I glance at my brother, communicating with my eyes.

He nods, instantly understanding. "Let me know if you need anything else."

"Thanks, brother."

He slants a concerned glance in Selena's direction, and a pained look shimmers in his eyes for a brief second before he turns and climbs the stairs to his bedroom.

I maneuver us into a seated position, tending to her injuries first before holding the mug of steaming tea to Selena's lips, helping her drink it. I've got it so bad because I can't tear my gaze away from her plump lips as she sips from the mug, remembering how amazing it felt to kiss her.

"Thank you," she whispers when she's finished.

I take the empty mug and place it back on the table. "Does your mom know where you are?" I ask, because it's dark out now and I'm sure Sandrine is expecting her to be home. I know she often used to work late, but I don't know if she still does that now I'm not there to keep Selena company on those nights.

The thoughts that someone else might have stepped into my shoes twist and turn in my gut, but I can't be selfish. Whatever is going on in her life, she needs me now, and I'm going to support her the best way I can.

"I..." She chews on the corner of her mouth and her brow puckers. "I don't know," she admits, her gaze raking over my face. "I don't even know how I got here."

That's worrying, but there's nothing I can do to change that now. "Let me send her a message so she knows you are okay." I pull my cell from my pocket and tap out a quick message to her mom. The phone pings almost straightaway with a response. I lift my head. "She's coming over. She was worried."

"I didn't mean to worry her. I just..." She trails off, snuggling back into me, her face pressing against the other side of my neck.

"It's okay, baby." I press a soft kiss to her temple, relieved when she doesn't push me away.

Touch has always been difficult for Sel, but when we became a couple, she grew comfortable with my touch, and I didn't have to be so careful. But it's been almost two years since we were together, and I don't know if things have regressed or if they are the same. I'm not taking any chances though, because she's calm now, and I don't want to do or say anything to send her spiraling again.

We don't talk for ten minutes, but it's not in any way awkward. Selena's not a big talker, and I'm used to comfortable silences. Getting to hold her is like a dream come true, so I'm not going to push it. But I don't need to.

"Keanu," she whispers a minute later.

"Yes, babe." I press another kiss to her temple.

"I'm scared."

"You're safe, Selena. I'm not going to let anyone hurt you."

A single tear trickles out of the corner of one eye. "He's here," she whispers, her voice cracking at the end.

Blood turns to ice in my veins, and I work hard to keep the panic off my face and from my tone. "Who's here?"

"The man who bought me." Her breath oozes out in panicked spurts. "The one I escaped from."

My lungs constrict, and I can't get enough air into my body. I stare at her, this time unable to keep the horror off my face.

"Don't let him take me, Keanu," she whimpers, curling into me and clinging to me so hard it's borderline painful. "Don't let him hurt me again."

I press a fierce kiss to the top of her head. "No one is taking you from me, and I would die before I'll let anyone hurt you like that again."

Chapter Five
Selena

"Can you tell me what happened?" he asks, failing to disguise the terror in his eyes. But there is determination there too, and although it feels weak to run straight back into his arms, I can't deny how much calmer I feel around him. I'd like to say I believe him. That he *can* keep me safe, but that's a stretch too far.

A shiver works its way through me, and I shake all over. He wraps his arms around me, holding me more closely but never too tight. Tears stab the back of my eyes, but these ones aren't unhappy tears.

I don't know any other guy our age who would've gone to so much trouble to learn how best to support his sick girlfriend. Keanu did everything he possibly could to learn about my condition so he could help me.

And I repaid him by cutting him loose and breaking his heart.

I shove that thought aside the instant it lands in my mind. Unable to deal with that guilt right now. My mind is too unstable and I need to get these words out. To tell him what went down today before I lose the courage.

I ease out of his arms, still sitting on his lap but putting a little bit of space between us. I draw a brave breath and summon the last vestiges of my strength. "My friend Kelly convinced me to attend a casting call for extras for that new show everyone is talking about," I start explaining in a wobbly voice, reaching under my sweater and clasping my fingers around the sapphire claddagh necklace I never take off.

Keanu bought it for me one Christmas. It was after I'd told him how it was the last gift I'd received from my birth parents.

Mom was of Irish descent, and she wore a similar necklace except hers had an emerald birthstone. She bought me one for my tenth birthday, and I never took it off. I don't know what happened to it after I was taken. All I knew was when I woke up in a strange room, and I'd reached up to my neck for it, it was no longer there.

A deep pain slices across my chest, like it does anytime I think of my family. Of my little sister. I gulp painfully, clasping the necklace tighter, fighting a fresh wave of tears. Keanu nods, his eyes dropping briefly to my necklace, before he gives me his full attention, his gaze locked on mine, encouraging me to continue.

I push back tears and clear my throat. "It was in a hotel in town. The director came onto the stage to address the crowd and ... it was *him*."

I had no clue it was him because all the clients used false names on the island. To me, he has always been Cassius because that's the name he chose to go by. It was only much later that I learned the significance of that name and how apt it was.

"You're one hundred percent sure?" A muscle ticks in his jaw.

I nod my head vigorously, as my fingers rub back and forth along my jewelry. "There's no doubt."

"We need to call the cops."

"And say what?" I softly ask. "That a well-respected film director, a man who has just established a new production studio and brought tons of new jobs to Boston, is a sick pedophile who buys little girls to torture and abuse?"

"Yes," he grits out. "We tell them exactly that."

I haven't been lucid long enough to think this all through, but I already know that kind of approach will not work in my favor. "I have no proof, K. It would be my word against his. And all it would accomplish is letting him know where I am. Giving him the means to take back what he believes he owns." I rub the necklace more vigorously, counting to ten in my head, working hard to keep myself calm.

His Adam's apple bobs in his throat, and his brow creases as he considers my words. "Fuck it. There has got to be something we can do. There are others who can confirm the condition you were found in. Maybe the timelines will stack up and they can place him in Texas at the same time as you. There are medical reports, and Denise can testify to your trauma as can your mom. Both are highly respected in their field. And you gave a statement back then. All of that has got to count for something."

"Maybe," I admit, because that will help corroborate my claims, but I know that's not going to be enough. He used condoms when he violated me, and he was careful not to leave any semen or DNA that could tie to him. "But without proof, the authorities can do nothing."

He peers deep into my eyes. "But if we put him on their radar, maybe they can uncover enough to make an arrest. Your case can't be an isolated one."

I wince as guilt blankets me. It's not like I haven't thought about the other victims over the years. About what happened to my best friend Juanita, kidnapped with me that day, and whether she is still alive or buried in an unmarked grave on the island. Or worse, whether that bastard sold her to the highest bidder too.

"I'm betting it's not," I admit in a whisper. "But if we go to the authorities, he will know where I live, Keanu. Where I go to school. Which modeling agency I'm assigned to and what shoots I'm booked for."

It's a miracle he hasn't discovered me before now. I remember Kelly telling me he's only recently moved into the area. I think the fact he was out of state must have helped keep me protected. That and most of my campaigns for KA were low-key, per my agreement with Alex.

"These men know how to abduct girls and make them disappear," I continue. "They did it to me once. What makes you think they can't do it to me again?" A sob bursts from my throat, and violent shivering racks my entire body. "I would rather die than fall into their clutches again," I admit on a sob, my hands dropping to my sides.

He hugs me to his warm body. "No one is taking you, Selena. I promise you."

"You can't make that promise!" I cry. "And we're not together. Why would you even want to?!"

"Don't do that." He leans back, latching pained eyes on mine. "Whether we are together or not makes no difference to how I feel about you. I will always care, Selena." His eyes burn hot, radiating the truth. "I will always want to protect you, and you are not shutting me out of this."

His words spread through me like sweet, warm honey, helping to ease some of the fear plundering my veins. "I don't want this for you," I whisper, averting my eyes. "You deserve better than me."

"Is that why you did it?" he asks in a calm tone.

I raise my eyes, locking on his comforting, familiar blue gaze.

I understand his need for answers.

How I left him feeling confused and betrayed.

I know I owe him a better explanation than the one I gave him, but I can only deal with so much. "I can't do this right now, K. I'm barely holding on as it is." Plus, I don't want to give him false hope. My head is a mess, and I don't want to drag him down again.

He nods slowly. "Okay, but we are discussing this when the time is right."

I nod my agreement, and my eyes well up again.

I can give him one truth. "I've missed you *so much*."

"Not a day goes by where you aren't in my thoughts," he simply replies, and my heart swells with love.

I have never loved anyone the way I love Keanu. I know I never will. My eyes drift to his lush mouth, and my lips tingle with a craving to kiss him. He was always so gentle with me. So considerate of my feelings, and kissing him was one of my favorite pastimes.

I miss kissing him.

I miss being with him.

I just miss him. Period.

But if I tell him that we'll end up back where we started, and right now, it feels like I've even less to offer him than before.

Was I wrong to come here? Not that it was a conscious decision, because it wasn't. But Keanu has always been my safe place, so it's no surprise I ended up here.

"I have a suggestion," he says, rubbing the thin layer of stubble on his chin. My eyes are drawn to the tattoos on his lower arms. He didn't have them when we were together. I never thought he'd be the type to get inked, but they suit him. With his dark hair, worn stylishly short at the sides and slightly longer on top, his ripped arms, chest, and abs, inked skin, and those stunning blue eyes that look like the ocean, he is hotter than ever.

I know his new edgier vibe has landed him some additional modeling gigs and tons of new fans. Every booker is crazy for his new look, and it's why he's so in demand. I'm very proud of him. Of what he's achieved in his career and that he's attending Harvard. He could have a full-time modeling career, but he's always aspired to more. I love how much dedication and focus Keanu puts into things he's passionate about.

He doesn't know this, but he's my biggest inspiration.

I peer into his beautiful face, encouraging him to go on with my eyes.

"Keven works for the FBI. I think we should talk to him. Off the record," he adds when he sees my eyes pop wide. "He can advise us what to do." He laces his fingers in mine. "But we would have to tell him the truth. He needs the facts if he's going to help us."

I take a few moments to mull it over, latching onto his hand, allowing warmth to seep from his skin to mine. I can't just rock up to the local police station and lodge a complaint. For all we know, that bastard has the cops on his payroll. Mom might have contacts who can help too, but the last thing I want is her career getting damaged by my past.

I trust Keanu.

Completely.

And if he says he thinks his older brother might help, then it's worth at least a phone call.

The alternative is I watch over my shoulder.

Become a recluse again.

And regress to the thirteen-year-old victim I've worked so hard to leave behind.

But I'm in no fit state to make such decisions right now. "It's a worthy suggestion, but I need to think about it. And I need to talk to Denise."

His tongue darts out, wetting his lips, and I stare greedily at his mouth, enjoying the distraction. "I understand, baby," he says, rubbing his thumb in soothing circles on the back of my hand. "But I don't like the fact he is out there and he might know who you are. How much information has he got on you?"

"I only had to complete basic details at the registration today. And I haven't provided any photographic ID yet." They wanted it, but I'm always cagey about handing over my ID, so I lied and said I'd forgotten it. I'd no intention of going through with this, and I was only attending to prove I could push myself out of my comfort zone and to support Kelly because I know she'd get a major kick out of it if cast.

"He knows me as Selena Smith, not Selena Douglas, so it's unlikely he's aware I'm here." I'm confident in my assessment because if he knew I was living in Boston, I wouldn't be sitting here right now. I'd be locked in some basement. Chained naked to the floor. Starving and drugged up with more scars covering my body and layered over my heart.

Although, now he's in Boston, it's only a matter of time before he finds me. The shoot I did for Miranda Fanning's new line will soon be splashed all over billboards. Yes, I'm older, and my hair is no longer dark, but I imagine my image is imprinted in his brain the same way his is in mine. He paid good money to buy me from Master Allen and Freddie, and I escaped the day after he claimed ownership of me.

It wasn't enough time to recoup his investment.

A monster like him would never forget the girl who played him for a fool and got away with her life.

A monster like him has been planning his revenge for the last seven years.

And I'm guessing he's only too eager to start exacting payback.

Chapter Six
Keanu

"How is she?" Sandrine Douglas asks me the second I open the front door.

I step aside, gesturing for her to come in. Dragging my hands through my hair, I exhale heavily. "She's doing okay now, but she wasn't in a good place when she arrived."

"Where is she?" Sandrine's concerned pale blue eyes flit around the room.

"In the bathroom. Come sit." I jerk my head toward the couch, and she follows me, sitting down on my right. I set my elbows on my knees, resting my head in my hands.

Now that I know the truth behind her panic attack, I am fucking terrified for Selena. My initial instinct was to whisk her out of the country in the dead of night and go someplace no one would ever find us. To hide her away until that sick bastard is locked up behind bars. But removing her from the safety net of her home, her mom, and her friends isn't the right thing to do either.

"What has happened?" Sandrine asks, and I lift my head up, staring into the troubled face of a woman I admire greatly. If Sandrine hadn't presided over Selena's case when she escaped the hell she'd been existing in for three years, I doubt she'd be where she is today.

Sandrine moved mountains to adopt her when it was discovered her family was dead. Murdered by the bastard who kidnapped her and her friend Juanita, when they were only ten. Although that case is still technically an open murder investigation, all the evidence points to that truth.

Sandrine saw something in Selena and made it her mission to adopt the frightened, fragile, broken little girl with the deep scar tissue. I'm so grateful she did. Not just because it brought her to Boston and led her to me, but because she has done so much to help bring her back to life.

Most people seeking to adopt want a cute baby. Not a troubled thirteen-year-old girl who had endured more horrors than any kid should have to live through. If Sandrine hadn't adopted Selena, she most likely would have ended up in a home or the foster care system, and neither scenario would have worked out well.

Sandrine stares impatiently at me, waiting for me to elaborate.

"It's not good, but Sel should probably be the one to explain." Or she should at least be given the option of deciding who tells her mom.

"Mom." Selena steps into the room, and Sandrine hops up, walking toward her with urgency.

She stops in front of her daughter, examining every inch of her, from head to toe, assuring herself that she's unharmed. Slowly, she opens her arms, and Selena steps into her hug. Her eyes find mine across the room, and she holds my gaze as she accepts her mom's comfort. My hands itch with a longing to touch her, to hold her, but I'm well versed in controlling my wants and needs around her. I'm used to letting Selena set the pace.

Selena shucks out of her mom's hold, walking to the couch and sitting down beside me. Her hand instantly reaches for mine, and I thread my fingers in hers, casually draping my arm around her shoulders. When she lays her head on my shoulder, it feels like I've died and gone to heaven.

Sandrine's delicate smile is a surprise. We've always had a good relationship, but Selena and I have been broken up for almost two years. I'd expected shock or maybe distrust, but she seems pleased her daughter has turned to me. We share a silent communication, and I nod, confirming she can trust my motives. Trust that I'll take care of her daughter.

"Are you okay?" Sandrine asks, clasping her hands in her lap.

Selena lifts her head, turning to face her mom. "I don't know," she honestly admits, and it's like someone has driven a dagger straight through my heart.

"Do you feel up to explaining?" she inquires, smoothing a stray strand of hair back off her face. I notice there are more grays threaded throughout her dark hair, but otherwise, she looks exactly the same.

Selena snuggles in closer, and I tighten my arm around her shoulders a little more, careful not to exert too much strength. Selena needs and deserves a gentle touch. Always.

I hold her close as she tells her mother what she told me a short while ago. I watch the same devastating emotions flit across Sandrine's face as I'd felt hearing the news. I know Selena needs time to process, but I've already decided I'm talking to Keven tomorrow. I trust him to keep it between us. Not to run straight to his bosses. And I need his advice on how best to keep the love of my life safe. There is nothing I won't do to keep her protected. Which is why I already sent a message to my brother asking him to locate a team of bodyguards for me. I didn't give him any intel except that it was for Selena and her mom and I needed them urgently.

Dad has a company he uses periodically whenever we need to step up security. Our family attracts a fair amount of media attention and the odd nutjob or two. While most of us don't have full-time bodyguards—except for Kaden's pregnant wife and their daughter and Kev's fiancée Cheryl, where it's necessitated because of recent run-ins with powerful figures in the criminal underworld—there are occasions where it's warranted. I know Keven is using a different company now, a company focused solely on celebrities and high-profile clients, and if he's deemed them suitable to protect Cheryl, then that's who I want watching over Selena and Sandrine.

I feel a little bit more secure knowing he's already setting that in motion.

But I won't feel happy until that pervert director Clive Lawrence is rotting in a jail cell. Or rotting in the ground. I'm comfortable with either outcome as long as he's off the streets and the threat is over.

Although, he isn't the only one we need to worry about.

But dealing with one pervert at a time is all we can do.

And we have no leads on Freddie, the bastard who kidnapped Selena and forced her into a nightmare. If that's even his real name. The authorities involved in the case at the start investigated, but they didn't have a huge amount to go on. Selena wasn't able to tell them much, because she was so traumatized and her kidnappers went to great extremes covering their tracks.

Sandrine cusses, and if the situation wasn't so serious, I'd laugh, because I've never heard her use profanity. At all. Like ever. "He's not getting away with this, sweetheart. I don't know how yet, but we are going to ensure he pays for what he did to you. And he's not getting near you or any other child ever again." Her voice resonates with steely determination, and I know she means every word.

"No cops, Mom." Selena shakes her head, sending strands of silky white-blonde hair tumbling over her shoulders. She dyed her dark hair blonde after we broke up, and I can guess why. But I love it on her. And she's so gorgeous she can pull off any look.

Sandrine sighs, clenching and unclenching her hands in her lap. "I hate to agree, but for now, that's the best course of action." I'm sure she's well aware how cops can be compromised and she's not going to take any action that might place her daughter in more danger. "I have a few trusted contacts I can reach out to. We need a plan, but it has to be a smart one."

"Keanu's brother Keven works with the FBI," Selena says. "And he might be able to help us. But I'd prefer if we didn't do anything tonight. I need to talk to Denise."

Sandrine nods. "I can take you tomorrow after work. If I didn't have this high-profile case, I would bring you first thing in the morning."

"I can take her," I blurt.

"I can go by myself," she says, thrusting her head up and her shoulders back, but I'm not sure I'm believing this show of bravado. "And I've already arranged a session in the morning."

"I don't want you going anywhere by yourself," Sandrine says.

"I agree." We trade another shared look. "And just to be up front, I've arranged for a security detail for both of you. Keven is setting it up right now. Bodyguards should be in place by midnight. You will both have twenty-four-seven protection."

Two pairs of wide eyes meet mine, and I hold their gazes with an unapologetic one. "That's the only way I'm letting either of you walk out of here tonight." Although, if I have my way, Selena won't be leaving anytime soon.

"Thank you." Sandrine reaches across us, squeezing my free hand. "There is no one I trust to look after my daughter more than you."

A lump the size of a ball lodges in my throat. "I would die before I let anything happen to Selena."

"I know, son."

Selena presses a quick kiss to my cheek, surprising the hell out of me. Her eyes are brimming with emotion. "I don't deserve your loyalty, but I'm grateful, and I won't turn it down."

"Good." My eyes lower to her mouth, and I want to kiss her so badly. "So, it's settled. I'll take you to Denise in the morning."

"What about your classes?" she asks.

"I can afford to miss a couple lectures."

"Okay. Thank you."

I'm relieved she's not fighting me on this. "And," I continue while I'm on a roll. "I'd like to suggest you stay the night here. I'd prefer to keep you close so I know you're safe." I glance at Sandrine. "We have a guest bedroom if you would like to stay too. Selena can take my room, and I can sleep on the couch or bunk in Kent's room."

"I don't want to put you out," Sandrine says. "And we can return home once the bodyguards are in place." She looks at Selena. "Selena might prefer the familiar surroundings of home."

"I want to stay here," she murmurs, looking sheepishly at her mom. She twists her head around, her eyes boring into mine. "I feel safer with Keanu."

I press a kiss to the top of her head. I can't help it. I just need her close. And I'm glad she feels safe with me. That she's letting me protect her.

"Okay, if that's what you want." Sandrine stands, pinning eyes on me. "While I would like to take you up on your offer, I know it's not necessary. That you'll keep her safe. I'd prefer to go home and make a few tentative inquiries." She holds up her hand as Selena opens her mouth, to protest, no doubt.

"Sweetheart." She crouches down in front of her daughter. "I will respect your wishes, and I won't make any plans until you have spoken with Denise and decided what you want to do, but it can't hurt to explore our options. I won't mention any specifics. I'll just sound out a few of my contacts." Her eyes flit to mine. "Then, maybe, we could meet Keven tomorrow night, and we can discuss the best way of handling this situation." Her eyes return to Selena, sheltering a world of pain. "I need to do something, Selena. You are my daughter, and I won't see those monsters cause you any more pain. We need to act fast. To put measures in place to properly protect you."

"Okay, Mom." Selena stands, kissing her on the cheek.

"I love you, sweetheart," Sandrine says in a choked voice. "And Keanu isn't the only one who would lay down his life for you. It's going to be okay." She moves slowly, pressing a gentle kiss to her forehead. "Please try not to let this undo all the progress you've achieved. I know that is easier said than done. But I also know how strong you are. How brave you are. And you are not alone. You have lots of people who love you and who want to keep you safe."

"I know, Mom," she whispers, and I watch helplessly as a single tear creeps out of the corner of her eye. "And I love you too."

"And eat something!" She smooths the tear away from her daughter's face. "You need to keep your strength up."

"I'll make sure she eats," I promise.

"Walk me out?" she asks, eyeballing me.

"Sure." I nod before facing Selena. "Why don't you run a bath? There's a bathroom with a tub on the next level up. There are towels and toiletries in the cupboard. Take whatever you need."

"That sounds good. Okay."

She gives Sandrine a quick hug. "I'll text or FaceTime you later and again in the morning."

"Okay, sweetheart. I'll talk to you then."

I watch Selena walk upstairs with a lump wedged in my throat. I love seeing her here in my space. I'd be lying if I said I hadn't imagined it countless times since we moved in.

"If you pack a bag for Selena, I'll have someone come by and pick it up," I say as I walk Sandrine out of our condo.

"An overnight bag, or do you intend for her to stay longer?" she asks, raising a brow as we wait for the elevator to arrive.

"That will be up to Selena, but if it was up to me, it'd be for longer."

I expect her to protest, so I'm pleasantly surprised at her reply. "I think that would be a good idea."

The door pings, and we step into the elevator. "You're okay with this?"

She pushes the button, and the doors close. "Make no mistake, Keanu, I am very far from okay. I am terrified for that beautiful girl upstairs but trying my best not to let her see that."

"I get that. I'm the same. But I'm not about to let anything happen to her."

"These people operate outside the law, Keanu. If that man finds out she is in Boston, there is nothing either of us can do to keep her safe, so we need to ensure he doesn't find her. And if he does, it's best she's not living with me." The doors open, and we step out into the corridor. She looks left and right, ensuring there is no one in the vicinity. "You two publicly broke up two years ago. As far as everyone is concerned, you have both moved on. This would not be the first place he'd come looking for her, which is why she is safer living with you for now." She folds her arms, slanting me a stern look. "Unless there is a girlfriend on the scene or some reason why she can't be hidden away here."

"There is no one else. There never has been. Selena has always been the love of my life, and I meant what I said back there. I would take a bullet for her. No one is hurting her again."

"She loves you very much," she says, patting my arm. "As I do. When she ended things, it broke my heart, because you were so good for her. But she needed to do things her way. She needed her independence."

"I would have given her anything she asked."

"Talk to her. Let her explain. She believed she was doing the best thing for both of you."

I struggle to see how it helped either one of us, but I keep that thought to myself.

We step outside, and I walk her to her car.

She lowers down the window once she's behind the wheel. "Please keep my daughter safe."

"I promise you I will protect her."

She nods. "You're a good man, Keanu. And I trust you with her life, but I have one piece of advice for you."

I quirk a brow, intrigued as to what she's going to say.

"Fight for her this time. If she tries to push you away again, which she might, don't let her. Convince her what we both know is true."

"Which is?"

"Her inner strength shines the brightest when she's with you."

Chapter Seven
Keanu

Selena is in the bath when I return, so I set about fixing dinner. Kent saunters into the kitchen as I'm stir-frying vegetables and chicken. "How's Selena?" he asks, moving to the sink and washing his hands.

"She's okay."

He dries his hands, leaning back against the counter, wearing an expression I can't read. "What's going on, Keanu?"

I toss the food in the wok, squeezing my eyes shut. I hate lying to my brother. Especially Kent, because he's the one who's been there for me the most these past two years.

Growing up, I was always closest to Keaton and Kent. It's a triplet thing. But during my earlier teenage years, it was Keats I was tight with. Kent was partying like crazy. Drowning in pussy and booze. Dabbling in drugs. And he rejected every attempt Keats and I made to intervene, so we stopped trying. Keaton was going steady with Melissa, and I had Selena. We just bonded more. I hated there was a divide between the three of us, but things are different now.

Now, Keats is the one I feel most estranged from. He chose to go to Berkeley instead of coming with us to Harvard, surprising not only

Melissa but Kent and me too. Kent has been the one supporting me as my world fell apart in the aftermath of my breakup with Selena. His advice might not have always been what I needed, but I can't fault how hard he's tried to pull me out of my head.

But even through all that, we're all keeping secrets.

Keats isn't happy. That much is blatantly obvious. But he doesn't volunteer the reason for it, and I don't pry. Because then, I might have to open up about my shit, and that's not something I find easy to do.

Kent isn't happy either. Sure, he disguises it better than Keats, but I know what I see. He's hiding something too.

We all are.

And it makes our previously unshakeable bond feel like a fucking lie.

I hate it, but I don't know how to fix things. Or if I should be the one to do it.

I tried to help Selena, and all that did was drive her further away.

"Earth to Keanu," Kent says, dragging me back into the present. "You hear me?"

I lower the heat on the stove and walk to the refrigerator, reaching in and removing two beers. I've been trying to abstain lately, but after today, I need this. I hand a bottle to my brother, popping the cap on my beer and taking a healthy glug before I answer him. "I heard you, but all I can say is there is a lot of shit going down and Selena will be staying with us for a while."

He pulls at his lower lip, eyeing me strangely. "What happened to her, it wasn't just today, right? Whatever it is, it's from her past, and you keeping her away from us, that was tied up with it too."

I'm dumbfounded at his astute observations. Because I've said jackshit about Selena in the past. Kept her away from my family because of her social anxiety and because she doesn't like to talk about what happened to her. Getting close to people comes with that risk. They want to know her story, and she's never been comfortable repeating it. Hell, it was months before she was able to tell me the truth although I had some inkling because Mom had given me a heads-up when I first started modeling with her. Mom wanted to ensure I didn't do anything to spook the timid girl with the long legs and big, sad eyes.

"Yes," I admit. "It's connected to her past, but I can't say anything more than that because it's not my story to tell."

He mulls that over in his head, slowly nodding, and I wonder where my brash, blunt brother has disappeared to. This is a side of Kent I don't see much of. "Is she in any danger?"

"Yes." My chest tightens in painful awareness. "And I'm not taking any chances. Kev is sending a security detail over, and I have a couple guys watching her mom too."

"Can I do anything to help?" he asks, bringing the beer bottle to his lips.

"Just be nice to her. Please. And don't touch her."

He scowls, and his nostrils flare. "Seriously, dude? I would never make a play for your girl."

I shake my head. "That's not what I meant. She's skittish when people touch her. I didn't realize how much we casually touch others until I had to be on my guard around her. No brushing past her. Patting her on the head or the arm or moving to hug her or kiss her cheek or anything like that."

He drills a hole into my head, and I know he's reading into what I've just said. "Got it. I'll be on my best behavior."

"And no parties or strange guys here. And when you bring fuck buddies home, I'd appreciate it if you'd keep it confined to your room, tone the noise down, and keep them away from Sel." I know I'm asking a lot, but if the tables were reversed, I would do it for him.

"Sure."

My eyes almost bug out of my head at how easy he agrees. I feel like a douche for not giving my brother more credit. I cross the room, grabbing him into a manly hug. I slap him on the back. "Thanks, bro. I appreciate it."

He pulls back, shoving me away with a grin. "She's your girl. I want her to feel comfortable here."

Pain splays across my chest with his words. I don't know what we are anymore, but I can't claim her as mine again. At least not yet. "She's my *friend*, Kent. There isn't anything going on."

"Yet." He smirks. "I saw the way you two were looking at one another. I think I get it now." I arch a brow. "She's your person, and you are hers."

My chest heaves as I stir the rice in the pot, turning the heat off. I glance over my shoulder at my brother. "Yeah. But it's complicated."

He bobs his head. "I see that."

The screeching of a stool ends our conversation, and both our heads whip around to the gorgeous blonde sliding onto a stool at the counter. Selena's cheeks flush a delicate shade of pink, and she lowers her eyes to the marble countertop.

"How was your bath?" I ask, removing three plates.

"Perfect," she softly says, gracing me with a shy smile when she looks up. Her hair is damp at the ends, her face scrubbed clean of makeup, and she takes my breath away.

Like every time I look at her.

"I made a chicken stir-fry. I hope that's okay?"

"Sounds good. Thank you." She purposely avoids looking at Kent.

"Can I get you a beer or something else to drink?" Kent asks in a much gentler tone than he normally uses, and I shoot him a grateful look.

She looks up at him through hooded eyes, her cheeks flushing a little. "Just a water. I don't drink alcohol."

"No problem." Kent grabs a water from the fridge, handing the bottle to her. "I'll set the table," he says, grabbing silverware and moving toward the small dining table behind us.

I lean my elbows on the counter, smiling at the love of my life. "I have a guy bringing a bag with your things. He should be here within the hour." I glance at her torn jeans. "I can give you a pair of my shorts if you like?"

"I'm good. I can wait."

Releasing Keanu

Dinner is a quiet affair, but it's not uncomfortable. After, Kent makes himself scarce, affording us privacy to watch a movie. I dim the lights and grab a blanket from my bedroom, and we curl up on the couch, me sitting with Selena's head in my lap. Even though there is so much we still need to say, we don't talk, and I'm okay with that. I'm content to have her snuggled into me, breathing the same air I breathe.

Her new bodyguards arrive a couple hours later, and they drop off her bags when making introductions. I take them aside in the hallway outside to explain her condition and ensure they know how best to help her if she has an anxiety attack. I want this to provide comfort and security, not add to her stress. I slip them a vial of lavender oil to keep in their car.

Selena has changed into cute pink and purple short pajamas when I return, and it takes colossal willpower not to stare at her slim legs or the taut peaks of her nipples, trying to poke a hole through her thin top. She lies back down on my lap, and I empty my mind of all horny thoughts, willing my semi to deflate.

A few minutes later, her breathing evens out and her arm drops to her side as she falls asleep.

I watch her like a bona fide creeper. Tracing every curve and dip on her face with my eyes. My gaze roams her long, lithe body under the blanket, and I make two silent vows to myself.

I will keep her safe.

And I'm going to make her mine again.

I carry her up the stairs, cradling her to my chest, my heart thumping wildly behind my rib cage, elated to have her in my arms again. I nudge the door of the guest bedroom aside, pleased I thought to turn down the covers earlier.

The second I place her down on the bed, she snakes her arms

around my neck. Her eyes are still closed as she sleepily murmurs. "Not here. Your room."

I falter for a second, unsure if she's aware of what's she saying. We have never slept the night beside one another, and I'm too weak in this moment to do the honorable thing. So, I lift her up again and pad to my bedroom, carefully placing her in my bed and tucking the comforter around her.

She reaches for me, and my heart soars. I press a featherlight kiss to the top of her head. "I'll be right there. Go to sleep, baby."

I get changed into a white T-shirt and pajama bottoms, take a piss, and brush my teeth so fast it's worthy of an entry in *The Guinness Book of World Records*.

I turn off the main bedroom light but switch on the lamps on either side of the bed. I put the TV on low, because I know Sel likes to sleep with it on.

Silence and darkness are triggers, and dimmed lighting and background noise helps ease her anxiety. I'm not sure if she still has recurring nightmares, but I'm assuming she does. I don't want her waking up in unfamiliar surroundings in the dark for fear of where it might send her. I crawl under the covers and scoot over to her side, gently curling my body around hers. Her body softens against mine, and a little contented murmur escapes her plump lips, and I relax, confident she's okay with this.

I watch her again, because, you know, I've got this creeper act down to a fine art form, and I can't contain the smile that breaks out on my face. I hate the circumstances that drove her to seek me out, but I can't deny how fucking ecstatic I am to have her here.

Chapter Eight
Selena

I bolt upright in the bed, my sleep tank stuck to my back, with high-pitched screams ringing in my ears. My heart is going one hundred miles an hour, and adrenaline courses through my body, making me feel antsy and on edge.

Movement beside me elevates my blood pressure to coronary-inducing levels, and the screams get louder, confirming they are emanating from me.

"Selena. It's Keanu. You're at my place. You are safe." His voice is calm and soothing, his reassurances determined and familiar. "It's okay, baby. I've got you."

My eyes drink in the strange room, and I jerk around, my shoulders slumping in relief at the tousled-haired form before me. "K." I fall into him, my hands fisting his shirt as I cling to him, sobbing.

Tentatively, his arms go around me, and he runs a light hand up and down my back. It helps calm me down, and gradually, my tears die out. "Sorry," I whisper, still clinging to him like he'll disappear if I let go. I hate feeling needy. Hate how it feels like it's undermining my hard-won independence, but I'm drowning, and he's the only one who can keep me afloat.

You're not weak. You're not regressing. There is a difference between feeling needy and needing assistance. You are seeking support in the right way.

The words reverberate around my head as if Denise was actually here speaking the words she's so often said. I try to keep that in mind. To remember all I've achieved. To understand coming here is not a show of weakness but a show of strength.

"You don't need to apologize. None of this is your fault." His chest rises and falls under my head. "And I like looking after you. I know you don't agree, but it's what I was put on this Earth to do."

"Stop being so perfect," I mumble against his chest, a slight smile tugging up the corners of my mouth when his chest rumbles underneath me.

"I will when you do," he teases, and I snort because we both know I'm as far from perfect as you can get. "Hey." He kisses the top of my head, and his next few words confirm how deeply connected we are. Keanu knows what I'm thinking because he knows me so well. "You *are* perfect to me, Sel. You always have been."

Tears sting the backs of my eyes, and I look up at him through blurry, hooded eyes. "Why don't you hate me?"

He places his forehead against mine. "I could never hate you. Never."

I shiver, and he removes his forehead from mine, slowly winding his arm around my back. "Let's lie back down. It's still the middle of the night, and you need to sleep."

I let him pull us down flat, and he tugs the comforter up over us. "You need to talk about it?" he asks, and I shake my head.

Discussing that nightmare will only induce a panic attack, and Keanu doesn't need to hear that shit. He's aware of my history, but I've never gone into graphic detail about all the things that were done to me because I don't want him suffering nightmares, and if he knew every sordid detail, it'd definitely keep him awake at night.

I twist on my side, snuggling into him, amazed at how okay I am with this. I've never slept in a bed with a man before, and I wasn't sure how I would feel. But I like this. I like how much closer I feel to Keanu. How protected I feel in his muscular arms. "K?" I snuggle closer to him.

"Yes, babe?"

I smile at his endearment. "I'm sorry I hurt you, and if it's any consolation, I hurt myself just as much." He doesn't say anything for a couple minutes, but his heart is thudding like crazy under my ear.

"I don't like hearing that, because if you were experiencing even a tenth of the pain I felt, I hate you felt that." His lips skim the top of my head again, and I melt into the mattress, my heart brimming with emotion. A shuddering breath leaves his lips. "I want to talk about it. Why you did it, but not in the middle of the night. And not when you've got this other stuff to deal with." His lips meet my hair again, and I squeeze my eyes shut, savoring the feel of him against me, comforting me, loving me.

"Okay," I concede, "but I just need to tell you one thing." I'm not sure where this courage is coming from, but I don't stop to question it. Angling my head, I stare up at him, and our eyes meet. "I love you," I whisper. "It was never about me not loving you." My lip wobbles as I watch his eyes turn glassy. My heart is whirling like an out-of-control spinning top on a bumpy surface.

"You mean that?" he asks, his voice thick with emotion.

I hate how vulnerable he looks and how much my actions have damaged what we share and made him doubt my true feelings. It doesn't matter that I did it in some misguided attempt to set him free, because it's crystal clear now that didn't happen.

"With my whole heart."

He wraps his arms around me, hugging me closer than ever. "I love you too. So fucking much." He eases his hold, tilting my face up with one finger. "I'm not expecting anything here, Sel. I won't put demands on you except for one thing." Vulnerability is etched across his handsome face. "Don't leave me again. We don't have to put any labels on this, but just tell me you won't push me away. I wouldn't survive it a second time. I need you in my life."

Everything is jumbled in my head, and I'm not sure I'm qualified to make such heady promises, but there is no way I'm refusing him this. Not after everything he has done for me. Not after today. He would've been perfectly within his rights to turn me away earlier. Or to get angry at me for the unfair way I've treated him. But all he's ever done is show me kindness and shower me with love. It's not his fault that I've abused that kindness and that I feel so unworthy.

"Okay," I whisper, trailing my hand up his chest to cup his face. "I won't leave, and I'll tell you everything. I won't shut you out."

Kent has breakfast waiting when we step foot in the kitchen the next morning. Keanu's brother's partying ways are legendary, so it's a shock to see him wide-awake at seven a.m. on a Friday morning, whistling under his breath as he cooks at the stove. I take a stool at the counter beside Keanu, trying not to focus on how fucking gorgeous he looks with his hair still damp from the shower and his big eyes bright with love as they study me.

"I hope you like your eggs sunny-side up," Kent says, sliding a plate with eggs, bacon and whole wheat toast across the countertop to me.

I drag my gaze away from Keanu. "You didn't have to do this," I reply. "But thank you. It looks delicious."

"You're welcome," Kent adds, offering me a tall glass filled with orange juice.

Keanu looks at his brother like he's grown wings or something.

"What are your plans for today?" Keanu asks him in between mouthfuls of the yummy breakfast.

"Catch a couple classes. Finish my assignment. Head to the gym, and I'm thinking of going to a frat party tonight," Kent says, sipping a mug of coffee. "What are you two up to?"

"I'm taking Selena to an appointment, and then, we'll probably just hang out around here," Keanu says.

"I wouldn't mind catching a yoga class later on," I say, because I know the studio I go to has a drop-in class on Fridays, and I could use the stress relief.

"Cool. I'll come with," Keanu says, readily agreeing.

Now, it's Kent's turn to look at his brother like he's grown an extra head. "You know yoga?"

"Keanu used to do yoga with me at home," I blurt.

Kent almost chokes on his coffee while Keanu playfully messes up my hair. "Thanks. That's just done wonders for my rep," he jokes, grinning at me.

Kent leans his elbows on the counter, and his blue eyes sparkle with mirth. Gosh, they are so alike with the same dark hair and mesmerizing blue eyes. But Kent is bulkier than Keanu, his hair is longer and stylishly messy, there is more facial hair on his chin and cheeks, and he has way more ink too. He's got that "diamond in the rough" look about him, and it's no wonder he has no shortage of women lining up to share his bed.

If I'm being honest, Kent scares me a little. I've only met him fleetingly a few times, but he always comes across as brash and intimidating and way too cocky. But he's been nothing but nice to me since I showed up here yesterday, so perhaps I formed the wrong impression of him. Or maybe, Keanu's influence is having a positive effect on him.

"What other things don't I know about my brother?" Kent asks, wiggling his brows at me.

"That's for me to know and you to find out."

Kent barks out a gruff laugh. "You're on, sister." He rubs his hands together. "I love a good challenge." He smirks at Keanu. "And I love winding this idiot up." He dumps his mug in the sink. "Bring on the fun times!"

I laugh, and it's nothing short of miraculous. Keanu's gaze dances between his brother and me, and a wide smile graces his lips. "It's okay, don't mind me," he drawls. "Continue to poke fun at my expense."

Kent slaps him on the back. "I think your ego can handle it." He waggles his fingers at me. "I'll get out of your hair. See ya later."

"He's not what I was expecting," I admit, pushing my half-eaten plate away.

"He's behaving himself with you here," Keanu says, frowning as he looks at my plate. "You need to eat, Sel."

"He gave me far too much. I'm full." I pat my flat stomach.

He swivels in his chair, and our legs brush, sending a jolt of heat through me. "How are you feeling?"

I shrug, wrapping my fingers around my claddagh necklace. "I'm okay." He searches my eyes for the truth. "I'm worried, but I'm in control. No meltdowns."

"And the nightmares? Was it new, or you still get them?"

"I still get them, just not as often." For years, I couldn't open up to Denise about the specifics of the things done to me. But part of my recovery these last couple years has involved me sharing more, and she's right. Getting it out has helped me work through the myriad of feelings associated with that very painful part of my past. And I found my nightmares reduced as a result. Go figure.

"So, things have been better since we split?" he asks, his tone and face tinged in sadness.

"Yes, but only because I've been making more of an effort with my recovery and stretching myself out of my comfort zone."

He's deathly quiet, and I know I've upset him again. "Keanu." I reach for his hand, but he slides off the stool.

"We better head out. I'm not sure what the traffic will be like."

I slip off the stool with my heart hurting, planting a fake smile on my face as I grab my bag and follow him outside.

Chapter Nine
Selena

"I overheard you and Kent talking last night," I say from the passenger seat of Keanu's pristine SUV en route to my psychologist's place. The traffic isn't too heavy, and we are making good time. "And I'm okay if you want to tell him about me."

His head whips around, his face showcasing his shock. "Which parts?" he asks, his eyes rotating between me and the road.

"All of it." I pin him with earnest eyes.

His jaw slackens.

"I'm not ever going to be shouting about it from the rooftops," I explain, "but I've spent too long a slave to my past. I want to lead a normal life. To let my loved ones in, and that won't work if I keep what happened to me a secret. So, I'm learning to open up about it."

But it takes enormous courage to go there, and I don't know Kent well enough to feel comfortable telling him directly myself. I worry my lip between my mouth as I phrase my words carefully. "It wasn't right of me to ask you to keep my secret. You basically lied to your family for me, and I shouldn't have asked that of you."

I glance out the window, the weight of all my past mistakes adding to my overall despondent mood since we left the condo.

"I never felt like that, and you shouldn't either," he says, his husky voice reclaiming my attention, reeling me in from the dark ledge I'm tethering to. "I was keeping your confidence, not lying. And no one would blame you for not wanting to discuss it or have others know. You were only a kid, Selena. You haven't done anything wrong."

"That's what Denise says." I turn to face him.

"I knew I liked her for a reason." He flashes me a panty-melting smile and I almost turn into a puddle of goo.

I quickly divert my gaze to the window again before I'm caught drooling, pulling my knees up to my chest, smiling at the woman with the small boy on the sidewalk as we pass by. The kid is holding a giant stuffed panda bear to his chest, and it's so large he's almost toppling over. I watch as his mother scoops him and the stuffed animal into her arms, holding him protectively and possessively, while rubbing his nose and making him laugh. The innocence and purity of the moment shine a light on the dark cloud growing inside me.

I need to know there is still innocence and goodness in this world. To know kids grow up the way they should: in a nurturing environment being bathed in love. Feeling secure and safe, learning and developing with the confidence and happiness that comes from a childhood filled with wonder and awe, not darkness and despair.

I have so few memories of the time before, because it's easy to let the darkness outshine the light. But I'm trying to reclaim those happy moments before my childhood turned into a horror story. To hold tight to the memories of my mom, dad, and little sister Carly. To remember the girl I was before I was forced to become someone else.

"Hey. Where'd you go?" Keanu asks, gently touching my knee, concern vibrating from him.

"I was just looking at that mom with her son back there, and my mind wandered."

He squeezes my knee, offering silent support, but no more words are spoken, because Keanu reads me perfectly and he understands I don't want to go there.

When we pull up at the curb outside Denise's house, he kills the engine and extracts the key. "Would it be okay if I waited inside?" His eyes drift sideways, and I watch as the car with my two new bodyguards glides into a space across the road.

"Of course. I'm sure Denise would like to say hello." Denise was always a big fan of my boyfriend.

Keanu gets out of the car first, running to my side and opening the passenger door. He takes my hand, helping me down, and he doesn't let go.

We walk up Denise's short driveway holding hands, and it's incredible how naturally we have slotted back into a pattern.

I guess it's like that when the other person is the other half of your body, heart, mind, and soul.

Keanu and I never needed labels because calling him my best friend or my boyfriend was never enough. It never conveyed everything he meant to me because he was always so much more.

Which is why it killed me to wrench myself away from him.

But my progress the last couple years is testament to the fact I made the right decision. Even if it hurt both of us, and though it might not seem like it now—in the midst of this crisis—I am stronger and more independent, thanks to the time apart.

Denise opens the door, not masking her shock and delight at seeing Keanu here with me. The instant we step foot into her high-ceiling hallway, she pulls him into a hug. "It's so good to see you."

"You too," he agrees, bundling her up into a big hug.

"Although it's completely unexpected," she adds, breaking away. "Because this little rascal didn't mention a word." She smiles affectionately in my direction.

"I didn't want to ruin the surprise." I grin. "I know how much you've been pining for him."

She lets loose a loud laugh. "Something tells me I might not have been the only one." She drills me with a knowing look.

"Oh, I was definitely pining for you too," Keanu says, deliberately misinterpreting her statement, and Denise laughs again.

"Don't be a stranger," she tells him, opening the door to the waiting room and gesturing for him to step inside. "And make yourself at home. You'll find nothing has changed since you were last here except we now have a new and improved coffee station, thanks to an anonymous donor." She's teasing, because the three of us know Keanu was the one who sent the gift to her. He did enough grumbling about the shit coffee for it not to be him.

"Can't wait to try it out." The laughter fades as he looks me directly in the eye. "If you need me to participate, just let me know."

Keanu has attended a few therapy sessions with me in the past, but I know this is one conversation I need to have without him in the room. "I'm good." On impulse, I stretch up and press my lips to his cheek. "Go test the coffee."

Denise ushers me into her front room, quietly closing the door behind me. I settle into the comfy gray velvet armchair while she makes the peppermint tea. The scent of lavender and sage wafts through the air from the diffuser she has lit. I survey the homey room as she sings softly under her breath, glad Mom found such an awesome therapist for me from the get-go.

I couldn't stomach the thought of attending meetings in a cold, clinical building or sitting in a crowded waiting room with a bunch of strangers. Mom inherently knew what I needed, and she interviewed tons of therapists before finding Denise.

Meeting her at her own home helps calm my nerves. That and her motherly demeanor.

She wears jeans and a soothing sea-green sweater today, with white tennis shoes. Her gray hair is pulled up in a messy bun, and her face is devoid of makeup. Coming here is like meeting a friend for tea. Except for the fact I pry my chest apart, rip my heart out, and spill my painful secrets. All in the name of healing. But I trust Denise, and she has been incredibly patient with me. Taking things in small baby steps. Helping me test my boundaries, reclaim my independence, face up to my past, live in the present, and prepare for the future.

I can't envision a time where I will ever stop meeting with her. I think I will always need her guidance and support.

"Drink up," she says, handing me the mug of peppermint tea. She sits down across from me, and we sip our tea in silence, like we always do. I sink back into my seat, gathering my thoughts and trying to make sense of them as I inhale the comforting scent of lavender in the air and drink the fresh, minty tea.

"Okay," she says when we have put our cups down. "Let's start with some meditation and deep-breathing exercises." We go through a familiar routine, and it helps ground me. Helps to keep my anxiety at bay.

When she is satisfied I am ready, she sits up straighter in her chair. "Tell me what prompted an emergency meeting today."

I kick off my ballet flats and tuck my legs underneath me. Clearing my throat, I tell her what happened yesterday with Clive Lawrence. My voice is clinical as I explain, but it's the only way I can get the words out without giving in to the fear bubbling under the surface of my skin since it went down yesterday. I toy with my necklace as I talk. We discuss my options and my feelings, and she coaxes information from me through skillful questioning that is patient and supportive.

"And what are your feelings toward Keanu?" she asks during the last part of the session.

"He makes me feel safe," I truthfully admit. "And I trust him, but I'm feeling huge guilt too."

"Why?"

"For pushing him away. For hurting him. For showing up on his doorstep after all this time and demanding so much of him."

"Demanding." She taps a finger off her lips. "That's a very strong word. Is it the right one?"

I think about it. "Not demanding. Asking." She quirks a brow, and I answer her unspoken follow-up question. "Okay, maybe not so much asking as him offering."

"And how does that make you feel?"

"Unworthy," I blurt, because it's the first word that springs to mind.

"Why do you feel unworthy?" she asks even though we've already discussed my feelings about Keanu at length.

"Because I'm not normal, and I can't give him the things he wants."

"The things *he* wants or the things you *think* he wants?"

"Aren't they the same thing?"

"Are they?"

"I'm selfish," I say after a few beats of silence. "And weak, because I ran straight to him without conscious thought."

"Do you think our subconscious knows our needs and desires better than our conscious mind?" she asks, tilting her head to the side.

"I don't know." I shrug. "I was on autopilot when I landed on his doorstep. I'm not sure I'd have made that decision if I hadn't been in the midst of a panic attack."

"And do you regret it?"

I shake my head. "No, even though it's going against everything I wanted to achieve when I broke things off with him. Even if it confirms I'm weak."

"Is it weakness or is it strength?"

We've debated this at length. "I honestly can't tell anymore."

"It is *not* weak to seek out support when we need it," she says, folding her hands in her lap. "It is *not* weak to lean on our loved ones when we need propping up." Her features soften as she leans forward. "Knowing when to rely on others is a strength, not a weakness."

"I relied on him too much before."

She nods. "And do you think this is the same? Are *you* the same?"

I contemplate her words for a few minutes, trying to organize my thoughts. "No. With him, I feel stronger, braver, more empowered, but I'm afraid of slipping into old patterns. It would be so easy because he's like a comfort blanket, and I know he wants to wrap me in his warmth and protect me from the cold. But I can't let him become my crutch again." I softly bite down on my lower lip. "I want things to be different this time."

"In what way?"

"I want it to be a partnership. I want to take care of him the same way he takes care of me. I want to show him I'm no longer that frightened girl who hid behind him, but I'm afraid I'm not fully ready. That I'm not strong enough to be who I want to be."

"For Keanu or for you?" she asks, glancing at the clock on the wall.

"For me," I say without hesitation, because that has always been the crux of the decision. "But also for him."

"It's one step at a time, Selena. And you have robust coping strategies. Look how well you are able to sit here today and discuss how your past threatens to impact your present and how self-assured you are when you discuss what you want and need from your relationship with Keanu." She beams at me. "You have come a long way, Selena, and you achieved it through tackling things one at a time. Don't overburden yourself. Don't put too many expectations on your relationship. Talk to Keanu. Let him know how you are feeling. Let him be a part of the decision-making process. And let him help you." She kneels in front of me, taking my hands in hers. "Your reunion may not have happened on your schedule, but that doesn't mean you aren't exactly where you should be with the person you should be right now."

"I know," I whisper, squeezing her hands. "I feel it in every part of me."

"It is not weakness to lean on loved ones in times of need. To let them support and protect us. You need him now, and you need your mom now. They love you and want to help you. Accept their help and their love and you will find the strength to handle what comes next."

"Thank you, Denise."

She stands. "I am here for you too. We still have our regular Wednesday appointment, but if you need to meet before then we can schedule another session. And I am always at the end of the phone. Call me anytime."

I rise. "Thank you. I will."

"You are going to be okay, Selena. And between all of us, we will ensure you get justice." She opens her arms, and I walk into her embrace. "Be careful and stay safe."

Chapter Ten
Keanu

"You okay?" I ask when we are back in the car, buckled in our seats.

"I am. Denise helped me process some things."

I'm so glad Sel has Denise in her life. Honestly, it's more than a patient-therapist relationship at this point. Denise has done so much to help her. "That's good." I smile over at her. "I know you're studying psychology," I add, because I might have checked up on her one or a hundred times during the period we were apart. "So, you're still planning on opening a sanctuary to help others?" Besides modeling, Selena's other goal is to open a haven where other victims of abuse can seek shelter and support.

"I am." Her voice resonates with determination. "Although it will take a while between my studies and raising the kind of money I'd need to turn my vision into reality."

"You know I'll help."

She beams at me. "I know."

Our eyes connect across the small space, and it's like looking into my soul. The air shifts in intensity as we stare at one another, neither of us saying anything, because we've never needed words to communicate.

Selena reaches out, caressing my cheek. "Thanks for being here for me, K."

"Always." I take her hand and gently turn it over, pressing a soft kiss to her wrist. A radiant smile lights up her face, and it's the little moments like this I've missed the most. Her cheeks flush, and she continues smiling as she removes her hand, tucking it underneath her legs.

"So, where to now?" I ask, turning the key and powering up the engine.

"Would you mind if we skipped yoga and went swimming instead?" she asks.

"A swim sounds good, but we'll have to pick up some gear."

"I use a private pool near Cambridge College, and I have a locker with extra towels, caps, and goggles. You can pick up a pair of swim trunks in the onsite store."

"Perfect. Let's go."

We arrive forty minutes later, separating to go into the male and female locker rooms after I purchase a pair of red swim trunks from the store.

I sit on the edge of a lounger, waiting for Sel, watching the five other patrons swim lengths up and down the pool.

This is an older facility, and while it's clean and well-maintained, it looks like something from the nineteen fifties. I can see why it suits Selena though. It's quiet, and the other members are older and stick to themselves. It gives her privacy in a less crowded space.

The door swings open and Selena appears in my line of sight. She's wearing a plain black swimsuit that reveals every angle of her lithe body. The curve of her small tits. The dip of her shapely waist. Those long, long legs that seem to go on for miles. Her hair is tucked up in a swim cap, and she has goggles resting on top of her head.

She walks toward me, carrying a towel, a cap, and a set of goggles, and our surroundings disappear as my gaze treks up every inch of her body. The scars on her upper thighs are only noticeable if you know to look for them, but I'm amazed at how confidently she is striding toward me, because she always shied away from displaying those marked parts of her body. She never liked me touching her in those places, and I always respected her wishes.

But something has definitely shifted.

And I'm so fucking proud of her for facing up to her fears.

For fighting so hard to overcome the trauma of her past.

If I didn't love her to the moon and back already, I surely would now.

Her full mouth broadens into a shy smile, but she keeps her gaze locked on me the entire time as she approaches.

"Hey." She perches on the edge of the lounger beside me, handing me the supplies.

"Hey yourself." I take the items from her, placing the towel behind me and wasting no time putting the cap on. I place my goggles around my neck, never taking my eyes off her. I swivel my legs, and our bare knees touch, sending delicious tremors ricocheting all over my body. "You look beautiful." I drink in her gorgeous eyes, noting the green and gold hues are more prominent today. She stares deep into my eyes, and a faint blush stains her pale cheeks.

"Thank you."

I reach forward, taking her elegant hands in mine. "I'm glad you came to me yesterday."

"Me too." Emotion swims in her eyes. "You could have turned me away, but you didn't. I appreciate that so much. I appreciate *you* so much."

Her tongue darts out, wetting her lips in an anxious tell, and my eyes latch onto her luscious mouth. We are leaning toward one another, our bodies straining for closeness, and I want nothing more than to bridge the gap and end this distance, claiming her lips and reminding her that she's mine.

But I can't be the one to do it.

She needs to be in control.

Not only because it helps keep her anxiety at bay, but because I need to know she wants this too.

Her eyes drop to my lips, and electricity crackles in the space between us. All the tiny hairs on my arms stand to attention, along with the snake in my shorts. My gaze wanders over her face, down lower, lingering a moment on the tight peaks of her tits evident through the material of her swimsuit. She sucks in a gasp, and I lift my eyes, watching her ogling the semi in my shorts with a look I've rarely seen on her before.

Selena looks aroused. And I've seen *that* plenty of times on her face. But this time it's not accompanied by sheer panic and fear. Her gaze rises to my face, and her eyes are darker, drenched in lust, and it turns the semi in my shorts to a solid block of muscle.

She shifts on her lounger, moving closer, and my heart is banging around my chest, looking for a way out. Sheer liquid lust fuels the blood flowing through my veins, and it makes a sharp detour, heading south, hardening my dick to the point of pain.

A part of me wants to grab her onto my lap and grind my aching cock against her sweet softness as I devour her mouth and caress every inch of her beautiful body. But we have an audience, and I would never treat Selena like that. She deserves the gentlest of touches. In familiar surroundings, where she feels comfortable and safe.

I hop up, discreetly adjusting the rock in my trunks, breaking the magnetic spell we're under. I extend my hand. "Let's swim."

Her soft flesh meets mine, and I guide her to the swimming pool, hastily thinking unsexy thoughts in a bid to deflate the monster erection I'm trying to disguise by hiding behind her body.

"I'll cook," Selena announces later that evening when we are back at the condo. We have a couple hours before her mom and my brother Keven are dropping by.

"I don't mind cooking," I protest.

"You cooked last night. It's my turn, and besides, I enjoy cooking. It helps me de-stress." She pulls her long blonde hair up into a messy bun and opens the refrigerator door, peering inside to inspect the contents. Her peachy ass is right in my face, molded to the skinny jeans she's wearing, and my boner is suddenly back in full force.

This is starting to become a problem.

"I'm going to talk to Kent," I blurt, needing to get out of here before I do something rash, like suggest we forgo dinner and lock ourselves in my bedroom.

Her spine stiffens, and she straightens, turning to face me. "You'll tell him?"

I step toward her. "I don't have to if you've changed your mind."

Her brief moment of doubt passes. She shakes her head, sending me a determined look. "I haven't, and I think it's best you tell him before Mom and your older brother arrive."

"Okay." I walk right up to her, slowly leaning down and pressing my lips to her cheek. The delicate fragrance of lavender and vanilla swirls around me, and combined with the feel of her silky-smooth skin, I'm a goner. "Sel," I whisper, drawing her in close but not too close, because I don't want the snake in my pants to scare her. "Have I told you how much I love having you here?" I whisper, and she shivers. I mentally fist pump the air. It's good to know I affect her the same way she affects me.

"You might have mentioned that on the way home when you convinced me to stay here for longer." I can hear the smile in her voice.

"It didn't take much convincing," I supply, raising my hand slowly and threading it through her hair.

"Because I love being here as much as you love having me at your place." She tilts her head up, and our noses touch. It would take very little to lower my mouth and brush my lips against hers, and I want that so badly. That same pulsing electricity is back again, humming and purring, almost taunting us to act on it. My hip nudges against hers, my erection prodding her stomach. I jerk back, instinctively, examining her face carefully, but all I see is the same wanton desire from earlier.

Her eyes burn bright as she stretches up, pressing her lips to the corner of my mouth.

I stop breathing, standing as still as a statue, shocked and elated she touched me so freely.

She kisses the other corner of my mouth, and I feel her body trembling. "Go talk to your brother, and later, I want to talk about us."

I press my forehead to hers, briefly closing my eyes. "I'd like that."

Her warm smile heats me from the outside in, and it's remarkable. Because her situation is fraught with danger, and she's clearly afraid, but she is holding it together, and that is *massive*.

I stumble from the room in a bit of a daze, shaking myself out of it when I approach Kent's room. I rap on the door, not daring to enter in case he's jerking off, watching porn, or has some fuck bunnies squirreled away in the master suite on the sly.

He opens the door, dressed in a pair of sweats, beads of water dotting his bare upper torso, confirming he's not long out of the shower. "Sup?"

"I was hoping to talk to you. About Selena."

"Sure." He leaves the door open, and I follow him inside, closing it behind me.

"What I have to say is some heavy shit," I supply, trailing him to the seated area at the back of the large room.

"Okay." He flops down on the couch, and I sit on the one across from him.

"I need to dial Kev in."

He arches a brow but passes no comment.

Our older brother answers on the fourth ring. "Keanu."

"Kev. I'm with Kent, and the stuff I need to tell him you need to hear too."

"Is this connected to what you need to speak to me about tonight? It's about Selena?" he asks as I put him on speaker.

"Yes."

"Okay. I'm all ears."

My foot taps idly off the floor, and bile floods my mouth as I prepare to explain. Kent eyes me intensely, but he doesn't rush me, and neither does Kev. "You can't share what I'm about to tell you with anyone. And I mean *anyone*. That includes the FBI and Cheryl, Kev."

While I'm hoping we might be able to get the FBI on the case to help nail that bastard Lawrence, I don't want my brother talking to anyone until after we've spoken later. Any potential discussions with the FBI will only happen when it's been agreed in advance and where Selena wants it.

This is her life. Her justice to claim. And none of us has a right to force her into anything she doesn't want to do.

"I don't like keeping secrets from my fiancée," Kev says through the line, "but there are certain things I can't tell her about my work, and she gets it. I have a feeling she would understand why I can't talk to her about this, so go ahead. I won't speak of this to anyone."

I know Kev won't. He's kept so many secrets for our family, and he's used to keeping things close to his chest.

Kent is a different story.

He's a bit of a loose cannon at times, and I need to know he can keep this to himself. I eyeball my triplet. "You cannot breathe a word of this to anyone. Not even Keats or anyone else in the family. Not unless Selena wants them to know."

"I promise I will keep this confidential." Sincerity bleeds from his tone and his face, and I nod.

"There's no easy way to say any of this, so I'm just putting it out there," I say, leaning my arms on my thighs. "When Selena was ten, her and her friend Juanita were abducted by pedophiles. They were split up, and Selena was taken offshore, to some island, where she was imprisoned for three years and kept as a sex slave."

Kent's face whitens, and his Adam's apple bobs in his throat. Keven is quiet on the end of the line. I guess, in his line of work, nothing has the power to shock him anymore.

I scrub a hand along my jaw, swallowing back bile. "She was regularly drugged, beaten, tortured, and raped."

"Shit." Kent sits upright, resting his elbows on his knees and burying his head in his hands.

"When she was thirteen, she was sold to a rich American prick. He took her back to the US, and she managed to escape from a motel in Texas, and the authorities were called. She discovered her parents and her younger sister had been murdered a few months after she was kidnapped. The same fate happened to her friend's family, leading the authorities to believe the men responsible for sex trafficking the girls were behind the murders. They have never been found. Never been brought to justice."

Pressure settles on my chest, compressing the oxygen in my lungs. I'll never forget the weeks after Selena told me what happened to her. The blanket rage that swept through me imagining the things she'd endured. She was only ten when she was taken. Her childhood ended that night. Her innocence was stolen. Her future irreparably altered.

I remember begging my mom to help. We had money, and I wanted to find those bastards who had hurt the girl I was in love with. Turns out, my parents had been working with Selena's mom, trying to track down the culprits. They had spent considerable resources between them, hiring PIs here and overseas and talking to various government bodies, trying to find the truth. But every lead was a dead end.

After that, they funneled their resources into charity work. Sandrine set up a charity that supports parents of kids who have been sex trafficked. It provides support and education. Gives them the tools they need to help their children heal and reintegrate into society after living through such trauma. Enables them to process their feelings and lean on others with similar experiences. Mom and Dad are their biggest donors, and they have worked behind the scenes to secure other donations. They haven't done it publicly for fear it would shine a spotlight on Selena.

I have so much love and respect for my parents for all they have done for her. They are good people. Not perfect, by any means, but their hearts are in the right places.

"I'm so sorry Selena went through that, Keanu," Keven says, his voice grave.

"Me too," Kent adds, looking over at me with tormented eyes. "I said some horrible things about her."

"You didn't know," I say, wanting to reassure him. "And I couldn't tell you because Selena could barely acknowledge it to herself, let alone discuss it with anyone. She suffers from PTSD. She has panic attacks, nightmares, social anxiety, and a host of other shit she's trying to handle." I grind my teeth to my molars as rage twists and turns in my gut. "Yesterday, she saw the man who bought her for the first time since she escaped from him."

Kent's eyes widen in alarm, and Keven cusses down the line. "This is why you need to talk."

"Yes. We need your help."

"I'm coming over now," he says. "See you soon."

He hangs up before I've had the chance to respond.

"That's why you said not to touch her," Kent says, dragging his hands through his hair.

"Yes. For the first year after she lived with her adopted mom, she screamed anytime anyone tried to touch her. She still doesn't like strangers touching her, and those close to her have learned to be careful around her."

"She lets you touch her."

"Yes, but I'm still careful to make no fast movements, to make her aware I'm going to touch her before I do, or to ask permission."

"Fuck, man. I had no idea." Kent shakes his head, and silence engulfs us for a few minutes. His eyes dart to mine. "That's why you were a virgin."

I shift uncomfortably on my seat. There are some things I won't discuss with my brother. With anyone but Selena. I toss him a curt nod.

"Aw, man." Kent slumps in his seat, squeezing his eyes shut. "I feel like shit for pushing you at that girl now."

"You didn't force me to lose my virginity, but I'd be lying if I said I haven't regretted it." It was a few weeks after Selena broke things off with me, shattering my heart, and I was a hot mess. My emotions were all over the place, and one night, in a fit of anger, and a haze of alcohol, I lost my virginity to some random girl I met at Torment.

It wasn't my finest moment.

My voice cracks as I admit the truth to my brother. "I was waiting for Selena. I would have waited forever," I truthfully admit. "And now she's here, and I know she still loves me like I love her, and I think we might have a chance of mending our relationship." I pin anguished eyes on my brother. "But if she finds out what I've done in the time we were apart, I'm afraid she'll want nothing more to do with me."

Chapter Eleven
Selena

"I made *coq au vin*," I tell the guys when they arrive downstairs an hour later. "It will be ready in thirty minutes."

"It smells delicious," Keanu says, smiling as he gives me a subtle nod, confirming he's spoken to Kent and all is okay.

"It's Mom's recipe. I remember how much you loved it." Heat creeps up my neck, onto my cheeks, and I drop my eyes to the floor.

"Sandrine's parents were French," Keanu tells Kent, tilting my face up with his finger. "And she's the most exquisite cook. Sel too." He softly cups my chin, his eyes conveying so much.

My heart grows wings, and I swoon at his complimentary words and his adoring gaze. I can't believe I am here. That the time apart feels like it never happened. That he looks at me the same way. Like I'm his everything in the same way he is to me.

The doorbell chimes, snapping me out of my romantic daze, and I pull away from him.

"That must be Kev. I'll let him in."

I stand rooted to the spot, watching Keanu sprint across the open living space toward the front door, failing to disguise my blatant ogling. From the way he looks in his skintight jeans and tight Travis

Scott T-shirt, which clings to his toned torso like a second skin, I'm practically frothing at the mouth. I thought Keanu only had tats on his lower arms, but the ink on his left arm now extends up under the edge of his shirt, indicating it stretches higher. I wonder if that's a recent addition. I've never really been keen on tattoos, but Keanu has changed my mind.

Or maybe it's just because the ink is on him. And he looks hot as fuck.

I didn't think it was possible to lust after him more than I already did, but this more grown-up version has me weak at the knees. Keanu was a few months shy of his eighteenth birthday, and only really starting to grow into his body, when we broke up, but now, at almost twenty, he is definitely all man.

And my libido has most certainly noticed.

Which is a welcome new development—even if it terrifies me as much as it exhilarates me.

Taking back control of my sexuality is another challenge I must face. One I haven't felt confident to tackle.

Until Keanu reentered my life.

It's crazy how comfortable I feel with him after twenty-four hours in his presence. But, honestly, it's like we were never apart.

A throat clearing draws my attention. "Selena."

I pin cautious eyes on Kent, anxiety simmering in my chest, hoping he's not going to discuss specifics.

"I'm so fucking sorry that happened to you, and I'm sorry if I've been an ass."

He's one hundred percent sincere, and I relax a smidgeon. "Thank you, and it's okay. I can only imagine what you must have thought of me." I cringe a little thinking back to the first couple of times I met Kent. How I stood there mute and frightened, clinging to Keanu and silently praying his brother would go away.

It's a timely reminder of how far I've progressed.

"I didn't know what to think," he says, shoving his hands in the pockets of his loose-hanging sweats. "I didn't understand it, but I do now."

"I'm trying to deal with my illness. Trying to open up more." I shrug, averting my eyes. "It's a work in progress."

"If I can help, you only have to ask."

I look up at him. "Thank you, and the best thing you can do for me is to treat me like you would any other girl."

His eyes pop wide, and I giggle. Yeah, I'm pretty sure Keanu would *not* appreciate Kent treating me like most of his girls. "Or maybe not." My laughter fades. "I just don't want any pity. I don't want my past to define who I am anymore."

"I think you're so fucking brave, Selena. I could never pity you."

Our eyes meet in shared understanding, and my heart stutters in my chest at what I see lurking behind his restrained smile. "Thank you."

I gulp, and Kent looks away. "What are you two goons looking at?"

I whip my head around, spotting Keanu and an older version of him staring at Kent like he's an apparition.

"Nothing much, jackass," Keven says, running his eyes along his brother's arms. "You got a fever or something?"

"Funny." Kent pouts, crossing his arms and glaring at his older brother.

"Sel." Keanu extends his arm, gesturing me forward. I step toward him, weaving my fingers in his. He pulls me slowly into his side. "This is my brother Keven."

"It's very nice to finally meet you, Selena," Keven says, his voice radiating warmth like his kind smile.

"You too." I lean into Keanu, smiling shyly at his hot, older brother. Although I've only met Kyler, Keaton, and Kent previously, I know all the Kennedy men are drop-dead gorgeous because there are photos of them plastered all over social media. They are a bit like living legends in the Boston area, and hearts break wherever they go. And even though Kyler, Kaden, and Keven have a different dad than

Kalvin, Keanu, Kent, and Keaton, they are all so alike with their dark hair, blue eyes, masculine jawlines, and tall, ripped bodies.

The doorbell rings again, and it can only be Mom. "I'll go."

Keanu releases me.

"Check who it is before opening the door," Kev advises.

"Selena is very security conscious," Keanu says, his eyes following me to the door.

I check through the peephole and open the door to my mom. She steps inside, and I shut the door before giving her a brief hug.

"You holding up okay, sweetheart?" she asks, unwinding the silk scarf from around her neck.

"Yes. I spoke with Denise and Keanu, and I went swimming, and then, we hung out around here. I'm fine." And I realize I am as the words leave my mouth, and I'm proud of myself.

"Sandrine." Keanu hugs my mom. "These are my brothers Keven and Kent."

Mom shakes both their hands. "It's nice to meet you. I've heard so much about all of you from your mom."

Keven and Kent trade surprised expressions.

"Ah, you're not aware." She removes her coat, and Keanu takes it from her, draping it over the back of a dining chair.

"Let's sit." Keanu ushers everyone to the couches, and I sink into the plush blue velvet, crushed to his side. Mom sits beside me, while Kev and Kent sit across from us.

"Your mother and I are good friends," Mom explains. "She contributes significantly to my charity, and she has shown untold kindness to my daughter, as well as fulfilling one of Selena's childhood dreams."

"Selena always wanted to be a model," Keanu confirms, jumping in before I can say it.

"It's how they tricked us," I croak. "The men who took us," I elaborate, knotting and unknotting my hands. "They stopped us on the street in Phoenix and told us we could be models. Gave us a card. Told us not to tell our parents, and we stupidly agreed."

Although, I remember wanting to tell my mom.

Feeling uneasy.

But Juanita was so excited. We had daydreamed about being models. About becoming the next Giselle Bundchen or Amber Valletta. So, I forced my gut instinct aside and went with my best friend that fateful day.

It was the last time I ever saw her. And not a day goes by I don't wonder what happened to her.

Becoming a model has been bittersweet, because it was something Juanita and I had planned together. And it took a long time for me to agree to model for Kennedy Apparel, because the thought of random men getting off to pictures of me has always made me sick. It's why I never do lingerie or swimwear shoots—well, that and the obvious scars on my thighs, stomach, and chest—and another reason why I don't do runway shows. I'm fortunate to be in a position where I can pick and choose what shoots I commit to. Ironically, limiting myself to modeling with KA, and only with Keanu, elevated my status, and brands are clamoring to sign me. It wasn't intentional. And I definitely didn't want or ask for the attention, but it's what has happened.

I was nervous about accepting Miranda Fanning's offer to become the face of her new collection because this level of fame comes with a price. But Miranda is the hottest new designer in the industry, and it would've been career suicide to turn her down. Besides, she has an ex-military brother-in-law who suffers with PTSD, and she's been supportive and accepting of my terms and conditions. I'm in safe hands with her and her team, and that is always half the battle for me.

But I'm concerned about the extra coverage and publicity, and I know it's only a matter of time before that bastard Lawrence sees me on a billboard or in a magazine and figures out who I am.

I knew this day might come when I accepted such a high-profile campaign, but I can't live my life in fear. I can't continue to let those bastards control who I am and what I become. I did that for far too long. Both when I was imprisoned and in the years after my escape when I withdrew into myself and hid away from the world.

It has to end.

I can't move forward until the past has been dealt with.

So even though I'm scared, one part of me is glad I stumbled across him at the casting call. Because now I have the upper hand. I know where *he* is. He doesn't know where I am yet, and that gives us an advantage.

Whatever we decide today, I'm not backing down.

I'm ready to fight. To take back control of my future and to finally kill the hold those sick bastards have over me.

Chapter Twelve
Keanu

"That was fantastic, Selena," Keven says, patting his full stomach as he pushes his empty plate away. "You'll have to email the recipe to Cheryl so I can bribe her into cooking it for me."

"You're welcome." She beams from ear to ear, and I could kiss Kev. He's been absolutely wonderful with her all night, and it warms my heart to see Selena like this. Yes, she's still shy and quiet, and she still sits close to my side, looking to me for reassurance on occasion, but she's comfortable around this table, laughing and looking relaxed, not stressed out or cowering behind me.

And I'm in awe of her.

Of how far she has come.

And I think I'm beginning to realize some truths.

Our breakup really had nothing to do with me.

She needed this. To find herself.

She moves to clear the table, but Kent and I won't hear of it. House rules. She cooked. We clean. I escort her to the couch, pressing a kiss to the top of her head as she sits beside her mom, and Kev plonks his butt into one of the low armchairs.

"I like her," Kent says, talking in hushed tones as we rinse and stack the dishwasher.

"I love her." I'm not ashamed to admit it. For years, I told my family nothing about the girl who had captured my heart. Now, things have changed, and I'm not going to hide her or my feelings anymore.

"I know, bro. I always have."

"I'm not letting her go this time," I say, wiping down the counter. "Selena is it for me."

Kent eyes me circumspectly. "You really mean that."

I toss the damp dishcloth in the sink. "Yeah. I do."

He thumps me in the shoulder. "Guess I've permanently lost my wingman, huh?"

"I was never a true wingman, and we both know it."

"Yeah. You were a miserable fuck most of the time. I've seen you smile more this past twenty-four hours than I have in the last two years."

"She makes my heart sing."

He sticks two fingers in his mouth, gagging. "Fuck no. Not you too." He shakes his head. "There is no one left. All my brothers have turned to the dark side."

Only Kent could refer to love as a darkness. Like it's an illness or something.

"Love isn't a burden, bro. It's the best feeling in the world. Even when the girl of your dreams yanks your beating heart out of your chest and stomps all over it, it's still worth every ounce of pain. Wait and see. You'll meet a girl, and she'll nail your heart to the wall, and you'll be powerless to do anything about it."

He shakes his head. "It's not gonna happen."

"Why the hell not?" I grab two bottles of water out of the refrigerator while I eye my cynical brother.

"Because we both know I'll somehow fuck it all up." He walks off, plonking down on the couch across from the women, and I wonder what happened that he's so hard on himself.

I sit down beside Selena, and I can't contain my shit-eating grin when she automatically takes my hand and leans into my side.

Keven smiles, his eyes full of approval, before he sits up straighter in his chair. "Selena and Sandrine were just bringing me up to speed on Clive Lawrence."

The smile drops off my face.

"I understand the need for the security detail after what happened yesterday, and I won't lie about the risk." He clasps his hands between his thighs. "I'm assigned to a high-profile team within the FBI investigating the criminal underbelly in MA. Since the death of Jeremy Garcia and the imprisonment of Daniel Stanten"—his nostrils flare at the mention of Cheryl's ex-fiancé who turned out to be the illegitimate son of Carmine Mancusso, the capo crimini of a powerful New York gang—"a bloody battle for control of the streets has ensued. We have undercover agents infiltrating the various gangs vying for ultimate control, and these guys are into everything. Drugs. Guns." His eyes flit to Selena. "Sex."

Selena stiffens beside me, and I slide a protective arm around her shoulders, offering her support.

"I can't go into the specifics, but Stanten was running a sex trafficking ring from Mexico and bringing girls illegally into Boston. Some were forced into prostitution here; others were sold. We've come across several organizations involved in other forms of sex trafficking. Mainly young girls and boys, and we're building a case. But it's slow, because evidence is lacking."

He runs a hand through his hair, softening his expression as he eyeballs Selena. "Lawrence is on our radar, even more so since he established his new production company right here, but on the surface, he is squeaky clean. I think we might be able to help each other, but it would have to be done formally. I'd like your permission to speak to my boss. To see what protection he can offer you in exchange for your cooperation."

"What good am I if there is no proof?" Selena asks. "It will be my word against his, and he has formidable friends. The men who frequented the island, the ones who bought girls to bring back to the US, were all wealthy, well-connected men. I only know this because Freddie loved to rub it in our faces. Telling us not to try and escape because these men were some of the most powerful figures and they had connections everywhere. That there was nowhere we could run, because they would always find us."

That bastard Freddie really did a number on Selena. That was the main reason why she was terrified to step outside her own door for years. Why she was homeschooled with a private tutor rather than attending high school. Why my mom arranged private escort for her to and from modeling shoots. Why we mostly spent time at her house rather than going out on regular dates.

"We'll find the proof, and I do have something I'd like to show you," Kev says.

This is news to me, and he should've run it by me first. "Why am I only hearing about this now?" My tone is sharp on purpose.

"Honestly, I wasn't going to go there, but I think Selena has a lot of the intel we've been searching for."

"I don't care," I snap. "This isn't about building the FBI's case. It's about protecting Selena."

"That is not what I meant, Keanu. Family is fucking everything to me, and I know that's who Selena is to you. I will help you keep her safe." He looks to Selena. "I've ordered a high-tech security system to install here. Keanu tells me you will be staying with him indefinitely?"

Her eyes widen as she stares at me, and I glower at Kev again. I never said *indefinitely* even though it's what I want. But we haven't discussed that yet, and I don't want to scare her away. She's agreed to stay here as long as that pervert is a threat.

"Uh, well…" Selena stammers, her cheeks burning up.

"I would like Selena to stay here until the threat has ended, but it's ultimately her decision." I drill Kev with a look that says "watch your fucking mouth."

Her shoulders relax. "I'll be staying here for the moment, but I will return to my mom's house at some point."

Keven looks to Sandrine. "With your permission, I'd like to install the same system at your house."

"We have deadbolts on all the locks and windows and security cameras on the exterior and interior of the house," Sandrine confirms. "I think we're adequately covered."

"Could I drop by sometime and inspect it? The latest systems are high-tech monitored systems that mean the police are notified immediately should anyone break in."

"I don't trust the cops," Sandrine says. "And I certainly don't want a system that notifies them if it's someone on their payroll who is the threat."

"You have specific cops you don't trust, or it's more of a general statement?" Kev asks.

"Boston has an extensive criminal history I'm fully familiar with. I know all the criminal organizations operating in our jurisdiction have cops on their payroll in most districts. That's enough suspicion to tell me we need to steer clear of local police."

"I understand, and it's undoubtedly a problem, but I still need to examine your security to ensure it's fit for purpose. We can't take any chances. I know you are already worried, and I don't want to add to it, but I won't lie to either of you." His gaze bounces between Selena and Sandrine. "These criminals tend to target the families. Using them to force their loved ones into backing down. If we go after Lawrence, he will be gunning for Selena, and that means you are at risk. A new high-tech monitoring system connected to a private security firm is my recommendation."

"Let Keven check out the house, Mom. Please."

Sandrine nods. "Of course. I'll do whatever is needed."

"With your permission, I would like to install tracking devices on your cells, phones, and cars. I will monitor it, and I'll also install the app on Kent's and Keanu's cells and computers so they have access to your whereabouts at all times."

"Do it," Selena says, removing her cell from her pocket and handing it to Kev. Sandrine does the same.

"Both of you too," Kev says, opening his palm as he drills a look at Kent and me.

"I also have some security chips I'd like you to embed in your shoes and on jewelry." He eyes Selena's necklace. "You can add one to that, and maybe your watch, Sandrine."

Some might think this is overkill, but I trust my brother. This isn't his first rodeo, and I'll do whatever he says if it keeps Selena and her mom safe.

Kev gets to work, making all that happen while Selena and I head to the kitchen to make coffee.

"Are you okay with all this?" I ask as I grab five mugs from the overhead cupboard.

"Yes." Selena pours water into the coffee machine. "I feel safer knowing someone knows where I am all the time."

Most people resent having bodyguards, and tracking devices, but I can understand why Selena feels comforted with the protection. And I'm glad. Because I didn't want to fight with her about this.

I rub my sweaty palms down the front of my jeans, holding Selena's gaze as I make a suggestion. "I was also thinking maybe you should learn to use a gun."

Her face drains of blood, and she shakes her head repeatedly. "No."

"You need to know how to defend yourself, and—"

"I know how to defend myself, K. I've been attending self-defense classes since I was fifteen."

I know that. But it's not the same. These guys shoot first and ask questions later. I've no doubt if they can't take Selena they'll kill her. Because she's a liability. A witness to their crimes and their depravity. Someone who can put them all away.

I walk toward her, invoking all my willpower to gently hold her to me when I want to crush her to my chest and never let her go. "I don't want anything to happen to you, and I'd feel more reassured if you had a gun and you knew how to use it."

My brothers and I all know how to handle a firearm. Dad brought us to the gun range as soon as we were old enough to learn. We've grown up with a spotlight on our family. Dealt with crazies and death threats and stalkers, and knowing how to use a gun is survival one-oh-one.

Faye, Cheryl, and Eva have all been kidnapped and held at gunpoint. I'm not overreacting. Being associated with me brings its own special brand of crazy. Add this very real threat to the mix, and I'd feel more assured knowing my girl can defend herself in multiple ways.

"I can't do it, K. I saw too much violence on that island. Saw girls I'd grown close to shot at point-blank range when they tried to escape or merely because they had outgrown their usefulness." She peers up at me with tears in her eyes. "Sometimes, they made us put on these shows, and if we didn't perform exactly as they had scripted it, they tortured us using weapons." A strangled cry escapes her lips as the horror of her words settles in my stomach like a dead weight. "Knives, guns, and other implements of pain," she adds.

Her many scars resurrect in my mind's eye, and I hold her closer, shutting my eyes as if that will ward off the pain. "I'm sorry," I croak. "I won't suggest it again."

We hug it out in the kitchen until I feel her relaxing against me, and when we're composed enough, we return to the others. They have been quietly talking while we've been in the kitchen. Sandrine questions me with her eyes, and I offer her a reassuring nod.

She never has to worry.

I've got our girl.

Always.

"All the tracking devices are in place," Kev says, handing Selena her cell and her necklace. I put the tray of coffees down on the coffee table and slip my phone back in my pocket. "Keanu knows how to insert these in your shoes." He passes a box of silver chips to me. "I'll come by one night this week to install the new security system."

"Thanks, bro."

"And I'll contact you to arrange a time to look at your place," he says to Sandrine.

"Thank you very much, Keven. I appreciate everything you are doing for Selena." Her gaze dances between me and my two brothers. "Everything you are all doing. You have my eternal gratitude."

"So that just leaves one last thing." Kev scrubs a hand across his prickly jawline. "I found some photos last year on a case, and I'd like you to take a look at them. If you feel up to it," Kev adds, peering at Selena. "It's completely fine if it's too much."

"What type of photos?" I ask, because there's no way I want her looking at gruesome pics. She has enough nightmares as it is.

"Photos of girls we believe were trafficked. There are a few men in the photos too. I wanted to see if Selena recognized anyone."

"They aren't—"

"They're not," Kev reassures me before I've even asked my question.

"I want to see," Selena quietly says, holding out her hand. I sit forward with her as she takes the bundle of dog-eared photos from my brother's outstretched hand.

Her body shakes as she starts looking through them, and I place a gentle hand on her knee, reminding her she is not alone. You could hear a pin drop in the room as Selena flips through the photos, pausing to examine a few in more detail. When she's looked at the last one, she lifts her eyes to Keven. "I'm sorry. I don't recognize anyone." She passes them back to him, and he puts them face down on the table.

"I have one more." He holds it up, with the back of the photo facing us so we can't see. Kev looks at me, and goose bumps sprout on my arms.

"What?"

He pinches his lips, looking a little uncertain. "When I first discovered this photo, I couldn't figure out why I was fascinated with it. Until I realized one of the girls looked familiar."

Nausea swims up my throat, and blood rushes to my ears. "No," I whisper.

"You don't have to look at this, Selena, but I think one of the girls in this picture is...you."

Silence engulfs the room, and tension hangs in the air like fog.

"I want to look," Selena whispers, her voice brittle, her body shaking.

"You don't have to do this, baby."

She looks deep into my eyes. "I know, but I want to. I *need* to."

"Are you sure, sweetheart?" Sandrine asks, sharing my concern.

She nods, and Keven hands it over.

Selena sucks in a gasp, and her hands shake as she holds the picture between trembling fingers. I look at it and stop breathing. The back of a long transport truck is wide open, and young girls are spilling out like sardines from an overturned can. Most are in skimpy dresses or dirty underwear, hair matted, sweat clinging to their over-heated skin. My eyes lock onto the two girls at the front of the picture.

The girl in the wrinkled black minidress staring into the camera with long, messy dark hair and big eyes is unmistakably Selena. I would know her face anywhere, even as a child. She is tall for her age, but her face is so young. Too young. Another girl is clinging to her arm, tears trekking down her face. Rage filters through my veins, and the urge to hit something is riding me hard. My body locks up, stress tying me into knots.

"No!" Selena cries, her voice laced with pain, as she jumps up, the picture falling through her fingers, landing on the hardwood floor. "Oh my God. No!" Her breathing becomes labored, and tears pour down her face. "No! No! No! No!" She sways on her feet as I stand, reaching for her. Her eyes roll back in her head and her eyelids flutter closed as her limbs give way, and she tumbles to the floor.

Chapter Thirteen
Selena

I slowly come to with the sound of voices shouting in the background. Opening my eyes, I look up into the concerned gray-blue eyes of my mom. My head is on her lap, and she helps me to sit up as I watch Keanu shoving Keven, screaming in his face. Keven has his palms raised, and Kent is between them, trying to keep them at arm's length.

"What happened?" I rasp, and Keanu stops berating his brother, spinning around on his heels and racing to crouch down in front of me.

"You fainted, sweetheart," Mom says at the same time Keanu asks, "Are you feeling okay?"

It all comes back to me in a rush, and my stomach lurches violently. Pushing Keanu and Mom away, I scramble to my feet, hand clasped over my mouth as I race toward the kitchen sink. I make it in the nick of time, hurling my guts up as tears roll down my cheeks.

Comforting hands scrape my hair back, keeping it off my face as I throw up the dinner I so lovingly prepared. When I've nothing left to expel, I rinse out my mouth with water before slumping against Keanu. His arms wrap around me, keeping me upright from behind.

Sobs rip from my tortured soul and I fall apart. He turns me around, holding me to his chest, and I collapse against him, soaking his shirt with my tears. "It's okay, baby." He smooths a hand up and down my back. "Let it all out."

The image plays on a loop in my head, and I squeeze my eyes closed, attempting to shut it down, but it doesn't work. Juanita is all I see in my mind's eye. My bestie was clinging to my arm, crying. The reel extends beyond what was in the photo, and tightness spreads across my chest. I struggle to breathe. My limbs turn limp, and my stomach churns as a stampede of butterflies invades my belly and flutters throughout my chest.

The scent of lavender wafts through the air as Keanu dabs some oil on my wrist. "Breathe, Selena." I inhale deeply, trying to control my anxiety as Keanu performs my deep-breathing exercises with me. Focusing on him and the familiar scent keeps the torturous images at bay. For now. Gradually, the attack passes, and I slump against Keanu again, clutching my necklace, physically and mentally exhausted.

"Selena, honey." Mom's troubled face lines up with mine. "How can I help? Do you want to come home?"

I shake my head, holding Keanu tighter. "I want to stay here, and I just need to sleep." It's the only way to blot out the pain of the recollection.

"Selena," Keven says, stepping into my line of vision, his face riddled with remorse. "I'm so sorry."

"I think you should go," Keanu says in a clipped tone before scooping me up into his arms. I rest my head on his shoulder, clinging to him, siphoning his warmth and his support.

"Do you want me to stay?" Mom asks.

"No. I'm good," I mumble.

"I will take care of her," Keanu promises, and no one doubts it.

Hushed conversation takes place around me, but I zone out, only resurfacing in the real world when Keanu deposits me on the bed in his room. "I'm running you a bath," he says before pressing a kiss to my forehead. I don't respond, curling into a ball as I attempt to ward off the images that are now imprinted on my brain.

Keanu returns, lifting me off the bed and carrying me into the bathroom. Floral-scented steam surrounds me, its tendrils enveloping me, helping take the edge off my panic. Keanu puts my feet on the floor, and my arms drop to my sides. My body feels heavy and tired as I stand in the steam-filled bathroom, as if I've just run a marathon. I'm depleted, and I can't even summon the energy to lift an arm, let alone undress.

"Do you want me to help?" he asks, and I nod, on auto-zombie mode. Slowly, he undresses me until I'm down to my panties and bra. "Are you good from here or..."

My eyes lift to his, and I silently convey what I can't articulate.

That I need him, because I've lost myself.

"Are you sure?"

I manage a barely there nod.

His hands shake as he unclasps my bra, his fingers brushing my arms as he pulls the straps down, letting my bra drop to the tiled floor. An involuntary shiver skates over my flesh, but I barely feel his touch because I'm only half here. He stalls, pinning me with panicked eyes, and I know he's terrified he's hurt me.

"It's okay," I croak, managing to force the words out while staring blankly at him.

He scrutinizes my face before nodding. His Adam's apple bobs in his throat as he hooks his thumbs in the sides of my panties, dragging them down my legs.

I hold on to his shoulders as I step out of my panties, letting him lead me to the tub and help me in.

The warm water sloshes around my ankles, and heat creeps up my legs, unthawing me, a little bit at a time. I sit down, briefly closing my eyes and sighing in relief as warmth surrounds me on all sides. Keanu keeps his eyes down, not looking at my naked body, and my heart kick-starts as my limbs unfreeze.

"Thank you," I whisper. "You're a good man, Keanu."

His eyes meet mine. "You're scaring me, Sel. I don't want to leave you in here like this. You're not going to…"

"No." I shake my head, knowing exactly where his head has gone.

In the weeks following my escape, after I discovered my family was murdered because of me, I contemplated ending it all. Tried a couple of times. Slit my wrists the first time. Tried to overdose on my prescription meds the second time. Put Mom through hell. A stint in a psychiatric unit helped pull me out of that suicidal abyss, and I haven't considered it again, promising myself I would fight to survive. To live.

But I didn't stick to that promise, and I've only really begun fighting back these past couple years.

As shocked as I am right now, killing myself hasn't crossed my mind. Although I understand why Keanu has expressed concern.

"Join me?" I ask, and he staggers back in shock, clutching the edge of the marble countertop.

"What?" he splutters.

"Hold me?"

He stares at me like he's imagining I've suggested this. And I get it. We've never taken a bath together. He's never seen me fully naked let alone held me like that. Although we have made out, and he has touched me, it never went very far because I was terrified of intimacy.

But I'm working through all that now, and in this moment, I want him in here with me. There isn't anything sexual in my need, but it's still a big deal for me. Because I have no fear. There is only determination. I know what I want and need, and I need this. My body needs this. And I'm letting those base instincts guide me.

This whole time, I'm staring at him, beseeching him with my eyes.

He pulls his T-shirt up over his head, revealing his ripped upper torso. "If you change your mind, at any time, you only need to say it."

"I trust you." And I really do. Keanu would never hurt me.

I look away as he lowers his jeans, and I scoot forward in the tub, trailing my fingers through the warm water, feeling its soothing power washing over me. The water sloshes as he steps in behind me, and I'm waiting for the panic or the terror to take control of me, but it doesn't arrive. When he's situated, I lean back against his warm, bare chest, resting my head on his collarbone. His hands land gently on my waist, and his touch ignites flames and fans the fire at the same time. Heating and cooling me both at once.

We don't talk for ages. We don't do anything except lie against one another, skin to skin, hugging and absorbing all the potent emotions swirling between us.

"The girl in the picture, the one holding onto my arm, was my friend Juanita," I say after a while. "You know I've wondered what happened to her."

"I remember."

"Something happened when I looked at that photo," I explain. "A flashback of sorts."

His entire body stiffens behind me. "What did you see?"

"I've always thought I didn't know what happened after that first night, when we were separated and taken away in different cars, but that isn't true." I know I have blanked stuff from my mind, because Denise and I have discussed this, and as I've begun talking about my experiences in more detail, other things have returned to me.

But I've never recalled anything about Juanita.

Until now.

"That picture was taken a few days after we were abducted," I say. "Freddie had drugged me. The last thing I remember was him shoving me in a black van, and when I woke up, I was in a seedy motel where he—"

Knots twist in my gut as I remember those early days. I remember waking up confused and dazed in a strange room. I remember my head spinning. How dry my mouth was. How I ached everywhere. I'll never forget the abject terror and the constant pain. I don't want to relive it, but I push through.

"He stripped me and sexually assaulted me," I whisper, and Keanu's arms move fully around my waist, as he hauls me closer.

"You don't have to tell me." I hate how his voice breaks.

"I want to," I truthfully admit. Keanu knows the basics, but I've never given him many details. "I've spent a lot of time going over stuff with Denise, and although it's painful, it helps me to process it." I angle my head, looking up at him, not surprised to see tears in his eyes. "I don't want to keep things from you, K. Unless it's too upsetting for you." I hate hurting him, and if the truth is too much, then I won't tell him.

"I've often wondered if it was better I didn't know too much or if it was worse because my mind has conjured up pictures of what they did to you anyway."

"I doubt anything you imagined is as bad as the reality."

"I want to kill them all," he says over a sob. "I want to fucking kill every bastard who put his hands on you without permission. Every motherfucker who hurt you."

"I want them to rot in jail, being raped and beaten by other inmates so they get a taste of their own medicine," I calmly say. "But more than that, I want justice for me and for Juanita and all those other boys and girls they tortured. I want to stop them from taking anyone else."

It's one of my biggest sources of guilt and regret. That it's taken me this long to get myself together. I should have helped the authorities more when I was first rescued. I could have done much more to help catch these fiends. It's why I won't hesitate now. If Keven's boss is willing to help, I will tell them anything I know. No matter how hard that will be.

"Juanita was taken by Freddie's right-hand man, Hudson. An evil piece of shit. She was assaulted too, but they didn't rape us because they needed us pure so they could auction our virginity for the highest price." Although I didn't know that at the time. "On the second night, we left the motel, and Freddie took me to an abandoned warehouse where I was loaded on that truck with a bunch of other girls. That's when I was reunited with Juanita and I found out what had happened to her."

I stop to draw a long breath, and Keanu kisses my temple. I lift my hands, linking them through his around my waist. "I can't remember everything. Just that it was hot as hell. We were hungry and thirsty and so fucking scared. Some of the girls were talking. Whispering about where we were going."

That's where I first heard mention of the private island that would become my own personal hell.

Tears prick my eyes as the memories float through my damaged brain. "Eventually the truck stopped, and we were told to get out. I don't know where it was, only that it was stifling. Hot and humid. There were several men there," I say, bile flooding my throat. "And we were separated into different groups." I gnaw on the inside of my cheek. "Juanita went crazy when they pulled us apart. She kicked and screamed and cussed when some guy with a bulging belly grabbed hold of her, trying to take her toward a red van."

My mind recalls it so vividly now. Tears streak down my face. "She kicked him in the balls, and he grabbed her by the hair, screaming at her in a foreign language. She spat in his face, and he shoved her to the ground, took out a gun, and shot her in the back of the head."

I'm full-on crying now, and Keanu turns me in his arms until I'm curled up against him. "There was blood everywhere, and all the girls were crying. I'd fallen to my knees, and I couldn't stop screaming. Until Freddie yanked me up by my shoulders and told me that would be me next if I didn't shut up and do what I was told."

My tears dry up, and I shudder in his arms despite the warmth of the water. "Something vital died in me that day." I stare deep into his devastated blue eyes. "A switch went off."

"You went into survival mode," he whispers.

I nod over the painful lump in my throat. "I was only ten, and I'd just seen my best friend killed, but somehow, I just knew that I had to do whatever they said to survive."

"It's why you are here today. It's that inner strength you've always had—even when you refused to see it. I've always known it resides in you."

"The trauma of that day forced the memories from my mind. Every day, for years, I've thought of Juanita. Wondered where she was or if she was still alive, when I've known all along that she was dead."

"Your mind was protecting you the only way it knew how."

"She was my best friend, Keanu. And I blanked how she died." I stare at him. "If I could forget that, what else have I purposely pushed from my mind?"

Chapter Fourteen
Keanu

Selena sleeps fretfully, waking up crying and screaming, shaking and clinging to me in the bed. I don't sleep a wink. I can't. I'm too worried about her. And I'm so fucking mad at my brother for showing her that picture. *What the hell was he thinking?* I know he didn't mean to hurt her, and in some warped way, it might have helped. But I can't agree it makes it okay. Not when my girl is in agony. Drowning under the weight of the new memories that have resurfaced.

I kiss the top of her head, inhaling the delicate scent of her hair. I still can't believe she let me take a bath with her. That she let me hold her and comfort her, wash and dry her, and help her into her sleep clothes.

I tried not to look. Not wanting to take advantage of the situation when she was vulnerable and broken. But it was hard. I'm a guy, and the girl I love was naked in my arms. I'm grateful I managed to control my cock and didn't harden against her. It wasn't challenging when she started talking because the horror of her abduction killed any lust lounging under the surface.

I want to take this girl and shelter her from the world.

If I could find a hideout where we could disappear to and live out the rest of our days in blissful ignorance and safety, I would do it.

But I know that's only a fantasy. That it's not what she needs. She can't run from her past, especially not when she's working so hard to confront it head-on.

I hate that Selena thinks she's weak when she's one of the strongest people I know. I've seen moments of clarity, where she believes that too, but her mind is struggling to hold on to that belief in the midst of what's happening now.

I want to be her strength until she's able to reclaim what's already inside her.

She stirs in my arms, whimpering as she wakes up. "Morning, baby," I whisper, pressing a kiss to her hair.

"What time is it?" she asks in a sleepy voice.

"Early. It's not even seven. You should go back to sleep."

"I can't." She shifts, and her leg slides in between mine.

Discreetly, I push my butt back, leaving more of a gap between our bodies so my morning wood doesn't poke her and make her uncomfortable.

"I was wondering if you wanted to get out of the city?" I ask, threading my fingers through her hair. It's in soft waves this morning because I only did a quick blow-dry on it last night after we got out of the tub.

She peers up at me, and my heart bangs around my ribcage. Selena is fucking gorgeous, and it's so difficult keeping my hands to myself. "And go where?"

"To my parent's place in Wellesley." A frown dents her smooth forehead. "The house is massive, and it's only Mom and Dad there. We also have a guest cabin on the grounds. We could stay there if you want complete privacy. It's nice and peaceful. We could go for a walk in the woods or take a swim, and we have a gym and a home theater."

I shrug, trying to downplay it, but I'd love to take Selena home. She's never been to the house. And I want to take her there. She already knows Mom and Dad, and they will stay out of our way if I ask them to.

"I think I'd like that," she says after a few beats, and I can't contain my goofy grin.

"Yeah?"

She smiles, and I want to kiss her so fucking badly. "Yes. Getting out of the city is just what I need."

"Cool." I continue playing with her hair. "I love this look on you," I admit.

"Thanks." She bites on the corner of her lip. "I wanted to change things up, and dying my hair was part of my plan of taking back control."

I nod, having already figured that out.

"And I thought it might help conceal my identity should I run into any of those monsters." She gulps, and her anxiety is palpable. "You know, it's always there." Her eyes fix mine in place. "The fear of them finding me. Or me bumping into them. I've lived with that every day since I escaped. But I learned to deal with it." She sighs, shaking her head. "And now, it's becoming reality." Her voice trembles, and I pull her into my chest.

"No one is letting him get near you, Sel. We're going to keep you safe."

We pack a bag and grab some breakfast, and I leave a note for Kent before we hit the road.

Selena is quiet on the journey, but she looks more relaxed, and I know this is the right decision. I've already texted Mom to let her know we're coming and not to make a big deal of it.

"Wow," Selena says as we enter the gates to my parent's large estate and I drive past the landscaped front lawn with multicolored flowerbeds and leafy shrubs. "I had no idea it was this big."

When Mom was at the helm of KA, she used to have flowerbeds

with the logo proudly displayed. In fact, Mom was a bit of a freak when it came to branded shit around the house. I can't tell you how often we got shade thrown at us in school. Since she sold the company, she's removed the branding and our house feels more like a home now.

"It's just home to me," I say, shrugging as I round the corner. The modern one-story property looms large in front of us, extending across the length of the estate, farther than the eye can see. Our house is composed of glass and wood with different angled roofs, and it's a sophisticated-looking building. Selena's eyes are out on stalks as we drive past the front of the house toward the garage, and I chuckle. That's usually the reaction when people see it for the first time.

I park my X5 and kill the engine. "You still okay with this?"

She nods, smiling. "Definitely. I'm glad we came."

My heart soars to bursting point. "I've always wanted to take you home. I can't describe how happy I am that you're finally here."

"I'm happy to be here." She leans across the console to place a kiss on my cheek. "Thank you for always being so patient with me. I know most guys would not have put up with the things I put you through."

"I'm not most guys," I say, cradling the back of her head. "And you didn't put me through anything." I rest my forehead on hers. "I was with you because I wanted to be with you. Because I love you. Every part of you. You have the purest soul and the purest heart, and I was drawn to you from the first moment we met."

Soft lips brush my mouth, and I gasp.

Selena pulls back, and her eyes glow with emotion as she brushes her thumb along my lower lip. "I felt it too," she says. "Although it confused and scared me." I nod, completely understanding. "But there is no other man I want by my side. There never has been. It's always been you." Briefly, I wonder about that Todd guy she was at Torment with. I want to ask her about him, but I'm fearful it will ruin the mood, and I just want to enjoy being with her.

Tears stab my eyes, and I can't speak over the messy ball of emotion in my throat.

"I love you, K," she whispers. "And I want to be with you—if you'll still have me."

I pull her over the console, settling her in my lap, and I hold her to me, feeling a deep sense of contentment that's been missing these last couple years. "I want to be with you too. I love you, Selena. For always." Most guys in my shoes would probably deny the girl who callously broke things off, stomping all over their heart. But I'm not most guys. And Selena's not like other girls. Our situation is different, and I'm not going to play hard to get just to get back at her.

We both want this, and while we still have stuff to discuss, I know we'll work through it.

I have faith in us.

Faith in her.

She won't hurt me again. I'm sure of it.

"We still need to talk," she says, resting her head on my shoulder.

"And we will. Tonight." I run my hand up and down her back. "But I'd like to enjoy our day. Just enjoy each other's company because I have missed you so much."

"I would love that too." She lifts her head, cupping my face. "But I'd like to request one thing."

"Anything. You know that."

Her hands drop from my face, and I instantly miss her caress. She worries her lip between her teeth, and I know she's nervous. She gulps, and I can almost see the cogs turning in her head as she considers how to say whatever it is she wants to say. I wait her out, not in a rush, letting her speak at her own pace.

"I've always loved how careful you are around me. How you ask permission before touching me. Or make slow, deliberate movements so I know what to expect." The little amber flecks in her hazel eyes flare brightly. "But your touch is soothing to me. More than that. I...I crave it, and I need it, and I don't want you to hold back anymore."

I frown, not quite sure I understand the point she's making. "What are you saying?"

"I want you to touch me freely, K. Whenever you feel like it. If you want to take my hand or wrap your arms around me or run your fingers up and down my arm, then I want you to just do it. Don't ask permission, and don't warn me. Do what comes naturally and I—" She gulps again, and a rosy-pink flush stains her delicate cheeks. "I want to be able to touch you too." Her cheeks flush darker. "I just want to be a normal couple."

"What about kissing? And other stuff?" I'm ecstatic at this change in direction, but I need to know the boundaries.

"Can we build up to that?"

"Absolutely." I don't hesitate to reassure her. And even though I long to kiss the shit out of her and do so many other things, I would wait for eternity if that's what she needs.

"Just so we're clear, I want all that with you." Her eyes turn glassy. "I'm ready to experience that with you."

Her small hands land on my chest, and I suck in a sharp breath. I can't believe what she's saying, because I've desired it for far too long. "So, I can casually touch you for now, and we'll build up to doing more," I say, wanting to ensure I've grasped it correctly.

"There is nothing casual about your touch," she says, "but yes. That's what I mean."

Her eyes drift to my mouth, and I think she's thinking about kissing me. Electricity sizzles in the space between us, and I know she can feel my cock hardening underneath her. I go to remove her from my lap, but she shakes her head. "Don't," she whispers. "I like feeling what I do to you."

"I want to kiss you so badly right now," I admit.

"I know," she whispers, caressing my face again. "But baby steps. And we need to talk. I need to explain before anything goes any further."

I nod, circling my arms around her shoulders and pulling her close. "I love you, and I'm never letting you go, Sel. Not ever again."

She doesn't reply to that, but it's okay. We'll have plenty of time to talk later.

Chapter Fifteen
Keanu

"Sweetheart," Mom says, beaming at Selena. "We're so happy to have you here." Behind her, my dad smiles warmly at me. My grin is so wide it's threatening to split my face in two.

"We're going to stay at the cabin," I say, holding Selena's hand more firmly.

"It was cleaned recently, but let me ask Lucinda to double-check. Ensure the bed linen is fresh," Mom says.

"Why don't we grab some coffee and sit out in the sunroom?" Dad suggests.

"That sounds great," Selena says, smiling shyly at my dad. Mom kisses me on the cheek, grinning as widely as me, before heading off in search of our new housekeeper.

"You two go sit down, and I'll make the coffee," Dad says, heading through the living room en route to the kitchen while I dump our bag underneath the sweeping staircase, leading Selena out the back way to the sunroom.

"I'll give you a tour after coffee, and then, we can drop off our stuff."

"Your house is beautiful," Selena says, glancing all around her.

"Mom has done a full upgrade on the interiors the past couple years. This place has been her testing ground for her interior design business."

Mom and Mrs. McConaughey, Brad's mom, set up a new joint venture a few years ago, and it's thriving. Brad is my brother Kyler's best friend, but he's more like a brother, having spent a lot of time in our house from the time they were young.

Mom and Brad's mom have ambitious plans to expand their business in the next couple years, and I'm happy for them. Mom needs to work. To have something to occupy her brain. And this time, she's going about it the right way. Employing a skilled team as she builds and grows the business so she's not working crazy hours or away from home very often.

When she was the majority shareholder and CEO of Kennedy Apparel, she traveled a lot. Both within the US and overseas. Dad was a stay-at-home dad, and we got used to Mom not being around. None of us liked it even though Dad did his best. I was luckier than my brothers because I worked at KA and got to see Mom there. But there are certain times when you need your mother, and there were plenty of occasions when she just wasn't there.

It caused some issues in our household growing up, and I know Mom feels huge guilt, but things are better now. We all have a much stronger relationship with her, and I love that she's close by whenever I need her. I also love her for caring about Selena so much. And I don't need to be a mind reader to know both my parents are delighted to see us here. Together. My parents know Selena has a beautiful heart, and I think Mom's always known she is the only woman for me.

In a lot of ways, Selena is like the daughter Mom never had. At least, she was until Faye showed up. Kyler's wife came to live with us when she was seventeen, and Mom is crazy about her. They are very close. More so than Mom is with her other daughters-in-law even though I know she loves all the girls with her whole heart.

"I see what you mean," Selena says as we walk into the sunroom.

She steps close to the window, staring at the grounds outside. The wide windows offer a perfect view over the sweeping landscape with expansive manicured lawns, a rose garden, tennis and basketball courts, putting green, outdoor pool and pool house, and the thick woods at the very rear of the garden. "This place is magical."

I come up behind her, about to open my mouth and ask before I remember the new rules. I'm still cautious as I wrap my arms around her from behind, but she doesn't flinch or give any indication she's uncomfortable, sinking into my embrace with a contented sigh. I rest my chin on her shoulder, momentarily closing my eyes as I enjoy the feel of her in my arms. "I love you, Sel."

She's smiling as she turns her head slightly to look up at me. "You just told me in the car."

I rub my nose against hers. "Is there a limit to how often I can tell you I love you?"

"Nope." She rubs her nose against mine. "No limit. I will never tire of hearing you say that, because I worried my actions had lost you to me forever. I will never take your love for granted."

My gaze lowers to her mouth before darting to her eyes, seeking permission even though I know she said we had to build up to this. If I don't kiss her soon, I think I'll combust.

"Keanu," she whispers, licking her lips as her eyes latch onto my mouth. "You make my heart beat so fast." Her eyes rise to mine, and I see the same desire reflected in her gaze. Her pupils are darker, burning with heat, and we move toward one another at the same time.

"Am I interrupting?"

We jerk apart at my dad's words, and Selena blushes.

"Awesome timing, Dad," I deadpan.

"Anytime, son," he teases, grinning madly as he places a tray with coffee and homemade cookies on the table in front of the wicker couch.

I guide Selena to the couch, sitting beside her as Dad takes the seat opposite us.

"Alex tells me you beat off some stiff competition to win the Miranda Fanning campaign," Dad says, mid-slurp. "Congratulations, Selena. That's an amazing achievement."

"Thank you." She blows on the top of the mug, and visions of her blowing across the tip of my cock surface out of nowhere.

Fucking hell. I have it so bad.

I dismiss the visual before I turn to stone in my pants.

"And congratulations to you and Alex. She was so happy when she told me you two were back together," Selena says, leaning back in the couch. I sling my arm around her shoulders, keeping her close.

"Life is good, Selena." Dad exudes happiness in spades. Both my parents do. My brothers and I are overjoyed they are giving their marriage another try. "I have the love of my life back in my arms. It doesn't get much better than this."

"Amen to that," I say, without hesitation, staring into Selena's gorgeous eyes.

"If Kent was here, he'd give both of us so much shit for that statement." Dad crosses one leg over his knee, grinning. "How is he doing?"

"He's good," I say, breaking a cookie in half and handing a piece to Selena.

Sel is naturally slender, and she doesn't have to watch what she eats like a lot of the models I work with. I've seen a lot of shit in the industry, and I'm glad Sel has stayed wholesome. That she doesn't snort coke like it's going out of fashion purely to curb her appetite and stay reed thin. That she doesn't purge after eating or refuse to eat at all. There is a lot I hate about the industry, and when I set up my own business, if I choose to set up a modeling agency, I plan to do things differently. "And he's agreed to stop throwing parties while Selena is staying with us so that can only be a good thing."

"All we need now is to find him a good woman." Dad waggles his brows.

"Find who a good woman?" Mom asks, joining us.

"Kent," Dad says, pulling her down onto his lap.

I beam at my parents, loving how readily they pack on the PDAs these days. Some might hate their parents pawing at one another, but I love seeing it. As long as I don't see *too much*, because that shit would be gross as fuck.

"It's going to take a brave, strong woman to tame my Kent," Mom says. "But I've no doubt the right woman is out there somewhere."

"He could have already met her," I say, draining the last of my coffee.

"Please, don't go there." Mom groans. "Whitney isn't right for Kent. They are not right for one another."

Whitney is Faye's half-sister and her and Kent had an on-off thing going for years whenever they saw one another. However, things were getting messy, and Kent put an end to it last year. I don't know if she's the one for him or not, because Kent won't talk about her to me, but maybe, she is. Maybe, they need to be apart too. Maybe, they'll find a way back to one another. Stranger things have happened.

"Maybe, the timing isn't right," Selena says, as if she has a hotline to my thoughts.

She has a hotline to my heart, and it's almost the same thing.

"Timing is everything," Mom agrees, pressing a soft kiss to my dad's lips.

"And that's our cue to leave." I stand, bringing Sel with me.

"Do you want to come by for dinner later?" Mom asks.

"Thanks, but we'll do our own thing," I say.

Mom nods agreeably. "Well, stay for dinner tomorrow then." She ruffles my hair. "We don't see enough of you with your busy schedule."

I glance at Selena, and approval is swimming in her eyes. "Sure."

"Perfect." Mom kisses my cheek. "We'll see you two later."

I give Selena a guided tour of the main house and the outer grounds before leading her out onto the path that runs through the woods and beyond to the guesthouse. We hold hands as we walk slowly through the forest, passing by the bungalow Lana and her parents lived in.

Lana is my brother Kalvin's wife, and she grew up with us because her mom was our housekeeper and her dad was the groundskeeper, up until a few years ago. Lana and Kal live in Florida now with their three-year-old son Hewson.

Sel and I shoot the shit as we walk, and I can't tell you the last time I felt this happy.

All thoughts of the danger Selena is in are firmly in the back of my mind, where I'm determined they will stay for the remainder of this weekend. Selena needs to unwind, and I want this weekend to be about her. About us. About reconnecting.

A blast of heat greets us as we step foot in the cabin, and the scent of fresh pine wafts through the air. A bag of groceries sits on the kitchen counter, and I smile at Lucinda's thoughtfulness. Or perhaps it was Mom.

I open the door to the corridor with the bedrooms, opening the second door to the largest room. "Are you okay to share with me, or do you want your own room?" I ask as I tentatively set our weekend bag on the floor.

"I want to share with you," she says, her eyes sweeping over the rustic room with the four-poster bed dressed in white and gold drapes with matching linens. "This room is pretty." She skims her hand along the wall, smiling, looking relaxed and happy.

We take a dip in the indoor swimming pool and unwind in the Jacuzzi, our hands and bodies never far apart. I feel like pinching myself because this doesn't feel real. It's like I've woken up in dreamland, because I've always imagined this with Sel, and I honestly thought it was out of reach.

Back at the cabin, we enjoy a late lunch of cheese, crackers, and fruit before curling up on the couch, watching back-to-back movies. I order takeout for dinner, and we resume cuddling on the couch as I scroll through the movie options, trying to find something more manly than the last two cheesy chick flicks we just watched.

Selena sits up abruptly, turning around and sitting cross-legged, her pretty face scrunched up in concern.

"What's wrong?" I ask, tossing the remote away and sitting up straight.

"Can we talk now?"

I examine the anxious expression on her face. "We don't have to talk if it's making you nervous."

"I want to get this off my chest. And you deserve the truth."

I switch the TV off and twist around on the couch so I'm facing her. "Okay."

She draws a brave breath and begins.

Chapter Sixteen
Selena

"The summer before senior year, I made a promise to myself that I wouldn't let my past control me anymore. That I was going to fight harder to claim the life I wanted. But with that decision came a hard realization." I move closer, taking his hands in mine.

This will hurt, but I can't lie.

"I hid behind you, Keanu," I softly say. "You sheltered me. You were my protector. Always jumping into battle for me. I didn't go anywhere or do anything without you, and I realized that I couldn't move forward if I didn't learn to do things for myself."

"I would have given you all the space you needed," he says.

"I know you would have, because you are selfless and you always did everything on my terms. But that was a problem too."

His brows knit together, and I don't blame him for being confused.

"Relationships are partnerships," I say. "And it doesn't work if one person is *taking* all the time and the other never gets anything in return." And, by default, that reality always made me feel weak, which fueled more guilt and self-loathing.

He opens his mouth to protest again, but I silence him by placing a finger to his lips. "I know you want to respond to this, but, please, let me tell you my side first."

I'm afraid I'll lose my nerve if I don't just get this out.

He nods, always so agreeable. Always trying to make things better for me. I don't know how I got so lucky to find such an amazing guy, and this time, I'm determined to hold on to him.

"That's how I felt. Like I leaned on you to do everything for me and that you gave of yourself when I gave you nothing back. And I love you so much I wanted more for you. I want to be your equal in every respect." I take his hands in mine, steeling myself for this next revelation. "You were saving your virginity for me, and I wasn't worthy, because I didn't know if I could ever be intimate with you. I didn't want to take that from you. You deserve a normal life. To go on dates without worrying about crowds or the possibility your girlfriend might have a meltdown in public. To have a normal sex life and not be afraid to touch your girlfriend for fear it might trigger something in her."

"What you and I shared was our normal, and I was more than satisfied with that," he says.

"But for how long, Keanu? How long would that have been enough? How long before the sexual frustration got to you and things became complicated?" I hold up my hand. "Those questions aren't meant to be answered. Maybe, I was wrong. Maybe, it wouldn't have come to that, but there was only one thing worse than imagining my life without you in it, and that was the possibility that my illness would tarnish the good years, mess up all the good memories I had of us together."

I chew on the corner of my mouth. "But that was only one part of it. The other was my need to move forward. To get a handle on my issues and start dealing with them." I slap a hand over my heart. "I knew I couldn't do that if I was your girlfriend. I knew I would continue to lean on you instead of pushing through my fears, pushing myself out of my comfort zone, and I knew if I was to be truly worthy of you that I needed to make a clean break. To set you free. And I hoped that by the time I was the woman I knew I could be, that it wouldn't be too late. That I would still own your heart in the way you have always owned mine."

"It still belongs to you, Sel. No one else has ever owned a piece of my heart," he confirms, moving closer to me.

"As mine still belongs to you."

His eyes penetrate mine, and that intense connection between us simmers and pulses.

"It took months before I plucked up the courage to end things," I continue. "I wanted to be completely truthful, but I knew if I told you these things that you'd never let me go. That you'd convince me we could do it together, so I lied. I told you I wasn't into it anymore, and all the time, my heart was ripping to shreds in my chest." I clasp his face in my palms. "It killed me pushing you away. I had a physical pain because it hurt so much. For the first couple of months, I picked up the phone to call you at least once a day. I regretted it as much as I knew it was the right thing to do. I was terrified I'd lost you forever, and *I missed you.*"

My voice breaks, and tears spill down my cheeks. "God, I missed you so much. It was like I was missing a limb. Like half my soul had disappeared. I didn't feel whole. I felt empty. And in those early months, my anxiety increased and I suffered more panic attacks, but gradually, it started to fade. I worked out a program with Denise, and she gave me little tasks. Things I had to do that would force me to engage with the outside world. Say hello to my neighbor instead of ignoring his greeting like I usually did. Go shopping on my own for an hour. Visit a museum or a café alone."

I rub circles on the back of his hand with my thumb. "It terrified me. I had the worst anxiety before I'd do each little task, but I did it, and I felt such a huge sense of achievement with each accomplishment. Denise insisted I reward myself for each milestone, so I give myself little treats. And we dug a new flowerbed in her garden, and for every task I achieved, I planted a new flower." I smile proudly. "It's almost overgrown now."

Emotion swims in his eyes, and he holds my hands tighter.

"I built up to bigger things over the time we were apart, and now, I can go for a swim or attend a yoga class by myself. I travel to and from school by myself. I attend classes and go to the library. I still struggle to make friends. Engaging in small talk with strangers is hell, but I met Kelly, and we became instant best friends. We do lunch and go to the movies and go shopping. I've been to nightclubs and bars. Still not my favorite thing to do, but it doesn't send me into a tailspin anymore. I do location shoots. I go to New York for shoots with Miranda. Mom usually comes with me, because I'm still not brave enough to travel there by myself, but it's one of my next goals."

"I'm so proud of you, Sel," he says, "and I have noticed the changes. I love seeing you more confident in yourself. More independent."

"Thank you. I'm proud of me too, but there is still more to do. I realize it'll most likely always be something I have to deal with. That the fear and guilt will always linger. That I'll have good days and bad days. But I'm confident I can handle it now in a way I couldn't when we were dating. I needed to learn to stand on my own two feet instead of letting you fight all my battles. Does that make sense?"

"It does, but at the time, I was blindsided and heartbroken. I just focused on us. I thought I wasn't good enough for you." His eyes scream an apology as he admits this next truth. "That I wasn't attractive enough in your eyes. I convinced myself that if I was hot enough you wouldn't have been able to resist me."

I hate that I caused him to have so much self-doubt. "Trust me, if you were any hotter, I'd spontaneously combust whenever I'm near you. You're so gorgeous, Keanu, and I *want you*, never doubt that. You are perfect, inside and out. Every single part of who you are is attractive to me. Sometimes, the sensations were so intense they frightened me to pieces. I didn't know how to process those feelings. My sexuality was, *is*, all tangled up. I'm trying to separate it now. To understand that what happened to me is completely different from sharing intimacy with the man I love."

I lean in and kiss the corner of his mouth. "In case you're still in doubt, that man is you."

"I believe you, and I can't believe I didn't see it."

"I didn't want you to see it. I wanted you to believe the lie because I wasn't strong enough if you tried to fight for me. I'm not proud of myself, and I hate that I hurt you, but we needed that time apart, Keanu. And not just for me. We both needed to grow and learn to live in a world without one another."

He reels me into his lap. "Please tell me we're done learning life lessons." He nips gently at my earlobe.

"I will never be done learning," I say, fighting a bout of delicious shivers. "But I'm done living in a world without you."

With my heart pumping wildly, I turn around and straddle him, placing my arms around his neck. "It was becoming increasingly difficult to stay away from you," I admit. "But I wasn't quite ready to come back to you. I was getting there, but events overtook me."

"I'm not happy you're in danger or that you're scared," he says, pressing wet kisses along the column of my neck. "But I'm thankful you came back to me. That we have this second chance. I understand now why you did what you did." With gentle hands, he turns my head so we're staring deep into one another's eyes. "You said earlier you wanted to be my equal, and I want you to know you already are. Your illness does not make you any less in my eyes. We were a team, Selena. We *are* a team. In any relationship, there are times when one partner needs the other more. And that's what a relationship is. Being there for one another. I see that with my brothers and their girls. Supporting one another at times of need is not a weakness. It's what you do when you love someone as much as we love one another. Right now, you may need me more, but trust me, there will come a time when I'll need to lean on you in the same way, and you will be there for me. Because you *are* my equal. In all the ways that count."

"I truly don't deserve you," I say through my tears. "You are the most amazing man, and I feel blessed that you are giving me, *us,* another chance."

"I'm not going to lie, Sel," he says, tucking my hair back behind my ears. "I've gone through stages where I was so angry with you I believed I hated you. And I can't say the hurt and anger have disappeared overnight because that kind of pain doesn't just evaporate, but I want this with you. I want to share my life with you. And I accept that comes with good and bad times, but I'm ready to weather that storm with you."

"I want that too, and I promise I will never push you away again or lie to you. I will always be honest and truthful."

"You can't make those kinds of decisions for me again, Sel. I need to be a part of it. I need to have a say. It's the only way it will work, and I want this to work." He kisses my cheek. "I want this to work so very much." He kisses my other cheek, and a trail of fiery tingles whip up and down my body, igniting a fuse deep inside me.

Instinctively, I press in closer to him, and butterflies flood my chest when I feel his hardness pushing against me.

He freezes, looking up at me with worry etched across his handsome face. "You turn me on so much, Sel, but I don't ever want you to feel pressured into anything. I want to make love to you, one day, but I'll wait as long as you need me to. That hasn't changed."

"I want that too. And I'm almost there."

"There is no rush and no need to set a timeline."

I smile at this sweet, sweet man. "I agree, and I want it to be natural and for it to happen when we are both in the same place." I tighten my arms around his neck, leaning down close to his face. "But right now, I badly need something else from you."

"Anything," he rasps, his eyes drenched with desire.

My eyes burn with need for him. "Kiss me, Keanu. I need to feel your lips against mine again."

Chapter Seventeen
Keanu

I've been dying to kiss her from the instant she reappeared in my life, so I'm not wasting another second. Angling my head, I close the small gap between our faces and press soft lips to her mouth. Her lips move more urgently against mine, and I let her set the pace, matching her kiss for kiss, so happy it feels like I could burst. Gently, I lap at the seam of her lips with my tongue, and she opens for me. I lick inside her mouth, our tongues softly stroking one another, and I instinctively pull her in closer to my body so we're flush against one another, chest to chest, hip to hip.

It takes mammoth effort not to rock my hard-on against her, but we're taking this one step at a time, and despite her earlier plea, I don't want to do anything that will startle her or upset her.

She runs her fingers through my hair as we kiss, and precum leaks from the crown of my cock. I swear I could come like this. When she moans into my mouth, I almost do, and my cock twitches, pressing against her of its own volition, my erection straining against the denim of my jeans. I still for a nanosecond, but her lips continue to worship mine, and I relax into our make-out session, kissing her like a starving man who has just stumbled across the most decadent feast.

I lose track of time, and I've no clue how long we kiss for, but eventually, we break apart, both panting and flushed with swollen lips and massive grins. "I've missed kissing you so much," I say.

"Me too." Her expression and her tone are dreamy, and I mentally fist pump the air.

Leaning in, I rub my nose up the elegant column of her neck, inhaling her signature scent. "So, it's official?" I ask against her throbbing pulse. "We are boyfriend and girlfriend again?"

"To me, we are way more than that. But officially, publicly, yes."

I lift my lips from her neck, staring into her gleaming eyes. "Publicly?"

She nods, smiling. "No more hiding, K." She pecks my lips, and a contented sigh slips out. "At least not from our families and friends. But I heard what Keven said last night and we can't go *public,* public."

I know what she means. We need to keep this private, within our circle, until the threat has passed.

"I don't want anything to happen to you," she adds. "And it's best we maintain separation in the public eye so you don't become a target."

"I can't wait for the day when I can shout from the rooftops that you are mine," I reply, "but I agree we need to keep this close for now."

Her cell pings, and she slides off my lap to grab it from the table. I immediately miss her warmth. "It's my friend Kelly," she says, reading a text. Her fingers fly over the phone keypad as she taps out a reply. "Would it be okay if she dropped by your condo tomorrow so I can fill her in?"

"Of course. But we won't be back until tomorrow evening."

"I'll tell her that."

We watch another movie, cuddling on the couch, and I can't keep my hands or my lips off her. We're kissing so much we miss huge chunks of the movie, but neither of us cares.

We're making up for lost time.

"It really is so peaceful here," Selena says, drawing back the comforter and climbing into the bed later that night.

I'm happy she's happy here. I was a little concerned the silence might trigger her, but she appears relaxed and content. I open my arms for her. "I love coming here. It's a welcome break from the hustle and bustle of the city."

"I love this cabin," she adds, turning on her side and snuggling into me. "It's perfect."

"This used to be party central when we were younger," I admit. "My brothers and I used to sneak out of the main house and throw parties here. There was a rear entrance my parents didn't know about, and kids from school sneaked in that way. I didn't attend often, but let's just say they were pretty wild."

"I didn't know that," she says, spearing me with an inquisitive expression.

"I never mentioned it because I knew you would never come. I didn't want you to feel bad. And I loved spending my weekend nights hanging out at your house with you. I've never been big into partying."

Except for the last couple years.

I punt kick that meddling devil off my shoulder even if that inner voice is right.

At some stage, I'm going to have to fess up to Selena. To tell her all the shit I've done in our time apart. My gut tightens at the thought.

What she thinks of me matters.

And she's bound to be disappointed.

A part of me just wants to get it out there, but I'm not telling her tonight. I don't want to ruin one of the best days of my life, and I know she'll be upset when she hears.

"Promise me, from now on, you'll tell me when there are parties or events." She cups my cheek. "I meant what I said. I want to do normal stuff with you. Don't shield any of that from me."

I press a kiss to her palm. "I won't. We're in this together."

"We are." A devilish smile graces her mouth. "Now, if we're done talking, I'm ready for you to kiss me again."

"Not sick of me yet?" I tease, clasping the nape of her neck.

"Never," she whispers over my lips. "I will never tire of you."

I kiss her with more determination this time, sweeping my tongue into her mouth, stifling a groan as she meets my determination with a level of her own. Soon, we are grinding against one another, our hands exploring with urgency, and I'm worried I'm passing the point of no return. My need for her is building to an all-consuming no-turning-back point, and she's not ready for that part of me yet. Reluctantly, I break the kiss, pausing to draw a breath and compose myself.

"What's wrong?" she pants.

"Absolutely nothing—except you're too fucking gorgeous and I'm having trouble controlling myself."

"Then don't," she blurts, her cheeks staining red.

"Sel." My face contorts in pain. "I know you said you wanted spontaneous, but I think we should plan the first time we make love."

"I agree," she says, nodding, "but right now, I want you to touch me and I...I want to touch you."

My cock, already down with this plan, throbs behind my pajama pants.

"You need to tell me where you want me to touch you." This is not something I'm comfortable second-guessing. I need clear guidance so I don't do anything that will upset her.

She takes my hand, pulling it down to her pajama-covered chest. "Touch me here."

"Lie flat on your back," I whisper, and she obliges. Her white-blonde hair fans out around her on the pillow, and she looks like an angel fallen to Earth. "You are so Goddamned beautiful, Selena." I graze my fingers along her face, then down onto her neck, across her collarbone, and lower. My pulse is pounding, my fingers shaky as I slide my hand over her tits, gently caressing them through the material of her sleep top.

A soft moan leaves her lips, and she arches her body into my hand. "More," she whispers, looking at me with complete trust.

I glide my hand down her stomach, slipping my fingers under the hem of her top, moving them up her soft silky flesh. Her breathing becomes exaggerated, and I keep my eyes on hers as my fingers reach the underside of her breasts. "Is this okay?"

"Uh-huh," she pants, and a smile tugs up the corners of my mouth.

I gulp back my fear as my hands aim higher, skimming over her tits, my fingers brushing the hard tips of her nipples.

"More," she says, her voice firmer this time.

Our eyes meet, and I read everything she's conveying. Blood rushes south, and I'm hard as steel in my pants. She sits up, lifting her arms, and I remove her top, tossing it on the floor by the bed. She lies back down, her hair spreading out around her like a halo, and my eyes roam her bare upper torso. Her tits are perfect handfuls. Small, soft mounds with neat, rosy nipples. The marks on her delicate skin are like battle scars—scars she wears more proudly now.

To me, they represent strength. Survival.

To Selena, they've always served as a reminder of a past she longs to forget.

Before, she would only let me touch her in the dark, so this is new. And further proof of how far along the road my girl has traveled. She is so strong. So brave. So inspiring.

"You're beautiful, Selena," I whisper, rubbing my thumbs back and forth across her nipples. Slowly, I bend down and take one puckered tip into my mouth. I lick the tight nubs with feather-soft brushes of my tongue, gently sucking, being careful not to be too hard or too rough, and I keep my eyes on her at all times. The second this stops being enjoyable, I will retract.

"Keanu." Her whisper is a desperate plea, and I arch a brow. "I'm aching for you." She bites down on her lip, spearing me with a silent command.

"What do you need, baby?" I ask, caressing her tits, trying to stop my rock-hard cock from poking a hole through my cotton pajama pants.

"Touch me down there," she says, and I almost tumble off the bed in shock.

I've never properly touched her pussy because the one and only time I tried to finger her, she broke down sobbing, and I never tried again. Nerves rattle my bones, and I'm not sure about this at all. "I want to, but are you sure, baby?" I clasp her face in my palms. "There is no rush."

"I need you, Keanu," she pleads. "And I promise if it hurts or I don't like it I'll tell you to stop, but I want you to try."

My heart is galloping around my chest and blood rushes to my ears as I peel back the covers, gripping the sides of her sleep shorts and pulling them down her long, lean legs. I spread her thighs ever so gently and start kissing my way up her leg, starting at her ankle. I alternate my gaze between her leg and her face, looking for any signs she's uncomfortable, but by the way she's writhing and mewling I know there is only pleasure. My heart surges with strong emotion as I kiss my way up her legs until I've reached her heavenly place.

I brush my fingers against her lace-covered core in a barely there touch, and she almost bucks off the bed. My eyes beseech hers.

"Please don't stop. This feels too good."

Encouraged by her words, I bring my mouth down, kissing her over her flimsy panties.

A guttural moan filters through the air, and I peel her panties away, leaving her exposed to me. I part her pussy lips, gently stroking her with my tongue, licking a quick line along her slit, watching her reaction carefully. I continue licking and stroking her with my tongue, and when she cries out for more, I suction my mouth over the bundle of nerves, sucking deep. I want to insert my fingers inside her, but I'm afraid, so I use my tongue to bring her to orgasm instead.

Her body bucks and thrashes as her climax consumes her body, and I keep my mouth on her, all the time watching for any signs I should stop. But there is no evident discomfort or upset, and my heart surges with joy at the obvious pleasure on her face.

I did that.

I put that look there.

And I want to continue doing it. To continue giving her pleasure. To show her how good it can be between us.

When her body quiets down, and I've milked every last drop of her arousal, I crawl up beside her, tugging the covers over us. "Was that okay?" I croak, stroking my fingers through her hair.

"Keanu." Her eyes open as she clutches on to me, and then, she starts crying.

Everything locks up inside me.

What the fuck have I done?

"Selena, I'm so sorry. I—"

She shakes her head, tears leaking out of her eyes. "Don't," she says. "Don't apologize." She presses her mouth softly and sweetly against mine, and I taste the salty tears on her lips. "That was the most amazing feeling ever." She smiles through her tears, beaming at me, looking at me with so much adoration it feels like I could conquer mountains. "You just gave me my first orgasm, and it was everything, Keanu. *Everything.*"

Chapter Eighteen
Selena

I wake the following morning tucked under Keanu's arm, feeling warm and safe, and I can't stop the giant smile that ghosts over my face as I recall last night. Yesterday was one of the best days of my life, and I'm still bathed in a happy glow. Keanu's soft snore confirms he's still asleep behind me, and I decide to take advantage of the fact I'm awake first.

He wouldn't let me reciprocate last night even though I wanted to touch him, to bring him the same pleasure he'd brought me, but he insisted it was all about me, so I want to do something nice for him today. I'm going to cook him blueberry pancakes and bring it in to him in bed.

I creep out from under the covers like a skilled spy, careful not to wake my Sleeping Beauty.

I stare at him for a moment, admiring his gorgeous form, and my heart is so full of love. His hair is all messy from my fingers, and the light layer of scruff on his chin and cheeks has me blushing as I remember how it felt brushing against the apex of my thighs. His lips part ever so slightly, and a pang of longing hits me in the chest. Keanu is an amazing kisser, and I don't think I'll ever get enough of his mouth on mine. He looks so peaceful and so young when he's asleep, and I want to capture the expression, so I take out my cell and take a sneaky pic of him, setting it as my screensaver.

I'm already dressed in my sleep shorts and top, having put them back on last night, but I grab my silk robe from our bag, tying it around my waist and padding out to the kitchen in my bare feet.

I put some music on my cell as I prepare the batter, keeping the volume down low so I don't wake my man, and I'm singing along to Ariana Grande when strong arms wrap around my waist from behind. I jump, startled, dropping the whisk in the batter. Keanu freezes. "Shit, sorry. I didn't mean to creep up on you."

"It's okay." I spin around in his arms. "Any boyfriend sneaking up on his girlfriend like this would make her startle." I shrug. "It's normal, and nothing could ruin my happy buzz today."

His answering smile melts me into a puddle of goo, and I fall even deeper in love with him. "Fuck. I love you." He swoops in, claiming my mouth as he bends me back a little, laying a passionate kiss on my lips.

"I love you too," I murmur, when we come up for air, circling my arms around his neck. "So, so much. You make me unbelievably happy."

"My mission in life is to bring you happiness."

"Well, you're damn good at it."

He chuckles. "Kent is going to give me shit when he sees how loved up we are."

"He can try." I slide out of his arms, returning my attention to my pancake batter. "But I think I have your brother wrapped around my pinkie already. I'll make him behave."

Keanu cracks up laughing. "I would pay good money to see that."

I playfully swat at his chest. "I accept your challenge," I joke. "Now, go shower, and when you return, I'll have breakfast ready."

"You didn't have to do that," he says, his eyes softening.

"I know. I wanted to. You always spoil me, and now, I want to spoil you."

He stares at me with glistening eyes. "This is like a dream come true. I wished for this."

Oh my. This guy. He slays me all the time. *How is he so sweet? So perfect? How is he mine?*

"You're the stuff dreams are made of," I say, stretching up to kiss him. "And I'm so happy we found our way back to one another."

After breakfast, we play some games on the Xbox and spend an amusing half hour looking through old photo albums. Keanu was such a cute baby, an adorable kid, and I especially love the photos of him as a young teenager because it reminds me of when we met. After, I spend some time helping Alex to prepare the family meal, enjoying listening to her talk about her new business venture, and her grandkids, and her plans for the renewal of vows ceremony which is taking place just after Keanu's twentieth birthday.

"Look who I found," James says, coming into the kitchen with Kyler and Faye in tow. Keanu appears from behind them, instantly moving to my side.

"What a lovely surprise!" Alex dries her hands on some paper towels before flinging her arms around Faye and Kyler, dragging them into a group hug.

"We were on our way back from the cabin," Faye says when Alex releases them. "And thought we'd stop by."

"I'd have been pissed if you didn't," Alex says.

"Hey, man." Kyler walks to us, pulling Keanu into a quick man hug. They slap each other on the back.

"Good to see you," Keanu says, sliding his arm around my waist. "You remember Selena?"

"Of course. It's nice to see you again." Kyler smiles warmly at me.

"You too," I quietly say.

"So, are you two back together?" he asks, quirking a brow at his brother.

"Oh my God." Faye rolls her eyes as she loops her arm through her husband's. "Ignore him. He has no tact."

"It's cool," I say, shooting Faye a smile.

"And yes, we're together," Keanu says, beaming at me. "Now and always." He links his fingers through mine. "Nothing or no one is separating us again."

"Aw." Faye places a hand over her heart. "That is so sweet and romantic."

"Maybe, now, you'll stop sulking like a toddler," Kyler says, smirking at Keanu as he leans around him, swiping a bread roll from the basket.

Keanu flips him the middle finger. "Bite me, asshole."

Alex swats the back of Keanu's head. "Language, Keanu. Especially in front of your girl."

I giggle, and Keanu's entire face lights up as he stares at me, his adoration clear to see.

"Man, you have it bad." Kyler chuckles, folding his arms, his gaze jumping between me and Keanu.

"Hey, you're in no position to throw shade. We all remember how googly-eyed you were over Faye."

"You mean how googly-eyed he *still* is." Faye slides her arms around her husband's neck, smiling up at him.

"Damn straight, babe." Kyler puts his hands on her waist, pulling her in for a kiss, uncaring that they have an audience.

"Love you," Faye says, rubbing her nose against his.

"Love you too," Kyler replies, cupping her face and pressing his lips to hers.

"This is so amazing! Everyone's in love," Alex says, and she's practically singing it. "And Kalvin and Lana are having another baby, and Eva is due to give birth just after Christmas. I'm so happy I think I might explode."

James pulls her into his side. "Please don't. I've only just got you back."

Keanu kisses the top of my head, pulling me around in front of him, and draping his arms around me. "You sure you're ready to be a part of my crazy family?"

"Nothing would make me happier," I say, realizing how true it is.

For years, I was afraid of people, afraid of what I'd say or how I'd behave around others, but being here just feels so natural and there is so much love in this room that it's impossible not to feel comfortable, to feel at home.

Faye and Kyler stay to eat with us, and they are the sweetest couple. Faye makes a huge effort to include me in the conversation, and she even invites us to come stay at their Connecticut cabin. She takes my cell number so we can make arrangements, and I can tell Keanu is pleased that I'm getting along with his family.

Faye and Kyler leave first, to head back to Harvard, and we stroll back to the cabin to pack up our things.

"We hope to see you again soon, Selena," James says a half hour later when we're ready to leave. Alex hugs Keanu, whispering in his ear.

"Thank you so much for having me. It's been a fantastic week-end." In more ways than one. My cheeks heat as my mind recalls the orgasm Keanu coaxed from me last night.

"It's wonderful to see a smile on Keanu's face again," he adds, glancing over his shoulder at his wife and son. "Kyler may have been joking earlier, but Keanu hasn't been this happy in a long time. You're good for him."

I blush profusely at his praise, but I can't deny how amazing it is to feel so openly accepted. "He's good for me too."

"Selena, honey." Alex slowly opens her arms and I hug her. "Thank you for loving my son," she whispers in my ear. "You've no idea how happy you've made him."

"Mom. Stop." Keanu gently pulls me from his mother's arms, reeling me into his embrace. "You're all going to scare her away. It's too much."

"It's good," I say, smiling. "I've had the best weekend. Thank you again."

"Hopefully, we'll see you soon," Alex says, "but, if not, we'll see you at the ceremony and party in November."

"I'll be here." I reconfirm what was already discussed and agreed around the dinner table.

"Are you sure you had a good time?" Keanu asks when we're in the car on our way back to Cambridge.

"I really did. The cabin was perfect, and your family was so welcoming."

He takes my hand, linking our fingers. "I always knew they'd love you. Well, Mom already did. You'll meet the others at the party next month, and they are going to love you too. Thank you for agreeing to come with me."

I tuck my hair behind my ears as I face him. "I told you. I'm with you all the way now."

Kent isn't at the condo when we arrive, so we have the place to ourselves. My anxiety levels increased the closer we got to Boston, and now I'm back here, I'm remembering all the stuff I'd successfully blocked this weekend.

"You look tense. What's going on?" Keanu asks, a frown appearing on his handsome face.

I rub the back of my neck. "It was nice to escape reality for a while, but now, I have to face up to it, and I'm already on edge."

"That's a normal reaction, babe." He holds my hips, pulling me toward him. "But we're being proactive, and this time next week, you'll feel much better with the new security system and the extra precautions at your mom's place. Plus, hopefully, Kev's boss will have agreed to help us and we'll have the FBI on board." He kisses my forehead. "It's going to be okay."

"I've been thinking about something," I say, hauling him over to the couch with me. We sit down, and he waits for me to speak. "You know how I recalled that memory of Juanita from the picture?" He nods. "Well, I've been wondering what else I might be blanking and if there is something I can do about it, like, maybe, undergo hypnosis."

"Is that something you've tried before?"

I shake my head. "Denise has mentioned it in the past, but I can't remember exactly what she said. I'm going to talk to her about it on Wednesday, and I'm going to do some research of my own."

"Maybe, if your brain has subconsciously hidden stuff, it might return naturally anyway?"

"I'd rather tackle it head-on than risk a memory coming back to me unexpectedly and me freaking out again."

"There's no harm in exploring options. Let's find out more, and we can take it from there," he says, and I love how he says *we*, confirming he's fully in this with me.

I leave Keanu downstairs for a while to do some yoga and deep breathing in his bedroom, and I'm surprised when I hear Kelly shouting up the stairs for me. The urgent quality to her tone has me jumping up and racing down the stairs in my sports bra and yoga pants. I slam to a halt in the living room, my mouth gaping open at the sight of Keanu with his hands around Todd's throat as he shoves him up against a wall.

"Do something!" Kelly pleads, her eyes beseeching me, and I snap out of it, rushing over to the guys.

"K!" I tug on his arm, trying to pry him away from Todd. "Let Todd go."

"What the hell is *he* doing here, Selena?" Keanu grits out, still holding Todd in his tight grip.

"He's Kelly's boyfriend! And he's turning blue. Let him down!"

"What?" Keanu lets go of him immediately, turning to face me. Todd slumps to the floor with a thud, and Kelly dashes to his side.

"Todd is Kelly's boyfriend." I know why Keanu has reacted like this. Clearly, he thought we were together at some point. I may have perpetuated that idea by not confirming Todd was only a friend. But last year, at the club, when we bumped into one another, I was in a panic, terrified I wouldn't be strong enough to stay away from him, so I used his confusion to my advantage. "Kelly was with us that night in

Torment, but she was in the bathroom when you and Kent approached us."

"So, you didn't date him?"

"No. I haven't ever dated anyone but you."

"Aw, shit." Keanu scrubs his hands down the front of his face before extending his arm to Todd. "Man, I'm sorry. I jumped to the wrong conclusion."

Kelly glares at Keanu, and I don't blame her. Todd takes Keanu's hand, letting him pull him to his feet. "It's all good, man."

"This is my fault," I explain to Kelly and Todd. "I should have told Keanu, but I wasn't aware Todd was stopping by too."

"We were late leaving Vermont," Kelly explains, "and I thought I'd drop by now rather than going back to the dorms and having to come out again later."

"Makes sense." I look at Todd, grimacing as he rubs his sore neck. "Are you okay?"

"I'll live." He eyes Keanu warily, and, if I'm not mistaken, with a little more respect.

"How about I make coffee? And Keanu's mom gave us some gorgeous chocolate cake." I eyeball my friend and her boyfriend. "Peace offering?"

"Deal," Kelly says. "But your boy can make it." She jabs her finger in the air in Keanu's direction, pinning him with a loaded look, daring him to argue. "Because you and I need to talk."

Chapter Nineteen
Keanu

The week passes quickly, and it's as if Selena has always lived with us. I love going to bed with her at night and waking up with her in my arms. I still have to pinch myself to believe it's real. Even Kent seems comfortable with her staying here, and he's taking the time to talk with her, to get to know her, and they are starting to bond in a way I never imagined happening.

Kev came over on Wednesday evening while I took Sel to her appointment with Denise. He had the new security system installed by the time we returned to the condo, and he explained how it worked to all three of us. We must set it every time we leave and put it on part guard when we head to bed at night. Should anyone attempt to get in, it will emit an internal alarm and notify Keven as well as Morgan Security, the company we are using for bodyguard protection. The guard on duty at night tends to rotate, so, this way, the security company will be aware, and they can touch base with whoever is on duty at the time.

It gives me peace of mind, because the longer that asshole is out freely roaming the streets of Boston, the more I worry. Sel is taking the necessary precautions though. She understands the risk, and she's fully cooperating. Her bodyguards go everywhere with her, and that's the only reason I'm not ditching my classes to shadow her.

On Friday night, we catch dinner and a movie after classes end, and it's past eleven by the time we arrive at our place. Sounds of female laughter tickle my eardrums as we approach our front door, and my jaw tenses as I prepare to face whatever lies in wait. I keep Selena behind me for protection as I tentatively swing the door open.

I suppose I should be grateful it's not a party. But the sight of Kent sprawled across the couch in only his boxer briefs with two half-naked chicks running their hands over every inch of him is still enough to fuel my anger.

He promised he'd keep this shit confined to the privacy of his bedroom. "What the actual fuck?" I snap, glaring at my brother. I should've known his saintly act wouldn't last for too long.

"What, dude?" He looks at me through unfocused, bloodshot eyes, a smug smirk plastered on his mouth.

Selena closes the door behind us, sliding around the perimeter of the room, making a beeline for the stairs.

"We had an agreement," I say through gritted teeth, watching my girlfriend lowering her eyes to the floor as she attempts to escape upstairs.

"Keanu. Baby." The brunette with the big, fake tits hops up, wobbling from side to side as she moves toward me in a barely there red lace bra and matching thong.

It's Casey.

Oh, hell to the no.

I glare harder at Kent. After my run-in with her at the last party, he promised me he wouldn't bring her back here again. She is a headache I most definitely could do without right now. Things have been going amazing with Selena, and this chick has the power to wreck everything.

Casey reaches for me, but I jerk back out of her hold. Selena stops at the base of the stairs, turning to stare at me with unspoken questions in her eyes.

I rub a tense spot between my brows, contemplating throttling my brother.

"Don't be like that, baby." Casey pouts, tripping over her feet and barreling into my chest. "You can join in. Like last time. It'll be fun."

"Yeah, Keanu," Blondie says, glancing over her shoulder and grinning at me as she strokes Kent's cock through his boxers. "Maybe, this time, you'll fuck my ass."

Selena's face drains of all color as I pry Casey off my chest. She's pawing at my crotch and yanking on the waistband of my jeans, trying to get her hands on my cock.

"Fucking stop!" I jump sideways before she lunges at me again. Panic jams my throat, and I glance at Selena, praying she'll let me explain. "Get your fucking hands off me!" I shout as Casey reaches for me again. "I am sick of repeating myself." I glare at her, a muscle ticking in my jaw.

If they fuck things up for me with Selena, I will go postal on all their asses.

"I'm. Not. Interested." I pin furious eyes on Casey and Blondie. "I have a girlfriend," I add, moving quickly to Selena's side.

Selena hasn't moved a muscle, like she's frozen in time. She's pale and painfully quiet, and I could fucking murder Kent for this. She flinches when I curl my arm around her waist, and it kills me, because she's trying to close herself off for the first time since she came back into my life. I'm not letting that happen, so I tuck her protectively into my side, keeping a firm hold of her so she knows this is where she always belongs. "And you are all being disrespectful to her."

Casey pouts, planting her hands on her hips, as she rakes her gaze over Selena. A sneer spreads across her mouth.

"Hey," Blondie slurs, continuing to stroke Kent's cock, "you're that model."

"So what if she's a model," Casey hisses, shooting daggers at Selena. "She's got no tits." Casey grabs her overinflated fake chest, squishing both breasts together. "And I remember how much you loved playing with these babies, Keanu," she says, pulling the cups of her bra down to expose her tits. "She can't satisfy you like I can."

Selena wrenches out from under my arm and races up the stairs without uttering a word.

I turn to rip Kent a new one, but he's already on his feet, a look of murderous rage on his face. "Get the fuck out, whore," he slurs, pointing at Casey. "And don't come back." He picks up her clothes, thrusting them at her.

"What?" she screeches. "You can't throw me out for telling the truth."

"Like fuck he can't," I say. "Get the hell out and stay out. You are not welcome here."

"You heard my brother," Kent adds. "Get lost."

"Screw you, asshole. You're not even that good of a fuck."

"Savannah. C'mon." She looks over Kent's shoulder at her friend.

"Who says I'm leaving?" Savannah says, licking her lips as she pushes to her feet.

"Me," Kent says. He runs his hands through his hair. "Both of you, get the fuck out."

"Assholes." Savannah glowers at both of us, but I couldn't give two shits.

My foot taps idly off the floor as I wait for them to get dressed. I need to go to Selena, but I want to make sure these bitches are out of here first.

I turn the full extent of my anger on Kent the second the door shuts behind them. "You promised me you wouldn't do this."

"We can't all be fucking perfect," he slurs, prodding me in the chest. "And I need sex. Fucking deal with it!"

"So, entertain your fuck buddies in your damn bedroom!" I roar. "Have you any idea how much you've upset Selena?"

"Fuck you, asshole." He drops back onto the couch, swiping his beer bottle off the floor, fixing me with a snide look I've seen countless times on his face when he's drunk. "Don't pin this on me. This is all *you!*"

"Tell me what you really think, *brother*." My fists clench at my side. I'm not usually the violent one in my family, but right now, I want to ram my fist in my brother's sneering face.

"You fucked your way around campus knowing that shit might get back to her." He swigs from his beer. "Not my fault you didn't come clean." He shrugs, and I want to punch him again. "This is my place, and I'll fuck *whoever* I want *whenever* I want *wherever* I want. You don't get to dictate to me." He points his beer in my direction, and I'm so mad I could spit. "You should've told her you turned into a man-whore after she dumped you. It's your fault she learned that the hard way."

"You're a dick," I seethe, hating that he's partly right. "I was going to tell her when the time was right." I stalk toward the stairs, stopping at the bottom and turning around. "I don't want to see either of them in here again. And next time, take your whores up to your room!"

I bound up the stairs, two at a time, approaching my bedroom with caution, knowing I need to have this conversation with Selena now, but I'm fearful she'll have a change of heart about me.

About us.

I take a few minutes to calm down, because bursting in there in a fit of rage won't help my cause.

She's in the shower when I enter the room, so I change into pajama pants and sit on top of the comforter with my back to the wall and my knees bent while I wait for her to finish.

Steam billows out of the bathroom when the door finally opens and she appears, dressed in pajama shorts and a thin pajama top. Her hair is damp, pulled into a loose braid.

When her anguished eyes meet mine, I wish I had a time machine so I could rewind the last half an hour. Screw that thought. I wish I could go back two years in time and wipe the whole slate clean. Erase all my mistakes and remove the reason she's hurting right now.

"I need to explain," I croak, patting the empty space beside me. "Come sit."

She pads around the bed, crawling up beside me but careful to leave a big gap between us. It feels prophetic. "I'm sorry about that."

"It's not your fault," she says in a quiet voice, tucking her legs close to her chest. "And you don't have to explain. We were broken up. You didn't do anything wrong."

I twist around so I'm facing her and take her hands, grateful when she doesn't resist. I need to be looking at her and touching her when I tell her this. "I know all that, but I still should've told you. I was going to, I swear, just not yet. We were only finding our way back to one another, and I was terrified my past actions might ruin everything. I don't want to lose you, Sel. I couldn't bear it again." I palm one side of her beautiful face. "I love you. More than I love anyone or anything in this world. Please tell me you know that?"

"I do." Her fingers curl around mine, and it's the encouragement I need to go on. To get this out.

"When we broke up, I was devastated, Sel. Heartbroken. Couldn't eat. Couldn't sleep. I was a wreck." I wet my dry lips, wishing I had done things differently. "But then, I got angry. I was mad at you for leading me on. Furious with myself for buying into your lies." Even though I know now they weren't lies, I was so confused back then. It was the only logical conclusion.

Fuck, this is so hard to tell her.

Although I want to avert my eyes, I keep them fixed on her beautiful hazel ones. "I got fed up feeling too many emotions, so I started going out with Kent, drinking to numb the pain. To help me forget." I could blame my brother for encouraging me to get under someone else in order to forget about Selena. But only a coward would do that.

It's all on me. And I need to own it.

"I always thought I'd lose my virginity to you. It's what I wanted. But then you broke up with me, and I was losing my mind, and I thought it would be a *fuck you* to you if I gave it to someone else, so I hooked up with this girl I met at Torment."

Tears well in her eyes, and I have a physical pain in my heart.

"She meant nothing. It meant nothing. And I regretted it straight away." Truth.

She swipes at her tears. "It's okay. I don't blame you."

"Don't, Sel. Please." This time, I do look away. I'm disgusted with myself. And I wish this was the worst of it, but there are more damning revelations to come. "I fucked up. I know I did, and I'm not proud of myself. I hooked up with other girls, thinking it would help me feel better. It didn't."

"And those girls downstairs?" she whispers.

I squeeze my eyes shut. "I've had a few threesomes and foursomes with Kent." I wince as the words leave my mouth, knowing how awful this is for her to hear. "We were with those girls one night, months ago. I told Casey I wasn't interested, but she doesn't take no for an answer."

"I see." Her eyes drop to her lap, and she tries to wrest her hands from mine, but I'm having none of it. I clasp her hands firmly, and she stops fighting.

"None of them mattered. I never dated or slept with anyone more than once. And I stopped it altogether after our family vacation to Nantucket in July because I realized how unhappy it was making me. It wasn't helping. It was having the opposite effect, because all it did was reinforce that they weren't you. And seeing my brothers in love—while I'm happy for them—only made me sadder. Made me miss you and our relationship so much. I felt even more lonely."

Silence engulfs us, and I couldn't hate myself any more in this moment if I tried. "Say something," I whisper.

"I will never be good enough for you," she says, and my heart cracks wide open. "How can I compete with girls like Casey?" She lifts her head, and tears spill out of the corners of her eyes. "I'm all screwed up, and sex will never be that uncomplicated for me."

"Sel." I cup her face, but she averts her eyes. "Please look at me, baby." Her tormented gaze slowly rises to meet mine. "You're not in competition with Casey. With anyone. Because there is *no competition*. Every girl pales in comparison to you. You are all I see. All I need. All I want." I press a fierce kiss to her forehead. "And I'll take complicated over any other girl any day. Even if we never have sex, you are the only woman I want. Please don't let what happened downstairs, or what happened while we were apart, ruin what we share. What we are building here, because that would kill me, Sel. I can't lose you again."

I pull her into my lap, relieved when she doesn't struggle. "I'm not proud of my behavior, and I wish I could go back in time and undo it all, but I can't. All I can promise you is that it's in the past. You are my present and my future. My everything."

Chapter Twenty
Selena

I wake up the next morning before Keanu, and I stare at his face for a long time while my mind churns with all he revealed last night.

I'm not an idiot.

Keanu is hot, sweet, sexy, and, most of all, *a guy*. A guy who has been deprived of sex and intimacy during his horny teenage years. I knew when I cut him loose that this would happen.

Releasing Keanu was not just for me.

It was for him too.

I was holding him back in a lot of ways but especially when it came to sex. I knew, deep down, that letting him go meant he would experience other girls. Experience sex without me. And I thought I'd made my peace with that.

But I haven't.

And I can't blame him. *I don't.* Like I told him repeatedly last night, he hasn't done anything wrong. I should be grateful all his hookups were casual and meaningless.

But I'm not.

For one, I'm jealous. The thought of other women with their

hands on him makes me green with envy. And all night, as thoughts of him having sex with other girls taunted me, I've been red with rage. Chastising myself for not being strong enough, brave enough, to have sex with him, at least one fucking time, before I let him go. Because those other women have experienced a side of him I don't know, and I hate that they shared that with him when I haven't.

But there's another part of me that's sad that all his experiences were meaningless. Because I didn't want that for him either.

Ugh. I scrub at my forehead, wishing I could yank all these thoughts out and make sense of them. I'm confusing myself, upsetting myself, when I'm the one who set this in motion. I'm conflicted and emotional, and today is the worst day to be dealing with this shit.

I stare at him again, watching his chest rising and falling, as he sleeps. I want to grab hold of him and keep him close. To lose myself in him. To experience what those women experienced. To show him I'm better than all of them. That I can pleasure him far better than they can. That I know everything there is to know about how to turn a man on because I was trained from age ten to please men.

And I need that affirmation to know I'm good enough for him.

My inner voice whispers my mind is warped for thinking these things, but I banish that voice, shutting off logic and acting on instinct.

Because I'm afraid now. Afraid I'm never going to be good enough for him. I know the kinds of needs men have. I stupidly thought it didn't matter when I was with him before because he was a virgin and he didn't know any better.

But he does now.

And I need to show him I can fulfil *all* his needs. That I'm the perfect girlfriend. That I'm not broken and vulnerable. That I'm strong and sexy and willing.

Before I overthink it, I slide down the bed, carefully pulling Keanu's pajama pants down, freeing his penis. All week, we've made out like demons, and he's gone down on me a couple other times, but he hasn't let me touch him.

That stops now.

His erection juts out proudly, and I lower my head, curling my lips around the tip and licking his slit. I take him deeper into my mouth as he stirs, hollowing my cheeks to take all of him into my mouth, feeling him hit the back of my throat as I suck his hard length in and out of my mouth.

He groans, and his hips thrust forward as he slowly starts fucking my mouth. I reach my hand under him, playing with his balls, and his entire body stills. His hips stop bucking, and I glance up at him, panic welling in my chest at the look of abject horror on his face. I loosen my grip on his erection the same time he pulls back with so much force and urgency he falls out of the bed.

My heart is pounding, and a thin line of sweat glides down my back. I gulp over the painful lump in my throat.

"Selena," Keanu rasps, pulling up his pants and slowly rising to his feet. He stares at me like I've just sprouted horns. "What...what are you doing?"

I sit up on my knees. "I want to make you come."

His Adam's apple jumps in his throat as he sits on the edge of the bed, turning to face me. "Why?"

"Why?" I frown, because isn't it obvious? "Because I want to please you."

He grimaces, and my heart lurches to my toes. "You didn't like it? It wasn't good?" Rejection takes a bat to my body, slamming into me and knocking all the air out of my lungs.

"Selena. No." He reaches for my hands, but I scoot away from him on the bed, swiping at the tears leaking from my eyes.

"Baby." He climbs over the bed, kneeling in front of me. "Don't think that. Of course, I liked it. I woke up to the love of my life sucking me off. And it was so fucking good."

"Why did you stop then? Why did you look at me like that?"

He brushes tears away from under my eyes. "You shocked me, baby, and it worried me."

I blink at him, not understanding. "Why? And were you like this with the other girls you slept with?"

He grimaces again. "Selena." He presses a lingering kiss to my forehead. "Firstly, you're the only woman I've ever slept in a bed beside. And, secondly, I'm not opposed to being woken up with your mouth on me, provided it's for the right reasons."

"I wanted to make you come. Isn't that the right reason?"

"C'mere, baby." He opens his arms and pats his lap. I crawl onto him, wrapping my arms around his neck and resting my head on his shoulder. "I need to ask you a question, and I want you to answer it honestly."

"Okay."

"Did you blowing me have anything to do with last night and what we discussed. Yes or no?"

I pause for a few beats. "Yes."

He tilts my face until we're eye to eye. "Talk to me. Tell me what's going through that beautiful head of yours."

I lift my head up fully, shifting on his lap so my legs are stretched out to the side. His penis is hard underneath me, reminding me of my epic fail. "I'm jealous of those girls," I admit after an eternity of silence when I've been battling with my response. But I won't keep secrets from him. I won't hide the truth. Even if I'm scared to admit my thoughts. "Because they've experienced parts of you I haven't."

"And what else?" he coaxes, threading his fingers in my hair.

"And I wanted to make you happy. To show you I know how to please you. That I can do it a million times better than they can."

Color leaches from his skin as pain washes across his face. Tears pool in his eyes as he moves closer, pressing his forehead to mine. "Jesus, Sel," he rasps, his voice cracking. "I don't need you to prove anything to me." Then he breaks down in my arms, sobbing as he clutches on to me, and I freeze. The only other time Keanu has cried in front of me was the night I told him what had happened to me.

And now, I feel like shit for upsetting him.

"I'm sorry, K," I whisper, as tears roll down my face. "I didn't want to upset you. I just wanted to make you happy."

"Selena." He lifts his head, peering at me as we both cry. "You make me happy every second of every day that you're by my side. You don't need to do...*that*, to do anything sexual, to make me happy." He chokes on a sob. "I love you!" he cries. "And getting to love you and to feel loved by you is all I need to be happy. I..." He wraps his arms around me, holding me close, and his body heaves underneath me, shuddering with gut-wrenching sobs. "God, Sel. I'm the one who's sorry. It's my fault for not saving myself for you. If I had, you wouldn't feel like this."

"No, Keanu!" I cry. "It's not your fault."

"But it is!" he says. "Now, you feel like you have something to prove, and I never want you to feel like you're forced into having sex with me!"

"I don't feel forced. I love you, and I want that with you. I want to make love to you."

He clasps my face firmly in his palms. "And I want to have sex with you. I want to *make love* to you. I crave it. But not like this! Not because you feel like you have to!"

"It's not like that!" I plead.

"Isn't it?" Pain shimmers in his eyes, and a wave of guilt sweeps over me.

I'm making a mess of everything. "No." I shuck out of his embrace, climbing to my feet. I pace the floor. "We're never going to get beyond this, are we? What's happened to me is always going to come between us. I will never be normal!" I cry out as tears stream down my face. I bend over, clutching my stomach, and my body throbs with pain. I feel it in every cell, every nerve ending, every molecule. "I will never be good enough for you."

I drop to my knees on the floor, sobbing.

Keanu is beside me in a heartbeat. "Baby, don't say that." He bundles me into his arms, and I collapse against his bare chest, crying tears all over his warm flesh. "We love each other, and we both want to take things to that level, but not like this." He kisses the top of my head. "It's going to work out, I promise."

"I feel like such a failure as a woman," I truthfully admit, snaking my arms around his waist and clinging to him. "Like I've failed you. I pushed you into those other women's arms because I couldn't give you what you needed."

"Stop it, Sel." Keanu forces my face up to his. "That is not what happened, and we both know it." Air whooshes out of his mouth as he stares at me. "I love you so fucking much. I wish I could open my chest, open my heart, so you could see how much. So you could know I would go to the ends of the Earth for you. Please don't give up on us, Sel. Please believe me when I say you are everything to me. You are the only woman that matters. And I want everything with you, but when it's right for both of us."

"Okay," I mumble, because I know he's right.

He carries me over to the bed, lying me down on top of the comforter. Brushing hair back from my face, he looks at me with so much love there's no doubt about the extent of his feelings. "I'd like to talk to Denise about this," he says. "Together." He links our hands. "Let's arrange a couple's session. We need to talk this through, to find our way to a place where we're able to make love for all the right reasons. Please?"

"You want to talk to her about something this intimate?"

"Yes. I trust her. And I know you do too. She'll help us figure it out."

"Okay." I nod. "I'll set it up."

Chapter Twenty-One
Selena

"Morning," Kent mumbles when I arrive downstairs in the kitchen. Keanu is taking a shower, so I'm cooking us a decent breakfast, because I don't know how long we'll be at the FBI offices for today.

"Morning," I reply, moving to the refrigerator.

"I'm sorry about last night, Selena," he says, watching as I remove eggs, onions, tomatoes, garlic, grated cheese, and spinach from the fridge.

"It's okay, Kent," I say even though it's really not okay.

I'm not okay.

Keanu's not okay.

But it isn't Kent's fault.

All of this would've come out anyway.

Although, having a visual of two of the girls Keanu slept with is something I could do without.

Nausea churns in my gut, but I force it away. I've enough anxiety about today as it is, without adding to it.

"No, it's not." He straightens up, pushing off the counter and grabbing a mug from the cabinet. "Coffee?"

I nod. "Thanks."

I start peeling the onion, chopping it along with the tomatoes and the garlic.

Kent hands me a steaming mug of coffee, and I force a smile out. "I'm making omelets. Would you like one?"

"Ugh." He rubs a hand over his flat stomach. "I'm sure it'll be delicious, but I'll pass. I'm a little delicate today." He waggles his brows, and this time, a genuine smile dances across my lips.

"I figured," I say, whisking eggs in a bowl. "I could smell the alcohol and weed the instant we stepped foot in the door last night." I worry about Kent. Especially with the drugs. I know how easy it is to become addicted, and that's not something I want to see happening to him.

"Not my finest hour," he admits.

"From what Keanu told me, that kind of stuff was a regular occurrence."

Kent has the decency to look sheepish. "Yeah."

I sigh, chopping the spinach more vigorously than necessary.

"Hey." Kent's voice softens. "What did the spinach ever do to you?"

I bark out a laugh, placing the knife down and rolling my shoulders, hoping to ease some of the tension sitting there. "Things are a little strained right now," I admit, sighing again as I clasp the mug between both hands. I lean back against the counter, mirroring Kent's position.

"That's my fault."

I shake my head. "It's not your fault or Keanu's. *It's mine.*" I shrug even though I'm locked up tighter than a bank vault. "It is what it is."

"If it's any consolation, he was miserable as sin the whole time he was apart from you. He adores you, Selena. You were all Keanu thought about that entire time. Trust me, he wasn't into any of those girls he hooked up with. Like, *at all*, and, to be honest, I pretty much pushed him into a lot of it." He rubs the back of his neck. "I'm a shitty brother."

"You're not a shitty brother."

He drops his eyes to the floor. "I am. For a variety of reasons."

"Well, if you're a shitty brother then I'm a shitty girlfriend," I blurt.

"Why would you say that?" Kent asks, genuine curiosity evident in his eyes.

I take a sip of my coffee, wondering if I should say this. But I'm guessing he already knows anyway. "If Keanu had been going out with any other girl, he wouldn't have still been a virgin at eighteen."

Surprise splays across Kent's face. "If you weren't ready, you weren't ready."

"It's more complicated than that."

He nods slowly. "I know that now." His tone is soft. "And Keanu doesn't hold it against you. He never has, and he never would."

"What if I'm never able to let it go, Kent? What if my past follows me around the rest of my life? How on Earth is that fair to him? To *me?*" I slap a hand across my chest, fighting a swelling of emotion. "Because I deserve to be normal. I want to make love with my boyfriend and not worry about falling apart!" I blurt.

Oh God. I can't believe I just said that. And to Keanu's man-whore brother of all people. I look away, embarrassed and pissed.

"Selena."

I tilt my head up.

"It'd be worse if you went the opposite way," he says. "If you used sex to try to fix the broken parts. You haven't done that, because you've got more respect for yourself and my brother."

I peer deep into his eyes, and I see so many hidden depths. Kent is nothing like I expected. I don't know if he's different with me because he thinks I'm that fragile or if he's showing me a part of himself he normally keeps locked up.

"I wish it was about respect," I say after a few beats of silence. "But it's more to do with fear and guilt."

We stare at one another again.

"What doesn't kill us makes us stronger, right?" he says, winking as he pushes off the counter, breaking whatever moment we were having.

"Yes," I whisper in agreement, long after he's exited the kitchen.

"Are you sure you don't want to postpone it?" Keanu asks again as we pull up outside the FBI offices in Chelsea.

"I'd rather get it over and done with."

"Baby." He takes my hand, rubbing soothing circles on my palm with his thumb. "We've had a rough night and a rough morning. We can move the meeting if you need more time."

"It won't make a bit of difference, K. I'll still be on edge tomorrow or next week or whenever I decided to do this. This isn't going to be pleasant or easy for either of us."

Pressure settles on my chest, pushing and pushing, until it feels like I can't breathe. I inhale deeply, drawing long breaths in and out, until the edgy feeling subsides. Keanu has already removed the lavender oil from his pocket, rubbing a couple drops on my wrist.

On instinct, I lean over and peck his lips. "You look after me so well."

"I love you, and I want to take care of you," he quietly admits. Worrying his lower lip between his teeth, he looks like he's contemplating something. "Forever, Sel. I want to take care of you forever. You get that, right?"

"Even if I—"

He places his fingers to my lips, shoving the words back inside. "Don't say it. We are going to have it all, Sel. I trust in us. In *you*. And maybe this hypnosis therapy will work."

I'd conducted some research on hypnotherapy before my Wednesday session with Denise, so I was somewhat informed. Denise explained hypnosis can help with unlocking traumatic memories and it might even enable me to process and heal in a quicker time frame, but it's not without risk, and it comes with no guarantees.

She has recommended EMDR therapy, which is a form of therapy that enables people to heal from the symptoms and emotional distress emanating from traumatic life experiences. She told me although it's widely assumed that severe emotional pain requires a long time to heal, this form of therapy has proven that the mind can heal from psychological trauma in the same way the body recovers from physical trauma. It's all centered around changing the neural pathways in the brain. She reminded me she had brought it up in the past, but I'd always dismissed it.

I don't remember that.

But I'm willing to give it a try now.

It might help uncover memories that will aid the FBI investigation. And it might give me some semblance of closure. Some peace of mind.

Denise said she had a patient who was a victim of sexual abuse as a child and the therapy made a vast difference in her healing. She recovered her memories and processed them, and it made a huge difference in her life. She couldn't go into details, for obvious reasons, but hearing that helped me make the decision to pursue it.

Denise knows a specialist who practices EMDR therapy, and she's arranging an initial consultation for me.

It's good to feel like I'm doing something. Because I need something to move forward.

I can't forget Clive Lawrence is in this city, not a million miles away from me, and he could discover me at any moment.

Although my bodyguards go everywhere with me and they drive me to and from school, yoga, and the grocery store, I'm still on edge. Still constantly looking over my shoulder. And I'm never going to move forward until I've dealt with him and other aspects of my past.

Which is why I need to do this today.

Keanu's troubled eyes meets mine as he waves his hand in front of my face. I zoned out, and now, *he's* panicking. "Sel?"

"I'm okay." I rub my thumb along his inviting lower lip. "I want them to catch that bastard so I stop worrying about him coming for me." Thankfully, Keven's boss agreed to investigate, and that's why we're here. I open the car door, glancing over my shoulder at my boyfriend. "C'mon. Let's do this."

"It's nice to meet you, Selena," Supervisory Special Agent Clement says when Keven ushers us into his superior's office a short while later. "Although I wish it were under more pleasant circumstances." He extends his arm to me, and I shake his hand.

"And you must be Keanu," the SSA says, and Keanu nods. "The family resemblance is striking."

"Thank you for agreeing to meet with us, sir." Keanu shakes his hand while keeping one arm locked around my waist.

"Please take a seat." He gestures toward a black leather couch at the other side of the room.

Keanu and I sit down on the couch while the SSA and Keven take two of the three chairs in front of us.

"We usually conduct these meetings in an interview room, but Sinead thought a more relaxed environment might suit better."

"Sinead, Agent Cunningham, is one of my colleagues," Keven explains. "She should be here any second now."

A sharp knock on the door heralds her arrival just as the words leave Keven's lips.

A slim woman in a gray pantsuit enters the room. Her dark hair is cut into an angular bob, framing a heart-shaped face and button nose. Her hips sway as she strides confidently to where we're sitting. She stops in front of me, placing a brown paper folder on the coffee table before extending her hand. "I'm Sinead. I'll be working on the investigation with Keven."

"I'm Selena, and this is Keanu." I take her hand, hoping she doesn't notice how badly I'm shaking.

"Thank you both for dropping by. I know this must be nerve-wracking," she says, sitting beside Keven. "But I want to reassure you anything you tell us will be treated with the utmost privacy. Our team has been working hard these past eighteen months to bring these criminals down, but we keep meeting roadblocks. We're hoping you might have some intel that will help us to break the case."

"I'm not sure that I do, but I'll tell you all I can." I clasp my necklace, tracing my fingers back and forth across the cold metal.

"Sometimes, even the smallest detail can matter," Keven says. "Some of these guys are already on our radar, but your knowledge could make all the difference."

Keanu takes my free hand, squeezing it firmly, and a layer of stress lifts off my shoulders.

"I thought it might be helpful to outline some of the background before we discuss the specifics of your case," the SSA says.

"Okay." I wet my dry lips, willing my heart to stop careening around my chest.

"If you need to take a break at any time, just let us know," Keven says, reassuring me with his eyes.

Another knock on the door elevates my blood pressure higher, and Keanu sits in closer, sliding his arm around my back, lending me more physical support.

A woman wearing a black skirt and white blouse enters the room, carrying a tray. She sets it down on the coffee table and leaves without uttering a word.

"Can I get you a coffee or some water, Selena?" Sinead asks.

"Water, please."

She pours water from a bottle into a glass, handing both to me. Kev pours Keanu and himself a coffee while the SSA and Sinead grab a water too. When everyone is settled, they begin to explain.

"There are several criminal organizations operating in the Massachusetts area," the SSA explains. "And their main sources of income are racketeering, drugs, guns, and the sex trade, specifically prostitution and the exploitation of minors."

"Like I explained," Kev adds, jumping in when the SSA looks to him to continue, "there's been an escalation in violence on the streets since Jeremy Garcia's death, Daniel Stanten's imprisonment, and Carmine Mancusso's passing. But it's still business as usual, and that means every week more girls are brought into the city and forced into prostitution. Sinead and I have been following the trail, and the supply is coming from two main areas. Mexico and Texas."

"However," Sinead says, picking up where Keven left off. "The operations in Mexico and Texas are supplying various different enti-ties, not just feeding the pipeline here in Massachusetts. We've heard rumors of an elite organization, headed by a powerful figure in the US political arena, that operates on a private island, off the coast of Florida."

My pulse thumps wildly in my neck, and sweat coats my palms. I sip my water, praying I keep it down.

"Our intel suggests this island is a haven for wealthy, powerful, well-connected men to indulge in illegal sexual activity with minors forced into prostitution," Keven says. "We are building profiles on some of these men, thanks to a few informants, and that is how Clive Lawrence first came to our attention."

"Does the name Gerald Allen, Junior mean anything to you?" The SSA asks as Sinead pulls a photo from the paper file now resting in her lap. "He's a senator from Florida."

My mouth turns as dry as the Gobi Desert.

"This is him," Sinead says, handing the picture to me. I put my water down and accept the photo with trembling fingers.

I stop breathing the second I glance at the photo. His mocking green eyes stare at me from behind a large, mahogany desk. His tailored suit and the expensive watch on his wrist, along with the opulence of his surroundings, convey power and confidence, and he looks like the classical definition of a successful businessman.

Except he's not.

He's a monster who preys on vulnerable children and exploits them for monetary gain.

My hand visibly shakes as I hold the photo, and I know everyone can see. My breath lodges in my throat and nausea churns in my gut as memories of encounters with that pervert flood my mind. Every muscle in my body is stretched tight, and a physical pain sits on my chest, compressing my air supply, making breathing difficult.

Keanu raises my wrist to my nose. "Breathe, baby. In and out. Nice and slow." I stare into his eyes as I focus on my breathing. Keanu's chest rises and falls in sync with mine, and his steady, supportive expression, as well as the scent of lavender on my skin, helps to quell the storm rising inside me.

"Are you okay to continue?" Sinead asks, and I'm grateful for the lack of pity in her matter-of-fact gaze.

I give a curt nod of my head, handing the photo back to her. "That's him," I quietly admit. "That's the man who owns the island."

"You've met him?" Sinead asks.

I nod again, looking down at my hand curled around Keanu's. "He came on the weekends when most of the parties took place," I explain. "Although, Freddie was the one who ran the island, ensuring everything went smoothly."

"So, you have been on the island?" Keven inquires.

"Yeah. When I was first taken there, I didn't know where I was. I could've been in outer space. We weren't allowed outside beyond the main facility, so I couldn't see for myself, but clients referred to it as an island, and when Lawrence took me with him, we went on a ship."

"Are you okay to look at some other profiles?" Sinead asks.

"Okay." I glance at Keanu, and he presses a kiss to my temple.

Sinead lays several photos on the coffee table. "Point to anyone you recognize. Anyone you remember seeing on the island."

I point out nine of the fourteen men in the photos.

The SSA and Keven trade a look.

"These men were on the island?" Sinead asks.

"Yes."

"You're sure?" she probes.

"I haven't forgotten any of their faces." Not when I've spent years regularly seeing them in my nightmares. "I'm sure."

"And what about these men?" Keven asks, laying another six photos down.

A violent shiver works its way through me as I stare into the face of pure evil. My stomach wrenches, and a strangled sound rips from my mouth. Keanu rubs my back, and I lean into him, needing his support. "That's Freddie," I croak, pointing at the man who made my life a misery for years. "And that's Hudson, his second in command," I add, pointing at the photo next to his. Another shudder whips through me, and I bite down on my lower lip so hard it's no surprise I draw blood.

"You're doing fantastic, Selena," the SSA says, nodding. "And this is already helping a lot. You've just identified a number of high-profile figures we suspected were involved, and you've pinpointed a number of men within the organization we've been watching and building profiles on."

Sinead gathers up the photos, putting them back in the file, and I slump against Keanu.

"If you feel up to it, we'd like to ask you some questions about the island," Keven says in a gentle tone.

Reliving my existence on that island is the last thing I want to do, but I knew coming here they would want to know. I've already warned Keanu this won't be easy to listen to, but I need to remind him again. I twist around, peering deep into his eyes. "Are you sure you want to stay for this?"

His eyes probe mine. "I'm going nowhere, Sel. Unless it'd make you more comfortable to talk about it with me not here."

I vigorously shake my head because nothing could be further from the truth. But I'm scared what he hears today might color his view of me.

As if he's read my mind, he says, "Nothing you say here will change how I think or feel about you, Selena. I know you were forced to do things against your will. I also know you survived because you are smart and strong and you did what you had to do." He brushes a stray hair off my face. "Say what you need to say, and if it gets too much, we can leave."

"I love you," I mouth even though the others can see.

"I love you too," he mouths back, reassuring me with his touch and his eyes and his cautious smile.

"Okay." I sigh heavily as I turn around. "What do you want to know?"

Chapter Twenty-Two
Keanu

I've never felt more helpless than I do as I sit listening to my girl explaining how life on the island worked. Or more sickened. But I deliberately force my feelings aside because this is about supporting Selena. And I know it's much harder for her to relive it than it is for me to hear it.

"When I first arrived, I was trained by some of the older girls so I'd know what to expect the first time I was raped. Master Allen sold my virginity at an auction." She visibly shivers, and I'm struggling to breathe. "After that, I was expected to become knowledgeable in all things sexual. We watched porn, watched others having sex with clients, and were made to have sex with the guards, all in the name of 'training.'" Derision drips from her tone and her expression. "The only positive to come out of it was after we were deemed skillful to let loose on the clients we were off-limits to the guards. Not that that stopped Freddie."

Her eyes darken, and she clenches her teeth. Every tendon in her body is locked tight. I smooth a hand up and down her back, but nothing relaxes her.

"We were pampered and well looked after, provided we cooperated," she says. Her eyes dart all over the room, and I know it's hard for her to relay this, let alone look these FBI agents in the eyes and tell them directly to their faces. "We had to look a certain way for the clients, so even when we were punished, they never marked our faces."

"And how often were clients on the island?"

"Most of the clients arrived on weekends, but some came for weeks at a time. Like a vacation."

My stomach tightens into knots as I exchange a loaded look with my brother. He's around this stuff all the time. He knows what kind of sick, twisted bastards prey on the weak and vulnerable, but I can tell this is especially hard for him. Because Selena is an extension of me—this hurts him too.

"And what happened when clients were there?" the SSA asks in a gentle tone.

"We were assigned certain clients," Selena explains in a neutral voice, and I know she's gone to that place inside where she shuts everyone and everything out. She's on autopilot mode, clinically explaining how things went down, while she keeps a tight rein on her emotions. It's the only way she can do this. I hold her closer, needing her to know I'm in this with her.

"Some clients would request certain girls. They had their favorites. On Friday nights, they held these massive parties in the large ballroom. Clients would get drunk and high and fuck their way through the room. There were no rules and no limitations. We did whatever was asked of us."

She stares off into space, and I think I might puke. Sel has told me some stuff, but she's never gone into detail, and I've never asked.

As she talks about orgies, double penetration, girl-on-girl action, and being tied up, I want to tear those fucking bastards who forced her into this from limb to limb. I honestly think I could murder these sick perverts and feel zero remorse. I'd be doing the world a favor wiping this scum off the face of the Earth.

They better hope I never face them because I'm liable to go

nuclear. The urge to annihilate these sick fucks isn't something that will disappear overnight. If ever.

I want to kill anyone who laid a finger on my sweet, innocent girl.

She was only *a kid*. She shouldn't have even known about this stuff, let alone been forced into doing it.

Tension is heavy in the air. Horror blatant on all our faces. When Selena starts describing the punishment Freddie and Hudson would dole out if she refused to do something, whenever she cried, or when she did something they deemed inappropriate, I can barely sit still. The need to hit something rides me hard. Pain spears my entire body like someone is stabbing me all over, pushing the knife in deep.

My eyes meet my brother's, and there is so much pain and sorrow in his gaze it almost undoes me. I grip Selena's hand harder, needing her touch to keep me from losing it. To remind me she got out. That she's okay.

"On Saturdays, we had to perform in these shows," she continues. "We had our roles and were given costumes, and if we didn't execute our parts perfectly, Freddie would punish us Sunday night when all the clients had left."

"Do you need to take a break?" Sinead asks after Selena finishes explaining exactly what these shows entailed.

Those disgusting bastards made her have sex with other kidnapped slaves on a stage for their sick enjoyment. I'm battling tears. And wild rage. And my heart is trying to beat a path out of my chest it's pounding so fast.

"I'm fine," Selena says in a monotone voice.

"How did you come to be sold to Clive Lawrence?" Keven asks, and I'm grateful he's switching the subject. Because I'm hanging on by a thread.

"As I got older, I became more disobedient," she says. "By that time, I'd pretty much lost the will to survive. Sometimes, I goaded the guards on purpose, hoping they'd kill me. I was in so much inner pain," she adds in a whisper, her voice all choked up as emotion breaks through the wall she's erected.

I close my eyes, laying my head against hers, inhaling her scent, and struggling to keep my composure. I wrap both my arms around her, hugging her tight.

She holds on to my arm, and she sounds numb again as she speaks. "Master Allen said I forced him into selling me. That I was his favorite and he would have kept me there longer if I had only behaved. But it was bullshit. The men that frequented the island liked them young, and as I was approaching fourteen, I knew my days were numbered."

I chew on the inside of my mouth to stop myself from shouting. Those sick, fucking, perverted bastards all deserve to burn in hell for what they've done to my gorgeous girl and to countless others.

"I was put up for auction again, and that asshole Cassius, I mean Lawrence, bought me."

"We know you escaped within twenty-four hours of landing back on US soil," SSA Clement says, flicking through the file. "So, I have to ask if Clive Lawrence touched you against your will."

Selena's eyes burn with anger as she glares at the SSA. "Have you not been listening?" she shouts. "He was a client on the island! I was his *favorite*," she spits out. "He was the first one to rape me, and he raped me repeatedly over the years I was imprisoned. He raped me on the boat on the way from the island to Texas, and he let his men take turns too. He—"

Nausea swims up my throat and I gag, halting Selena mid-sentence. Kev slides a trash can underneath my face, and I hover over it as my stomach churns and my heart pounds. When the nausea passes and I don't think I'll puke, I stand, needing to get out of this room. I need air. I sway as my legs threaten to go out from under me. Kev reaches for me, offering a steady arm.

"Keanu." Selena's anguished tone guts me. I hold onto my brother's arm as I face the woman I love. She rises, pain etched across her beautiful face.

"I'm sorry, Sel, but I can't listen to this anymore."

She cups my face. "I'm sorry. I—"

"Do not apologize," I roar, shaking her off as I lose control of my tenuous emotions.

"Keanu." Keven's tone warns me to keep it together.

"Shit, Sel, I'm sorry." I rest my forehead against hers. "I'm not angry at you. I just... I need some breathing space. I need to clear my head. I—"

"I understand. It's fine." She takes my hands, squeezing tight. "I love you, and I hate seeing you in pain. Take whatever time you need."

"We can stop, Selena," Sinead says. "Reconvene another day."

She shakes her head. "No. I'd like to continue. I'd prefer to tell you everything now."

"Okay. If you're sure."

"I'm sure." Selena eyeballs Keven, and some silent communication passes between them. Then he's steering me out of the room, thrusting a bottle of water in my chest and telling me to follow him.

I don't know how I manage to put one foot in front of the other, but I do. I've no clue where we're going, but I follow my brother to an impressive gym on the top floor of the building, slurping water as I walk.

Kev strides toward the punching bag, holding it as he turns to face me. "Go for it. Let it all out."

I drop my jacket on the ground and rip my shirt up over my head. It floats to the floor as I pummel my fists into the bag, hitting it over and over, allowing my frustration and rage to fuel each punch.

By the time I'm done, sweat drips down my face and covers my back and I'm breathing heavily.

"Better?" Kev asks.

I shrug. "For now." Because, honestly, I don't know how I'm going to process these latest revelations.

"Come with me," Kev says, tossing my jacket and shirt at me.

I follow him through a side door, up a flight of stairs, and out onto the roof. The weather is still mild, even though we are into October now, but there's a decent breeze at this height, and I welcome the feel of it ghosting over my sweat-slickened skin.

"Selena is one of the bravest women I've ever met," Keven tells me as we stand shoulder to shoulder, staring at Boston Common in the distance. "And that is one of the most shocking stories I've ever heard. And, trust me, I've heard some bad shit."

He looks sideways at me. "I'm guessing this played a part in your breakup." I nod. "But you're back together now," he adds. "And it's the real deal."

"It is," I say, using my shirt to mop my damp brow. "She's the one."

"Then, you need to talk to someone, Keanu." His eyes bore a hole in mine. "She's not the only one who needs to process that fucked-up shit."

I sigh, knowing he's right. "I need to be there for her."

He grips me by the shoulders. "You already are. But you're no use to her if you can't get a handle on your own feelings. Anyone would be the same in your shoes." He lets go of me. "Hell, I want to destroy these fuckers for what they've done to her, and I barely know Selena. I can only imagine the shit going through your brain."

"We've never talked about it in detail," I admit, sliding my arms into my shirt. "And I used to wonder if my imagination was worse than knowing the truth." I swallow the hard lump in my throat as I button my shirt. "Now, I know it wasn't, because I had no clue it was that bad."

I hold my jacket to my chest, facing my brother head-on. "That fucker needs to pay. They all do, but we'll start with him."

"Agreed. We've just placed someone on the inside with Lawrence. We *will* get that sick bastard, but we need to find hard evidence or catch him in the act. It's going to take some time to build a rock-solid case against him. And we can't guarantee he won't discover she's living in Boston in the meantime."

"He can't get to her, Kev. I will fucking take him out myself before I let him anywhere near Selena."

"No heroics, Keanu. The last thing Selena needs is you locked up for murder. We'll keep her safe. I promise. Morgan Security is the shit, and those guys would die before they'd let anything happen to her. And my boss is assigning an agent to her full-time. He's also got an undercover guy and a full-time agent on Lawrence. Plus, the guy's a public figure and he's got cameras on him twenty-four-seven. He won't be able to do much without someone capturing it on film." He grips my shoulders again. "He's not getting near Selena, brother. And that's a fucking promise."

Chapter Twenty-Three
Selena

I meet with Denise every morning the following week as I spiral in the aftermath of the FBI meeting. I'm proud of myself for telling them everything, but reliving it all has brought everything to the forefront of my mind again, and I'm struggling to cope.

Keanu provides steady support, reassuring me he's going nowhere, that he doesn't feel any differently about me, and holding me in the middle of the night when I wake up screaming, but he's quieter than normal, and I think he's struggling too.

My natural inclination is to dive deep into myself. To lock out the world. Hold onto the pain and bury myself even deeper. But I'm trying not to do that.

For me.

For the man I love.

For my sanity.

Hence, the daily therapy sessions, and I'm going about my routine as usual. Attending classes, swimming, going to yoga, talking with Mom, and hanging out with Todd and Kelly.

But it's difficult because that monster is still out there. Way too close for comfort. I'm on edge. Constantly looking over my shoulder. Waiting for the moment he finds me.

So, when my agent Jessica calls, asking to reschedule my shoot with Miranda Fanning to this weekend, I jump at the opportunity to get out of the city. Now that Keanu's schedule has been cleared, he is free to come with me, and I'm excited for our weekend in the Big Apple.

Keanu canceled all planned shoots last week, telling his agent Frankie he wasn't available for the foreseeable future. He wants to be there for me, but I wasn't comfortable with him sacrificing his career until he explained he's not that into modeling anymore. That he's considering quitting for good. It would be a shame, because he's such a natural in front of the camera, but if he's not feeling it, he's not feeling it. No one should be forced to do something they don't enjoy, and Keanu is fortunate he has the financial means to follow his heart. He's also decided he doesn't want to set up a modeling agency when he graduates Harvard. He has set his sights on creating his own fashion label. It's a great idea, and I told him that.

"Thank you so much for agreeing to fly us," I tell James, Keanu's dad, as we board the Kennedy family jet. Although, calling it a jet isn't doing the plush plane justice.

"It's not a chore. I love flying, and it's my version of Dad's taxi," he quips, chuckling. "Make yourself at home," he adds. "We'll be taking off shortly." He walks off in the direction of the cockpit.

"Wow." I turn around, gawking at the lavish interiors. "I wasn't expecting it to be so big."

"That's what all the girls say," Kent supplies, cupping his crotch and thrusting his hips forward.

"Jesus fucking Christ, Kent." Keanu drags his hands through his hair. Irritation is transparent on his face as he gestures in my direction.

"K, relax." I place my hand on his arm. "It was funny, and Kent didn't mean any harm."

I know Keanu is only trying to protect me, but he can't jump down everyone's throats any time they make a suggestive comment. I'm determined to be more chilled out, because I know my mood is impacting my boyfriend. And he's already dealing with the fallout from my revelations. I want him to relax and enjoy himself this weekend. For us to leave all the stress and tension on the tarmac and be a normal couple living it up in New York.

I run my fingers up his chest, locking my hands behind his neck. "We're going to New York for the weekend." I smile as I stretch up and press a quick kiss to his lips. "And it's going to be awesome."

"Damn straight," Kent says, flopping in a chair behind us.

"You better not make me regret inviting you," Keanu grumbles, sitting in a chair across from his brother, pulling me down beside him.

"You make it sound like I'm the antichrist," Kent complains, reclining in his chair and kicking his feet up.

"Close, brother," Keanu says, grinning. "Very close."

"I'm beginning to think 'supersize me' is your family's motto in life," I tell Keanu after he's given me a grand tour of the plush penthouse apartment the Kennedys own in New York. It's prime real estate, overlooking Central Park, and only a few blocks from Miranda Fanning's offices.

"Go big or go home," Kent says, sauntering into the living room with a beer already in hand. He's shirtless and shoeless, and I work hard to avoid ogling my boyfriend's brother, but it's hard because Kent is seriously ripped. Boy works out a lot, so I'm not surprised.

"You've got a fascination with all things big, huh?" I joke, accepting the bottle of water he offers me, while Keanu swipes his beer.

"She finally understands." Kent faux rolls his eyes before winking. The second the bottle leaves Keanu's lips, Kent steals it back. "Get your own beer, asshole."

"Did someone say beer?" a strange male says, and I scream as a tall good-looking guy with blond hair steps into the room.

"It's okay. Brad's a friend," Keanu says, instantly hauling me into his side, running his hand up and down my spine.

"Sorry," Brad says, stepping sideways to let a gorgeous brunette into the room. "I didn't mean to startle you."

"Looking sexy as fuck, Red," Kent says, unashamedly eye-fucking the brunette.

"I'm convinced you have a death wish." Brad shakes his head. "Quit hitting on my woman, or I'll lay you flat on your ass."

"I'd love to see you try," Kent says, grabbing the brunette into his arms.

"Get your hand off my arse, Kent, or I'll be the one laying you out flat." The brunette pins him with a challenging look, and Kent grins like all his Sundays have come at once.

"I'll get flat on my back for you anytime, Red." He wiggles his brows. "You only have to ask."

"Control your mongrel," Brad says, spearing Keanu with a look. "Before I muzzle him."

"Down, boy," Keanu says, tugging Kent back. "Don't tempt me into giving McConaughey the green light."

"What are you guys doing here anyway?" Kent asks, flipping his brother off.

"We've been in town for a couple days. Rachel had some meetings," Brad says, slinging his arm around the woman's waist. "Ky said it was okay to stay here, but we can check into a hotel if we're in the way."

"It's cool, man," Keanu says. "There are plenty of bedrooms."

"Is that really the truth, Red?" Kent smirks at the woman who I assume is Rachel. "Or did you find out I was hitting New York for the weekend and you just had to be here."

Rachel rolls her eyes, shucking out of Brad's hold and walking toward us. "If your ego gets any bigger, you'll orbit into space," she says, shoulder-checking Kent as she makes a beeline for me.

He laughs. "There's nothing wrong with my ego, Red. It's just your eyes that need examining." He wraps an arm around her from behind. "When are you going to ditch that pussy and date a real man?"

"My man is all man," Rachel purrs, slanting lustful eyes at Brad. "We'd be happy to give you a demonstration anytime. You could use the pointers."

"Now, I know you're just yanking my chain," Kent says as Brad grabs him into a headlock.

"That's it. I'm throwing you off the balcony," Brad jokes. Or at least, I think he's joking.

"I'd like to say they're not usually like this," Rachel says, smiling at me. "But you're living with Kent, so you get it."

"She's not living with *Kent!*" Keanu protests, sulking, and I can't help laughing.

"Oh, man. Don't you start." Rachel rolls her eyes, thrusting out her hand. "Hi, Selena. I'm Rachel."

It all clicked into place when I heard their names. I know who they are. Rachel and Brad are best friends with Faye and Kyler, and Brad basically grew up with the Kennedys. Now, Rachel's accent makes sense because I remember she's Faye's Irish friend. I've heard Keanu mention them over the years, but I've never met either of them.

"You're the one who's going to be working with Miranda." Keanu told me about Rachel securing a much sought-after internship with Miranda Fanning. She's moving to New York after graduating from design school in the summer, and Brad is moving with her.

"That's me." We shake hands briefly. "Miranda showed me some of the clothes she's chosen for you to wear at the shoot tomorrow, and oh my God, they are amazing." She enunciates the last word, rolling it off her tongue. "You're going to look so hot in them!"

Her excitement is infectious, and I smile. "I can't wait."

Kent heads out to a party, having made plans to meet up with some girl he hooked up with the last time he was in New York. I really hope he steers clear of drugs tonight. Despite his protests, I worry it'll extend beyond recreational use. That he'll become addicted. Those bastards who kidnapped me spent years shooting shit into my veins and I'd become dependent. Getting clean was sheer hell, and I wouldn't wish it on anyone.

I've shared my concerns with Kent, but he told me not to worry.

That he has it under control.

Only, I know better.

We probably should have gone out with him tonight, but I don't want to because I have an early start in the morning. So, we stay in with Rachel and Brad. We order takeout, chat for a while, and watch a movie. It's nice. Normal. And I'm feeling way more relaxed now that we're out of Boston.

"I like Rachel and Brad," I tell Keanu as I crawl under the covers beside him a few hours later.

"They're good people," he agrees, opening his arms for me.

I snuggle into his side, pressing my lips to his warm, inviting chest. He moans, so I dot more kisses all over his chest, enjoying the way he responds to my touch. I make my way up his neck, peppering his smooth jawline with more kisses, teasing him by kissing the corners of his mouth.

"I need to kiss you, Sel," he rasps, curling his large palm around the nape of my neck and drawing me close.

The instant our lips touch, fireworks explode, and I see stars behind my closed eyelids. I angle my head, deepening the kiss, and I'm clawing at him, needing to get even closer. He licks the seam of my lips, and I open for him, welcoming his tongue into my mouth.

I climb on top of him, straddling his hips, feeling the hard bulge in his pants pressing against my ass, and I whimper into his mouth, grinding on top of him as primal need swamps my body. I ache down below, my body demanding release, and I rock my hips against his, showing him what I need.

I love the sensations Keanu evokes in me. He barely touches me, and I'm a quivering mess. I love how naturally my body responds to him, and it's how it should be when you love and desire someone as much as I do him. The normalcy of my responses encourages me, making me feel bolder, allowing me to take control of my sexuality.

"Sel." He drags his lips from mine, palming both sides of my face. "We should slow down."

"I don't want to slow down." I genuinely don't. I'm so wet for my man, and there's nothing wrong with that. I weld my lips to his again, and we get lost in one another.

In a flash, he flips me over, his lips never leaving mine as he covers me with his delectable body. Very gently, he eases down on top of me, softly jerking his hips into mine, and my eyes roll back in my head. I lift my legs, locking them around his waist, pulling him down firmly on top of me.

He stiffens, and his lips stop moving against mine as I grind against him, needing the friction, as my impending release climbs higher and higher. "Keanu, please."

"Baby." He nips at my earlobe, tugging it gently between his teeth, and I cry out in raw need.

He sits up, leaning back on his heels, as his hands roam my body. "K."

"Shush, baby. I got you," he says, hooking his thumbs in the band of my sleep shorts.

I push off my elbows, locking eyes with him, as he pulls my shorts down my legs. "I need you inside me, K."

He stops with his hands on the sides of my panties, staring deep into my eyes. "We need to talk to Denise first, babe. I already told you. I don't want to hurt you."

We were due to have a couple's therapy session on Thursday, but I canceled it, because I could see Keanu was hurting from the previous weekend's revelations and neither of us was in the right frame of mind to stir up another hornets' nest. But now, I'm kicking myself that I didn't go through with it.

Because *I want him.*

I want to feel him moving inside me.

Loving me with his mouth, his hands, and his penis.

But I can't be pushy.

Because I know how important it is to him to do this the right way. I see how he's torturing himself now, because he wants this as much as I do, and I know he hates saying no to me, but he doesn't want to risk doing something that might trigger me.

And how can I ever be mad at him for that?

I can't. No matter how badly I want him to make love to me now, it will have to wait. "Okay, babe."

He climbs back up my body. "I love you so fucking much, Sel."

I run my fingers through his silky, dark hair. "I know, and I love you too." I send him a cheeky grin. "But I'll love you even more if you make me come with your mouth. I ache for you, K."

He rubs his thumb along my swollen lower lip. "As I ache for you, pretty girl." He kisses me softly and sweetly, and I melt into the bed. "And I will never leave you wanting."

He moves to slide down my body again.

"On one condition," I blurt. "You let me reciprocate this time." He hasn't let me touch his penis, and I'm done with inequality. I can tell he's going to shoot me down again, so I crawl into his lap, circling my arms around his neck. "Baby, please. I need to touch you. I want to make you come. I want to watch the pleasure on your face, knowing my hands and my mouth did that to you. Please let me." I clasp his beautiful face in both hands, basking in the glow of love emanating from his gorgeous blue eyes. "Please let me love you."

"I'm afraid if I let you do it once, I'll want it all the time," he admits, his eyes blazing with desire.

"I fail to see the problem," I tease.

"I never want you to feel obligated."

"Are you going to force me?"

"What!" Disbelief and anger flood his features. "Why the hell would you ask me that?!"

"Baby. Calm down." I peck his lips, clinging to him tight. "I'm sorry. Poor choice of words. You're not going to make me do anything

I don't want to do, so can we agree if I touch you it's because I want to make you feel good?"

His features soften as he nods, and a layer of stress lifts off my shoulders. "And if you don't want me to, you only have to say it. I never want to make you do anything you don't want to do either."

He chuckles, pressing a feather-soft kiss to the underside of my jaw. I shiver all over, and my core throbs with fresh need. "What's so funny?"

"The notion that I'd ever not be in the mood," he replies. "I'm a guy, and you turn me on so much, Sel. I'll never get enough." He grabs the hem of my top, pulling it up my body. "This okay?" he asks.

"More than okay," I pant, as I let him remove it.

"I love your body," he murmurs, kissing the swell of my breasts. I'm on his lap, my chest at the perfect position for his hot mouth. "And I love these," he adds, caressing my tits in his big hands. I cry out when his mouth suctions on my left breast while his hand fondles my right.

Then he guides me down flat on my back, nipping, licking, and sucking his way down my body until he reaches my panties. I arch my hips and lift my butt off the bed so he can remove them. And then, his mouth is exactly where I want it. Lapping at my most intimate part, his tongue licking a line up and down my folds. When his tongue pushes inside me, I almost buck off the bed. The intensity of the sensations rippling throughout my body is out of this world. I know I'm not going to last long, and I want his fingers in me. I know he's afraid to do it, because of what happened that one time we tried, but I need to feel his fingers in me now.

"I want your fingers, K." I prop up on my elbows to look at him. "Please. I promise it will be okay."

He glances at me through hooded lashes, and it's so carnal watching the man I love with his head between my thighs, staring at me with so much lust and love in his eyes. "Tell me if it hurts or you want me to pull them out," he croaks after a few moments of intense staring.

"I will."

Slowly, he inserts one finger, moving it carefully in and out of me, watching for my reaction the whole time.

"More," I whisper, loving the feel of his finger inside me.

"Fuck," he hisses when he inserts another digit and my muscles clench around him.

"Faster," I pant, arching my hips as I ride his hand. Pressure is building and building, and I'm on the edge of something monumental. He pumps his fingers a little faster, still cautious, but when his tongue flattens on my clit, I explode around his fingers and his tongue, crying out as the most incredible wave of pleasure consumes every part of me.

He rides it out with me, only withdrawing his fingers when my sated body has collapsed against the bed. "Oh my God." I giggle, grabbing him to me. "That was amazing." I kiss him hard. "I love your magical fingers." I giggle again, and I want to bottle this feeling. This moment.

"I love you," he simply says, taking my hand and bringing it to his mouth. "More and more every day."

"I love you beyond anything humanly possible," I say. "Beyond words. Beyond logic. Beyond space and time." He bends down to kiss me, but I slip out from under him, pushing him down onto his back. "And now it's time I showed you."

Chapter Twenty-Four
Selena

I waste no time removing his pants, freeing his penis, leaving him completely bare. And he's magnificent. Broad, smooth chest. Chiseled abs with a tempting line of dark hair trailing down to his long, thick erection. I fist my hand around his hard length, stroking him in firm, long strokes, watching as his eyes roll back and his shoulders melt into the bed.

"Faster, please, babe," he murmurs, and I increase my pace, pumping him up and down, enjoying the look of intense pleasure washing over his face. I bend down, and my tongue darts out, licking the bead of precum on the tip of his penis. He groans. A deep, primitive groan that sends heat to my core and puts a big smile on my face.

I love making him feel good.

And I love that I love doing it.

There is no doubt and no hesitation.

Keanu has spent years worshiping and caring for me, and it's time I reciprocated it in more ways than one.

I worship his penis. Licking, nibbling, and sucking on it until his hips are bucking and he's writhing in need. I open my mouth and take him deep, hollowing out my cheeks as I suck, watching him come undone with every swipe of my tongue.

"Sel, I'm going to come." His eyes penetrate mine.

I keep sucking, deep throating him as I encourage him to keep going with my eyes. I'm not stopping now. I want him to come in my mouth.

"Agh, Sel." His hips thrust faster, but I can tell he's holding himself back, not wanting to do anything to hurt me. God, I freaking love him so much. He always puts my needs above his own. I could live a million lifetimes and never feel worthy of this man.

I slide my hand between his thighs, fondling his balls, and the instant my finger tentatively nudges against his puckered hole, he detonates in my mouth, shooting streams of hot, salty cum directly down my throat.

I keep my mouth latched onto his penis until I've sucked him dry, then I release him with a loud popping sound. He instantly lifts me up into his arms, cradling me against his solid chest. "Holy hell, Sel."

"I think you liked that," I say, smiling up at him.

"I fucking loved it." He caresses my face. "Are you okay?" Worry radiates from his eyes.

"I'm perfect, K." I kiss him softly. "I love doing that to you."

He kisses me back, slow, long, and deep, and I sigh contentedly when he finally breaks our lip-lock. "Let's talk to Denise this week."

"I'll message her now," I say, reaching for my cell, because I'm as eager as he is to set it up. The sooner we air our concerns, the sooner we move forward, and I'm ready for Keanu to make love to me. I want him so badly I could scream.

Although we argue about it, Keanu comes with me to the shoot the following morning. We're supposed to be keeping a low profile in public, but he's adamant that he's not hiding this weekend, and I don't argue too much. Because I can't bear to be apart from him for any length of time.

Yes, we really are one of those annoying couples, joined at the hip, blissfully happy in one another's company.

The shoot goes well. It helps that my partner on this campaign is Stephen Dillon. An up-and-coming new face on the scene. A guy who happens to be openly gay, so there's no sleazy talk, no flirtatiousness, and Keanu has no reason to be jealous.

If anyone has a right to jealousy, it's me, because Stephen spends half his time drooling over my man. But he's respectful, and he never crosses a line. Content to sneak sly looks at Keanu whenever he thinks we're not looking.

I'm exhausted by the time the shoot ends, and when we get back to the penthouse that evening, I take a nap for a couple hours before we head out to dinner with Rach, Brad, and Kent.

After dinner, we meet up with some friends of Keanu's and Kent's at a local bar before moving on to a club.

"We can leave whenever you want," Keanu says as soon as we are seated in a booth in the VIP area.

"I know, and I'm good. I'm enjoying myself."

While I've attended clubs in the past two years, I've never been totally relaxed. Until now. Because Keanu makes me feel safe and protected, and I genuinely have no issue being here. I like this crew, and nothing could dampen my good mood.

I stick to water while Keanu slowly sips a beer. Rachel isn't drinking either, but Brad and Kent have been downing the beers since we arrived. Brad's a little tipsy, but Kent is definitely drunk, unashamedly groping the petite redhead who somehow found her way onto his lap.

"Let's dance," Rachel says, taking my hand.

Keanu opens his mouth, to object on my behalf, no doubt, but I beat him to it. "I'd love to." His jaw hangs open, and I giggle. I kiss him quickly. "I won't be long."

Rachel leads me to the edge of the dance floor, in full view of our table, and we put on a little show for our guys. The rhythmic beats infiltrate my limbs, and I sway my hips in time to the music, getting lost in the movement of my body and the hypnotic melody of the song. Rach is a fantastic dancer, and her lack of inhibition encourages me to shake off the last vestiges of self-consciousness. I move my body freely, throwing my arms in the air and shaking my booty as the song changes and the tempo picks up pace.

"You are sexy as fuck," Keanu rasps into my ear, coming up behind me.

"Right back at ya," I say, spinning around in his arms.

He pulls me in flush to his chest, and we grind our hips together, moving in sync with one another and in time to the music.

We dance for ages. Until my dress is glued to my back and damp tendrils of hair cling to my brow. My jaw hurts from laughing and kissing, and I'm high on life right now, and it feels amazing. I never want this feeling to end.

We leave the club a couple hours later. Kent and the redhead are all over one another in the back of the taxi while the rest of us pretend not to notice. Keanu is scowling at his brother, and I rub the tense spot between his brows. "Relax, babe. It doesn't bother me." And it doesn't. They're both into it, so where's the harm in that?

We say good night to the others when we arrive at the penthouse, heading to our bedroom. The second the door is locked, Keanu is peeling my dress off and carrying me to the bed where we spend another few hours exploring every inch of each other.

"Can't we stay here forever?" I grumble the following afternoon as we prepare to leave for the airport.

"I wish we could," Keanu says, reeling me into his arms. He plants a passionate kiss on my lips that leaves me weak-kneed and aching. "I'm glad you had a good time. We should do this more often."

"Definitely," I agree, taking his hand as he grabs our bags and mentally preparing myself for the trip back home.

Releasing Keanu

We meet with Denise after school on Thursday for our first couple's session in years. I'm nervous. Keanu's nervous. But Denise helps put us at ease.

"My understanding from talking with Selena is that you two want to progress your sexual relationship, and you have some concerns, Keanu," Denise says. "Is that correct?"

"Yeah," he says, clutching my hand more tightly.

"Tell me how you are feeling about it. What specific concerns do you have?" she asks, smiling at him in encouragement.

"I want Selena to enjoy it, but I'm afraid of doing something that might remind her of her past. Or trigger her to remember something traumatic. I don't ever want to hurt her or make her feel uncomfortable."

"How do you feel about this, Selena?" Denise asks.

"I love that Keanu is so concerned about my needs and that he wants it to be good for me. I wish I could tell him that his concerns are without foundation, but I won't lie." I wet my dry lips, gazing into my boyfriend's eyes. "I can't guarantee there won't be times where something happens that triggers a flashback, because I don't have control over it."

"And that's why I'm worried," he says, rubbing his thumb back and forth across the back of my hand. "That'd kill me, Sel."

"Are there specific things you don't want Keanu to do, Selena?" Denise asks. "It's best to be completely up front before you make love. To let Keanu know if there is something you won't like or won't be comfortable with."

"Denise and I have discussed sex and my sexuality a lot over the past two years," I tell him, so he knows how much thought I've given this. "I've been reading up on healthy sexual relationships, making a list of my sexual goals, and trying to figure out how I can take back more control. Modeling has helped, because *I'm* calling the shots. I'm deciding how others see me and what images are portrayed. Feeling good about myself in shoots, feeling sexy and desirable, has empowered me. Because *I'm* in control. I decide who sees my body. I will never do lingerie or swimwear campaigns. Not because of the scars on my body, but because I don't want any stranger objectifying me in any way."

I sit up straighter, angling my body so I'm facing him. "The only one who will see my body, apart from me, is you. And I've already trusted you with that." My cheeks heat a little. I trust Denise, and I trust Keanu, but it's still awkward having this conversation. Talking about something so private with others stretches me out of my comfort zone. But I also know myself well enough to understand that this is the right way to do this. Keanu may have been the one asking for this meeting, but I would've suggested it if he hadn't.

"When we were together the last time," I say, "I got scared as we became closer. The more we made out, the more I wanted to take things further, but I was terrified of your touch too." His face drops, and I hate that he's hurting, but this won't work without complete honesty, without full disclosure. I've been in therapy long enough to know that. "I realize now it's because I wasn't ready." I squeeze his hand. "But I am now."

"How can you be sure?"

"Because I can't keep my hands off you and I want your hands *on me* all the time. And yet, it's not enough. I crave every part of you. And although I already feel so close to you, I want to feel closer. I want to feel you moving inside me. I want to feel you worshiping me completely. I want there to be no more barriers between us." I stare deep into his eyes, wanting him to really hear this next admission. To feel it deep in his bones for the truth it is. "I want to give you my virginity."

He blinks, staring at me in shock and confusion. I glance at Denise, and she nods, reassuring me, silently telling me to keep going.

"I know that might sound strange to you, but I read this article online recently. It was written by a woman named Veve Bee. She's a child abuse pediatrician. Her words really resonated with me." I memorized them so I could repeat them to myself whenever I need reminding that I have the power and the control over what happens to my body from now on.

"She said, 'Virginity is not a physical entity. It's not something that can ever be taken from you. It's a concept, a mental and emotional decision you make to give of yourself when you are ready, and not when someone decides to be violent with your body.' I can send you the link. It's a really powerful article, and it has helped me enormously." He nods, and I know he'll read it.

I look at Denise, and she nods encouragingly. "Being raped is not the same as having loving, consensual sex." I palm his face. "I've never had that, so this will be my first time. I want *you* to take my virginity. I want you to be my first."

I smile at him. The words breathing new life into me. I'm not lying when I say stumbling across that article helped me. Denise had been saying similar things to me over the years, but her words didn't get through. Maybe, it was just the timing, or maybe, it was the way the author articulated her thoughts, but it hit home. Injecting me with courage and confidence.

I'm making this decision now to give myself to my boyfriend.

Freely without hesitation.

Because I love him.

I clasp both sides of his face, eyeballing the man I love with determination, hoping he hears this. Sees this. "I want you to be my first and last, Keanu. And I'm done waiting to experience that with you. I don't want to wait anymore. I'm ready." I caress his stubbly jawline. "If you are."

Tears roll down his face as he pulls me into his arms, hugging me.

It's a significant moment in our relationship.

A definite turning point.

I feel the air changing around us.

The dynamic shifting.

My future coming into focus.

He eases back, staring into my face. "I wish I could explain how full my heart is right now."

"You don't need to explain," I reply, placing my hand over his heart. "I already feel it."

"You know I want this with you," he adds. "And I want it to be perfect."

"It will be," I reassure him. "Because I'll be with you."

"I need you to guide me. To tell me what feels good. What feels uncomfortable. And if you want to stop, at any time, you just say the words, and we will. You are in control, Selena. Always."

Happy tears prick my eyes. "I've always felt safe with you, Keanu. And I promise I'll tell you if I don't like something, or I have a flashback, or I want you to stop."

His Adam's apple bobs in his throat. "Is there anything specifically you don't want me to do?"

"I'm not sure about anal. We'll need to work our way up to that."

"Jesus, Sel." He runs his fingers through his hair. "That's not... I would never expect that of any woman." His cheeks flush. "And that's not something I've done."

I can't contain my grin. "I like that I'll be the first." If I can get to that point, because that may be a hard limit for me.

"Is there anything else?"

"Just don't be rough or aggressive, and I don't want to be tied up."

"I would never be rough with you. I only ever want to treat you with the softest touch. To cherish your body as you deserve."

"Okay, then." This has actually gone better than I expected. I'm smiling as I turn to face Denise.

"I'm very proud of you both," she says, beaming at us. "And I'm here for you. This might not be plain sailing, but just keep doing what you are doing. Talking to one another. Keeping the communication channels open."

"There is one other thing," Keanu says. "Should we plan this, or should it be spontaneous?"

"Selena." Denise defers to me. "What do you want?"

I look into Keanu's eyes. "I know I said I wanted it to be normal, which implies spontaneity, but I think, for my first time, we should plan it. So I can prepare. Every step of my recovery has involved planning, and I think this should be the same so there are no surprises."

"I'm more than okay with that," he agrees.

"A lot of couples plan their first time," Denise says. "It's not always a spur of the moment thing. You'd be surprised."

Denise hugs us warmly as we leave, and I feel so much lighter stepping out of her house than I did when I first arrived.

"You sure you're okay with everything?" I ask him when we're in the car en route home.

"Absolutely." His answering grin is wide. Reaching over the console, he takes my hand, lacing his fingers in mine. "I'm glad we did that. And I'm glad we can talk about this. I feel more relaxed trusting you'll tell me if I'm doing something you don't like. And I'm glad that we're going to plan it, because I want it to be special, Sel." His eyes well up again. "I want it to be a memory you will cherish for eternity."

"I already know I will, K," I truthfully admit. "Because you're the only man who will ever own my heart, mind, body, and soul."

I'm floating on a cloud the following day, and it feels fantastic to finally be making progress in my life. I have my first session with the EMDR hypnotherapist next week, and Keanu and I are going to sit down this weekend and work out the details of our first time.

I'm excited and happy and a little distracted as I edge out of the row in the auditorium, which is why I don't spot him loitering just inside the door of my developmental psychology class until I'm almost on top of him.

My eyes do a double take as I stare at the man who played such a huge part in my destruction.

Cassius.

My stomach lurches violently, and I clamp a hand over my mouth to stop myself from throwing up.

Clive Lawrence is dressed casually in jeans, Vans, and a college sweater, and he's wearing a ballcap, keeping his head down low, trying to blend in.

But his gaze is zeroed in on mine. His dark eyes are glinting with righteous indignation. The wicked gleam promising all types of punishment. A knowing sneer pulls up the corners of his mouth as he pushes off the wall.

Panic consumes me, and my stomach heaves again. I clamp my lips shut as my feet root to the floor. All the blood drains from my face as his lips kick up higher and his eyes trail the length of my body.

My classmates push past me, laughing and gossiping as they stream through the doors, oblivious to the monster in their midst.

The crowd surges toward the exit, and my brain reengages.

I can't be left alone in here with him! There is safety in numbers, and I need to move!

My limbs are jittery as I force them into action, walking up the steps and trying to finagle my way into the middle of the crowd where I'm less vulnerable.

But he predicts my response, moving quickly along the side, sliding past bodies to intercept me. His arm juts forward, and he grabs hold of my wrist. I open my mouth to scream when he presses the muzzle of a gun into my side. "I wouldn't do that if I were you," he warns, close to my ear.

"Let me go." I attempt to wrest my arm out of his solid grip. My skin is crawling at the feel of his fingers around the bare skin of my wrist, and nausea lodges in the back of my throat.

"Never." His fingernails dig into my sensitive flesh, and I swallow my cry of pain.

His dark chuckle sends shivers down my spine as he forces me up the last few steps, discreetly pushing the gun into my lower back. The crowd is his shield as he leads me to an inevitable fate. None of them is paying us any attention, so I can't even attempt to silently communicate a plea for help. He's almost flush with my body at the back, and the feel of him up against me sends me into a tailspin. My body is on instant high alert. Fear and nausea taking control. My breathing becomes labored, and blood rushes to my head, making me dizzy.

I try to calm down, but I'm so fucking scared, and my heart won't stop thumping loudly in my chest.

"Did you miss me, whore, because I sure missed you." His warm breath skates over my ear, and a whimper flees my mouth. Every muscle in my body is on lockdown, and if he wasn't pushing me forward, I doubt I'd be able to put one foot in front of the other.

"You won't get away with this," I say, hating how my voice cracks. I'm barely caging my hysteria, and I hate that he most likely knows it.

I just need to get him outside to the main lobby where my bodyguards are waiting.

Inhaling and exhaling deeply, I force myself to calm down as I quicken my pace, praying I can keep my panic at bay for another couple minutes. I just need to stay within the safety of the crowd and lead him to the lobby, and then my bodyguards will do their job.

If he gets me alone, all bets are off, so I need to stay the course.

He prods the gun into my back. "You're mine," he whispers in my ear, and another whimper flies out of my mouth before I can stop it. Adrenaline stampedes through my body, and I'm trembling all over. "I own you," he adds. "And you're going to fucking pay for running away from me. Even if it's the last thing I do."

Chapter Twenty-Five
Keanu

"They're here," Kent says, pointing at the camera which shows the exterior view of the building.

I race out of the room, out of our condo, forgoing the elevator and taking the stairs two at a time as I rush to get outside.

A black FBI SUV pulls up to the curb behind the bodyguards' car just as my foot hits the sidewalk. Ignoring the FBI, I dash to the open rear door of the other car. "Get out of my way," I snap, shoving Ray—the older of the two bodyguards tasked with keeping Selena safe—out of the way. He's crouched down in front of the back seat, so he falls back on his butt when I barrel past him.

But I have zero fucks to give.

I'm paying these assholes to protect her, so how the fuck did Lawrence get anywhere near her?

I want to tear through them for placing her in harm's way, but I need to focus on my love, because she's the priority, and right now, she needs me. Selena is curled into a ball on the back seat with her fingers clasped around her necklace, rocking back and forth, in obvious pain.

I glare at Ray and Paul. "You're both fired," I snap.

"Keanu." Kev appears behind me. "Let's not be hasty until we know what happened."

"He approached her in the auditorium," Paul says. "And our agreement was to wait outside for Selena. We didn't know, man."

Ignoring all of them, I climb into the back seat, shoving my frame into the space between the front and back seats. "Selena. Baby. It's Keanu. I'm here." It kills me to see her like this. She hasn't had an anxiety attack in weeks, and this has set her progress back.

I remove the vial of lavender oil from my pocket.

"We tried to do that," Ray says, sounding remorseful. "But she wouldn't let us touch her."

"No shit, Sherlock." I glare at them over my shoulder as I edge closer to Selena's face. She's staring vacantly into space with a glazed look in her eyes. "Sel, I'm going to touch your wrist, okay?"

Her eyes flit to mine for a brief second. A flare of recognition lighting and extinguishing almost as fast. I dab the oil on the inside of her wrist, rubbing it in before bringing it to her nose. "Inhale, sweetheart." She breathes in and out. "That's it. Long, deep breaths." I perch on the edge of the seat, lifting her up a little as her posture relaxes. When she leans into me, circling her arms around my back, pressing her face into my chest and holding on to me for dear life, I close my eyes, thanking God for looking after her today.

I won't ever forget getting that phone call from Ray. Or the terror that pierced my heart when he told me how close I came to losing her again.

I am not leaving her side for a single second.

Not until that bastard is behind bars or festering ten feet under.

"We need to get you inside," I say after a few minutes. The FBI agents on the sidewalk are drawing attention, and some of our neighbors have come out to find out what's going on.

She nods, clasping my hand and letting me help her out of the car. I tuck her in to my side, pushing her head down so the nosy onlookers don't frighten her, and guide her inside the building and up to the condo.

I grab a blanket off the back of the couch before sitting down with Selena in my lap. Then, I cover us both as Keven, Agent Cunningham, and another guy I don't know come into the apartment, followed by the two bodyguards.

Keven closes and locks the front door as Kent approaches us, handing me a mug. Minty steam rises from the top of the drink. "It's peppermint tea," he confirms, crouching down in front of us, looking at my girlfriend with clear concern. "You like that, right, Selena? It helps calm you down." I don't know when she told him that, but I'm grateful he remembered.

"Thanks, bro."

"Thank you," Selena whispers, reaching out to touch Kent's hand.

Kent sits on the arm of the couch, pinning me with troubled eyes. He's come to care about her, and he doesn't like seeing her like this.

I know, man. I feel it too.

"What happened?" I ask in a clipped tone. Although my question was meant for the two idiots charged with protecting the love of my life, Selena is the one who answers.

"He was in my class, K." Her hands cradle the mug. "I didn't see him until the very end, and by then, it was too late. I couldn't avoid him."

"How the hell did he get in there without anyone seeing?" I direct my question to the three men in the room who are all supposed to have eyes on my girl.

The dark-haired FBI agent, who looks kinda familiar, clears his throat. "I'm Colin. I'm the FBI agent assigned to Selena," he says.

"Awesome fucking job, dude," Kent says, sneering.

Colin sends Kent a pointed look before returning his gaze to me. "Lawrence arranged a meeting with the head of the psychology department. Said he was looking for a consultant to work on his new show and he thought one of the professors might be able to help. He used that as an excuse to gain access to the building. He took the internal staff stairway to get into the auditorium. It bypasses the main hallway and lobby where we were waiting for Selena."

"I thought an agent was watching Lawrence too?" I ask, looking at my brother.

"There is an agent assigned to him, but Lawrence came out a back entrance in a different car with tinted windows."

"How did he know Selena was there?" I inquire.

Kev folds his arms across his chest. "We don't know. There was nothing in any of his calls or emails to indicate he's been looking for her or that he'd found her. Most likely, it was the billboards."

A week ago, a host of billboards featuring Selena and Stephen as the new faces of Miranda Fanning's label went up around Boston.

"Or he somehow found out from registration records for the show," he adds.

Sinead sits down beside us. "What did he do, Selena? Did he say anything?"

She pushes hair out of her face, biting on the corner of her lip for a few beats before she tells us how it went down. I hold her tighter as she talks, feeling so helpless, hating the vulnerability in her voice. "If the department head hadn't shown up, he would've gotten me out of there the same way he came in." She glances at me. "It was pure luck that he arrived, and he was surprised to see Lawrence there."

"Please tell me he saw him holding you at gunpoint?" I ask.

"Cassius is a sly bastard. He slipped it back in his jacket super-fast. I thought of saying something to the department head, but I just wanted to get away from that monster, and I wasn't convinced he wouldn't take the gun out and shoot the guy."

"You made the right call," Sinead says.

"And we're going to bring the college into our confidence now," Keven says. "To ensure that man isn't allowed back on the campus, or anywhere near you."

"It won't matter," Selena says. "He knows I'm in Boston now. He'll track me down."

"Not if you're out of the country," I say, voicing the thoughts that have been going through my mind the past hour.

Selena pins her gaze on me. "What do you mean?"

"I think we should go overseas. We can both keep up with classes and assignments online. Neither of us have any important shoots coming up. We can make this happen." I eyeball the FBI agents in the room. "Selena won't be able to relax in Boston after this. She was already on edge, and now, it'll be ten million times worse. We all know she can't report this. It will be his word against hers, and although the department head saw him with her today, she didn't tell him it was against her will, and he didn't see the gun. Lawrence will just bullshit his way out of it."

"I'm not sure taking Selena out of our jurisdiction is the best way to keep her safe," Colin interjects.

"Because you all did a stellar job of that today," I snap. I'm being unfair, but I don't care. This is Selena's life we're talking about.

"I think you might be onto something," Kev says, looking contemplative. His gaze bounces between his colleagues. "Think about it. Lawrence's new show is all anyone is talking about. He's already committed to shooting it here, and filming starts next week. He'll have the eyes of the nation on him. Even if he discovers she's left the US, he won't be able to go after her."

"That doesn't mean he can't send someone else after her," Colin supplies.

"Agreed, but if we go somewhere remote and hidden, and there is no log of our travel, he'll be hard-pressed to find us," I say, already having a place in mind. "And we'll have a private security detail with us, and I'll be with her twenty-four-seven. I know how to use a gun, and I'm not afraid to do what's needed," I add.

"Taking the law into your own hands will not end well for anyone, Keanu," Sinead warns.

"I don't hear anyone else offering options," I snap.

"I want to do it," Selena says. She's been quiet while we've been discussing it. "I want to put as much distance between me and him as possible. And I trust Keanu and my bodyguards to keep me safe." She addresses me head-on. "Today wasn't their fault. No one could have predicted he'd do that." She lifts her eyes to Ray and Paul, before lowering them back to me. "I don't want them fired. We've gotten used to one another."

"Fine, baby. If that's what you want." I shoot daggers at them. "But you don't get any more chances. No more fuckups."

"It won't happen again, Mr. Kennedy." Ray's expression is solemn.

I nod, exhaling heavily. "Okay."

"We'll need four more men," Keven says to Paul. "Make the call." Paul nods, removing his cell from the inside pocket of his jacket. Keven sits on the coffee table in front of us. "I'm coming too."

"I don't think—"

Kev silences his colleague with a deadly look. "You really don't want to finish that sentence, Colin."

Colin throws his hands up, shaking his head.

"I can't see Clement signing off on this," Sinead says.

"That's for me to fix, and it's not like I can't work remotely." Although Kev is a field agent now, he started as a technical specialist, and that's where his real skill lies. "And I've a bunch of vacation time to use if it comes down to it."

"You don't have to do that," Selena says. "I don't want you to waste all your vacation time protecting me."

"You're family, Selena," Keven says. "And we protect our family. It's not up for debate." He swings his gaze to me. "Right, brother?"

"Right." Only an idiot would turn down such an offer. I'm not that stubborn to refuse my brother's offer of help or too proud to accept it. Keven has done more than anyone to keep our family safe over the years, and I trust him with my life.

With Selena's.

And I could use the backup.

I know who we're up against. And the truth is, Lawrence won't stop until we stop him. If he can't grab Selena, he'll try to take her out, because she knows too much. She's a liability, and we all know it.

I'm not about to sit around waiting for him to come at her again.

"You got someplace in mind?" Kev asks.

I bob my head. "I do."

My lips tug up into a smile as I tilt Selena's face to mine. "Wanna take a trip to Greece with me, baby?"

Chapter Twenty-Six
Selena

"This place is breathtaking," I admit, as we travel by private car from Thira International Airport in Santorini toward the house that will be our new home for the next couple months. It's so unbelievably quaint here with all the traditional chapels, white-washed low-rise houses—some capped with vibrant blue roofs—beautiful little towns, stunning crystal-clear sea, and the rugged terrain on all sides as the car drives toward our destination.

"I can't wait to explore the island," Cheryl says. "I'm going to get some amazing shots here."

Keven's fiancée, Cheryl, is a very talented photographer. She's in the process of setting up her own studio in Beacon Hill, while finishing up her contract with Sara Lewis, a well-known Boston photographer.

"I knew it wouldn't take much to twist your arm into coming," Keven says from the front passenger seat, grinning over his shoulder at his fiancée.

"Are you kidding?" Cheryl arches a brow. "Have you seen how beautiful this island is? Wild horses wouldn't have kept me away.

Besides, you know I hate it when you have to travel for work. I don't like being apart from you for that long."

"I'm glad you're here," I tell her, snuggling into Keanu's side. "Helps balance out all the testosterone." With six male bodyguards, Keanu, Keven, and a local male driver who's been hired to take us wherever we want to go, I need another female for moral support.

I only met Cheryl an hour before James jetted us out of Boston, but I've already warmed to her.

Cheryl and Keven were childhood sweethearts, and she was over at the Kennedys a lot when Keanu was younger. I remember him mentioning her and how much he liked her. They only reunited last year after a few years apart, but Keanu assured me she was easygoing and that I'd like her, and he was right.

It already feels like I've known her forever.

And this from the girl who finds it hard to make friends.

I'd completed some research on Santorini over the past few days, while the guys made plans and set everything in motion, but nothing prepared me for the real live experience. It's beautiful here, and I can't wait to explore.

Santorini was the site of one of the largest volcanic eruptions ever recorded, and the population lives at an elevated position with a sheer precipice on all sides.

We are staying at a house Keanu has visited before. He actually did a shoot here last year. Friends of his parents own the property, but they only use it a few times during the year, and, thankfully, no one was scheduled to come here at this time, so they readily agreed to let us rent it for the next couple of months. We'll return to Massachusetts next month to attend James and Alex's marriage renewal ceremony, but we'll come back here after unless there has been progress in the case against that bastard Lawrence.

The second his name lands in my head, my body turns rigid. I have barely slept a wink since Friday, and any time I've managed to fall asleep, I've woken up screaming as my nightmares have returned with a vengeance. I can't even think about how close I came to being kidnapped again, because I've had multiple anxiety attacks since my run-in with him.

But I refuse to let him set me back.

I refuse to let fear and panic take root within me again.

I have the tools I need to manage my anxiety, and I'll still have my weekly therapy sessions with Denise over FaceTime.

I'm determined to leave him behind in the US and just focus on healing and spending time with my guy, trusting the FBI to deal with Lawrence while we're gone.

SSA Clement thinks me leaving might push Lawrence into making a hasty decision that will lead to his eventual arrest. He was supportive of Keven's plan and has agreed to let him work from here. He's my official FBI bodyguard while we are in Greece, and he'll also be using his technical know-how to dig deeper into Lawrence's world. To hopefully find something they can use to put the bastard away.

While it's hard for me to put my faith in the authorities, because they have failed me so far, I trust Keven. And I trust Keanu.

And leaving the US was the right decision.

So, I toss all thoughts of that monster from my mind. Because he's not ruining this experience for me. For us. I'm going to make the most of my time while we're here.

We're both able to watch videos of the classes we miss, and we can submit assignments digitally, so schoolwork should only take up a few hours a day, leaving us plenty of time for fun.

"Wow," Cheryl exclaims as we drive through the gated entrance to the property a short while later.

We climb out of the car, gawking at the beautiful villa in front of us.

Situated on the cliffs of Oia, it occupies a coveted position on the edge of the caldera, and it's not that far to the historic town. The capital city, ferry, and airport are all in proximity, should we need to make a fast exit. This place offers us privacy while still being accessible, so it ticked all the boxes.

Oia is the most historic town on the island, and this property was built on the grounds of a former captain's house. It was owned by a wealthy shipowner back in the day. The current owners have expanded and modernized the house, and it is simply stunning.

The one-story whitewashed villa is set on an expansive plot. It has five en suite bedrooms, four reception rooms, including a home theater, and an abundance of outdoor space. It offers sensational views of the caldera, the volcano, and the Aegean Sea.

"C'mon." Cheryl takes my hand. "Let's investigate." We all but skip around the side of the house, slamming to a halt at the spectacular view awaiting us.

"Oh my God. I think I've died and gone to heaven." My heart is in my throat as we walk toward the massive infinity pool disappearing over the edge of the cliff.

Gray slate tiles cover the entire outside space, and there are multiple seated areas. On the far left, in a little alcove, is a long dining table and chairs with a full bar at the back. Over on the other side is a separate section with outdoor beds covered with flimsy white drapes and a covered seating area resplendent with potted plants and patio heaters. Another bar completes this space, and I'm already imagining nights out here, cuddling with Keanu under the peaceful starry night sky.

"I thought I was used to the Kennedy opulence, but this place is something else," Cheryl says, as we stand side by side staring at the breathtaking view. The sea is placid today, barely a ripple in the water. A couple of boats linger in the distance, and I wonder if that might be something we can do while we're here.

"Hey." Keanu pokes his head out a window at the back of the house. "Come inside. It's every bit as impressive as the exterior."

We walk inside, our mouths trailing the ground at the pristine white walls and matching white furniture. The only color in the space is the gray and blue accents used for fittings and furnishings.

"Our bedroom is this way," Keanu says, appearing from a hallway and taking my hand. "Yours is on the other side, Cher bear." He jabs his finger in the opposite direction.

"Cool." She gives me a quick hug. "I'll just unpack, and maybe, we can head to the store then."

"No need," Keanu says. "The housekeeper already stocked up. I emailed her a list. We're good."

Cheryl ruffles his hair. "You're so organized. And so thoughtful."

"He really is," I agree.

Keanu shrugs, but I can tell he's happy with the compliment. We separate, leaving Cheryl to catch up with Keven while Keanu shows me the huge open-plan kitchen and living room, home theater, small gym, and dining room.

"What do you think?" he asks, opening the door to our bedroom. It's not the biggest bedroom I've seen, but it's perfect. The king-sized bed is dressed in crisp white linens, and there is a large en suite off to one side and a walk-in closet on the other. But it's the area outside the double glass doors I'm most interested in.

"I love it," I exclaim, stepping outside, my mouth hanging open again. We have our own private plunge pool, a Jacuzzi and two loungers. "This feels like a dream!" I whirl around, falling into his arms. "I'm so happy we're here."

"Me too," he agrees, pressing his velvety soft lips to mine. "And I promise you're safe. The guys are working shifts. Three on daytime. Three on nighttime. They will sleep in the small gatehouse we passed at the entrance. Those on night duty will guard the house and the entrance gate, and Kev and I have guns too. Cheryl also knows how to shoot. So, you are well protected."

"Thank you. I love you." I kiss him for a few minutes before pulling away. "I promised Mom I'd FaceTime her. She wants to see the place." I check my watch, mentally calculating the time differ-ence, happy I can catch her just before she leaves for work.

The next couple weeks fly by, and we settle into a comfortable routine. We get up early, attending to classwork by lunchtime, so we have the afternoon free to explore the island. Cheryl takes off most afternoons to photograph different places, and we usually tag along. She's been teaching me how to use her camera, and her enthusiasm is rubbing off on me. I'm seriously considering getting my own camera.

At night, we either eat out at one of the local restaurants or cook on the outside grill. But we always end up outside, sipping sangria, with the pool lit up and the dark sky littered with strips of orange and violet creating a vibrant canvas overhead.

"I'm so happy Cheryl and Keven came with us," I tell Keanu as we get ready for bed.

"Me too," he agrees, slipping under the covers in his boxers. "Kev is the least intrusive of my brothers. Well, besides Keats."

"What do you think Kent is getting up to in our absence?" I ask, wiping the cleansing milk off my face with some cotton pads.

Keanu snorts. "I'd prefer not to think about that. I've no doubt it's party central at the condo. Thank God, I remembered to lock our bedroom door and take the key."

"I bet he misses you," I say, switching off the overhead light and crawling into bed in only a silk tank and my panties. Keanu already has the bedside lamps turned on, bathing the room in a subtle glow.

He shrugs. "It's hard to tell with Kent sometimes."

I throw my leg over his, pressing my side into his body, my breasts smooshing against his hard, warm chest. "I want to make a plan, K," I say, knowing he will get what I'm referencing. "I need you," I plead, tracing circles on his hot flesh with the tip of my finger.

"Twice-daily orgasms aren't doing it, huh?" he teases, threading his fingers through my hair.

I lean up and peck his lips. "I'm not complaining. And the orgasms are mind-blowing, but as much as I love your hands and your mouth, I need more." I prop up on one elbow, my hair tumbling over my shoulder. "I need all of you. I'm ready." I cup his gorgeous face. "Are you?"

He twists around so we're both on our sides, facing one another.

He takes my hand, joining our fingers. "I am, and I think this is the perfect place to make love for the first time."

"It is. I'm comfortable here. Happy here." He nods. "But?" I ask, sensing there is one.

He drags his lower lip between his teeth, peering intensely into my eyes. I don't know what he is looking for, or what he sees, but I notice the moment he makes his decision. "Close your eyes."

I frown. "What?"

"Just close your eyes, baby. For one minute." He kisses me.

I've no idea what this has to do with the discussion we were having, but I trust him, so I close my eyes. The bed shifts as he moves, and then, I hear the opening of a drawer.

"You can open your eyes now," he says. I blink my eyes open and stare at him. He's kneeling in front of me on the bed with his hands behind his back.

Shit, he's not going to tie me up or something, is he? A prickle of unease sweeps over my suddenly overheated skin. But I dismiss that thought the second it invades my mind. Keanu would never suggest that.

"Sit up," he croaks, and I do as he says, resting my back against the headboard. He clears his throat. "I've waited a long time to make love to you, Selena, and I know you're ready. But something was holding me back, and it wasn't what I thought."

I'm not following, and if he changes his mind, I'm going to be so disappointed. But I will never hold it against him. He has waited years for me to reach this point. And I can wait longer if that's what he needs.

"Coming here helped make it clear in my mind." His eyes glisten, and I reach for him the same time he places his arms out in front of him. I gasp as he pops the lid on a small blue box. "I want to make love to you, Selena. But I want to do it as husband and wife. Will you marry me?"

Chapter Twenty-Seven
Selena

Istare at the ring with my mouth open, my eyes wide in shock. My heart is thumping wildly behind my rib cage, and butterflies invade my chest, celebrating like it's Mardi Gras.

"Say something," Keanu pleads.

I lift my blurry eyes to my boyfriend. His eyes betray his vulnerability, and I need to put him out of his misery.

I don't need to think about this at all.

Not for a single second.

"Yes," I say, as tears pool in my eyes. "Yes, I'll marry you." A sob bursts from my mouth, but it's all good, because it's a happy, emotionally charged sob. My heart soars, and I've never felt so happy in my life. This is everything. *He* is everything.

Keanu crashes his mouth against mine, and our lips and tongues tangle in a frenzied marriage of lust and love. "I love you," he pants when we finally break apart.

"I love *you*." I smile so wide my jaw hurts.

With trembling fingers, he takes my hand, sliding the pretty ring on my ring finger. "I'll get you a proper ring when we get home," he says, as I lift my hand, admiring the sparkling green stone set on a plain platinum band. It's a little loose but not enough that I can't wear it.

"Why would you get me another one?" I ask, dragging my eyes from my finger to my boyfriend's face.

My fiancé. I autocorrect myself, and another mammoth smile spreads across my mouth.

"Because this is the best I could find on the island, but it's not even a diamond. I don't know what that stone is, only that it reminded me of your eyes." His cheeks flush with that admission, and I swoon. "It's only temporary until I can take you to Neil Lane to get a custom ring designed."

I examine the ring on my finger in closer detail, marveling at the little amber flecks underneath the green stone. I've never seen anything like it, and I already love it. I cup Keanu's face. "I don't need a big, expensive diamond. I love this ring. Even more so because you chose it for me."

"A queen deserves an engagement ring fit for a queen, and you're *my queen*, Selena. I'm buying you a new ring." He pins me with a determined look. "We can get a replica of this ring if you like it that much, but you're getting another one."

"How did you even manage to get this?" We haven't spent much time apart since we got here, so he must've been sneaky.

"Remember that morning last week I said I had to help Kev with something?" I nod. "We went ring shopping. He helped me choose it."

"You both have great taste. It's stunning."

"That settles it. We'll get a replica of this one," he says with finality, holding my hand and running his finger over the top of the ring.

I could argue, but Keanu can be stubborn when he fixates on something. And I'm too Goddamn happy right now to risk anything bursting my bubble. I shrug, smiling. "Whatever you want."

A radiant smile graces his gorgeous mouth, and I can't believe this beautiful, thoughtful, selfless man is going to be my husband.

He rests his hands on my waist, and we're grinning at one another like idiots, but I couldn't care less. "I was thinking we could get married here," he says. "As soon as we can arrange it, and then, we can plan another wedding back home, whenever we feel the time is right."

I circle my arms around his neck. "I love that idea. But what about your family? Will they be mad?" Keven obviously knows, and I'm betting he told Cheryl Keanu was planning to propose. It's only natural they'll be in attendance. But will the rest of his family be pissed? What about Keaton and Kent? I don't want to cause problems for him.

"Nah." He shakes his head. "They'll be happy for us. And Mom'll be cool once we let her design your dress and help us with the planning of the Boston wedding." He runs his hand up and down my back. "What about your mom? If you want her here, I'll make it happen."

"I would love her to be here, but it's not going to work. She won't be able to get time off from her job on short notice, and if that monster is watching the house, it's too risky. He could track her to here."

Keanu scrutinizes my face. "I'm desperate to make you my wife, but we can wait if—"

I press my fingers to his lips, shushing him. "I don't want to wait. I want to marry you as soon as possible. I'll call Mom and tell her the good news. She'll understand, and she'll be happy for me. For us."

"You sure?" he asks, tucking my hair behind my ears.

"Positive." A squeal of sheer happiness emits from my mouth, and I bounce up and down. "We're getting married!"

"Believe it, babe," Keanu says, grabbing me by the hips and sliding off the bed, swinging me around in his arms. "I can't wait to call you Mrs. Kennedy."

It's amazing what money can do. If you asked me a few days ago if we could pull off even the simplest of weddings in less than a week, I would have told you you were cray-cray. But here I am. A mere five days since Keanu proposed, getting ready to walk down the aisle of the cute little chapel perched on top of the hill in Oia.

Keanu and Keven arranged everything with the local priest. Luckily, early November isn't a popular time for weddings, so we didn't have to worry about securing a date, thanks to the local ruling that only permits a small number of weddings per day.

The guys also bought our wedding rings, and they reserved a table at the best restaurant in town for after the small ceremony. Dan Evans, the Kennedy family lawyer, organized all the paperwork, using his contacts in the US to pull it off in record time.

Cheryl came shopping with me, so we could both pick dresses. Luckily, the guys already had pants and dress shirts to wear. The local flower shop provided simple bouquets of white and pink bougainvillea, wrapped in ribbons. Cheryl has her camera, and Paul is going to record the ceremony on his iPhone so we can send it to our families afterward.

With the exception of the crew we have here, only Kent, Keaton, and my mom know about today. Mom was ecstatic as I knew she would be. She already loves Keanu like a son. While I know she wishes she could be here, she didn't want us holding back on her account. She made me promise to send her pictures and the video.

Keanu had to tell Kent and Keaton. They're triplets. And it wouldn't have been right not to tell them.

It also wouldn't have been right for Keanu to get married without them by his side. Which is why, with Keven's help, I arranged for them to be here as a surprise. The look on Keanu's face yesterday when he opened the door to Kent and Keaton was priceless, and I'm so glad I went behind his back to do it.

In order to hide their travel plans, we had them fly from Boston to London and from London to mainland Greece. Then, they were transported here between cars and boats. Neither of them complained, understanding the need for subterfuge, and I can tell they're as happy to be a part of this as Keanu is to have them here.

"Any cold feet?" Cheryl asks as we stand outside the wooden door to the chapel.

"Definitely not." I smooth a hand down the front of my plain white dress. We found it in a small bridal boutique in Fira, Santorini's capital city. It's a simple design, but it's exactly my taste, and I knew this was perfect the second I spotted it on the rack.

It's a halter-style dress that flares out at the waist, and it's cut out at the back, showcasing some skin. The only embellishment is a silk sash that ties around my middle that's held together at the front with a small gold, patterned metallic strip. Strappy gold sandals, with a low heel, complete the look. We found a white chenille wrap in another store, which I'll use after the ceremony. Although it's still warm for November, it tends to get a little chilly in the evenings and at night.

"You look stunning, Selena. Keanu is a lucky man."

"You look stunning too," I truthfully admit. Cheryl choose a light-green silk dress that hugs her gorgeous curves. It dips low in the front, and it's cinched at the waist. The material is delicate, and it sways with her body as she moves.

"Thank you for helping with my hair and makeup."

I've also kept that simple, and my hair is styled in soft waves cascading down my back. Cheryl did my eye makeup with rich golds and browns and lashings of black mascara which make my lashes appear longer and fuller. The light-pink blush on my cheeks matches the delicate pink gloss on my lips.

"It was my pleasure." She gives me a careful hug. "Thank you for letting us be a part of your special day," she adds, fanning her face as tears prick her eyes. "I think what you are doing is beautiful."

I squeeze her hand. "Thank you." I draw a brave breath as butterflies flutter in my chest.

"Ready to get this show on the road?" she asks.

We've broken with tradition, and no one is giving me away today. I'm walking up that aisle by myself, with Cheryl at my rear, because I'm the one giving myself to Keanu today of my own free will, and nothing feels more empowering.

I nod, letting a natural smile break free. "Let's do this. I don't want to make my man wait a second longer."

Cheryl opens the door, stepping aside so I can enter first.

Traditional Greek music accompanies us up the short aisle, performed by a guy on a guitar and a woman with a sweet, lyrical voice. The six bodyguards turn around in their seats, in the second row, smiling as we approach. Paul is holding up his iPhone, capturing every moment, just like he promised.

Keanu waits in front of the marble altar with Keven, Kent, and Keaton by his side. The celebrant stands on the altar, book in hand, smiling warmly as we make our approach.

My husband-to-be is wearing a crisp white long-sleeved button-down shirt and khaki pants. But it's the awestruck expression on his face and the naked emotion in his eyes that draw my attention. My eyes remain locked on his as we walk.

Keven leans in, kissing me on the cheek as Cheryl takes my bouquet, and they both take seats in the first pew. Keaton and Kent kiss me on the cheek next, smiling warmly as they claim seats beside Cheryl.

The whole time, my eyes haven't strayed from my groom.

"You take my breath away," Keanu says, clasping my hands and drawing me in close to his body.

"I love you," I say, my voice thick with emotion, my eyes brimming with tears of joy.

"Love you too."

We face one another and hold hands throughout the ceremony. The priest speaks in Greek, and I don't have a clue what he's saying, but it's okay, because I doubt I'd hear the words even if they were spoken in English. I can't take my eyes off my groom, and my heart is fit to burst.

When it comes to the vows, the celebrant speaks in broken English, and it's so unique and romantic. The others chuckle under their breath, and we smile. I know I will cherish this moment for the rest of my life. We repeat our vows, and my hands tremble as I slide the platinum wedding band on Keanu's finger. His eyes shine with love as he slides a matching wedding band on mine.

Our lips collide in a passionate kiss when the celebrant pronounces us man and wife, and I cling to my husband, my heart overflowing with emotion.

After the ceremony concludes, Cheryl takes a ton of photos, and then, we make the short journey to the restaurant, accompanied by our bodyguards.

The guys reserved a gorgeous private alcove which overlooks the sea. A couple bottles of champagne are already chilling on the table, and Keven pours six glasses as the security team takes positions at a table next to us. As they are on duty, they are all sticking to water, but they'll share the same meal we're having.

Keanu picks up a card from the table as he wraps his arm around me.

Kent hands me a glass of champagne. "Thanks." I graciously accept it from my new brother-in-law. I don't usually drink, but I've let down my guard a little here. Firstly, it's legal, and secondly, Keanu is here to make sure I'm safe and that nothing happens to me. So, I feel comfortable relaxing. Although I haven't gone overboard, sipping one glass of sangria at night. This is my first time tasting champagne, and the crisp, amber-colored bubbly glides effortlessly down my throat. "Oh, wow, this is yummy."

"It's from Ray, Paul, and the other bodyguards," Keanu says, passing me the card.

I read their kind words with a lump in my throat. "That's so sweet."

We smile and raise our glasses at the guys.

"This is from the four of us," Keats says, gesturing at Kent, Keven, and Cheryl, as a waiter brings a small two-tier wedding cake to the table. It's covered in white icing with a pink bow around the base of the top layer. An edible rendering of a man and woman embracing rests on top of it. I hope it tastes as yummy as it looks.

"It's just a token gift," Kent explains. "We'll give you your main present when we get back to the US." Kent, Keven, and Keats exchange a conspiratorial smile, and I wonder what they are planning.

"Thank you so much." I hug all of them, and Keanu slaps the guys on the back and kisses Cheryl on the cheek.

"These are from your mom," Cheryl says, handing me a massive bouquet of blue, pink, and purple flowers.

I bury my nose in the delicate, fragrant scent, inhaling deeply.

"I need to call her," I say, but Keanu is already handing me his cell. I press my lips to his. "Love you, husband."

"Love you, wife," he says, hauling me against his warm body. His hands land on my waist as he lowers his mouth to mine. He deepens the kiss while his brothers and the table of bodyguards whoop, holler, and break out in a round of applause.

We separate eventually, and my husband laughs at my fire-engine-red cheeks. I swat his arm. "Don't start."

We call my mom and Denise in between drinking champagne and eating the delicious food they bring out. Then we FaceTime James and Alex and break the news to them. Their obvious delight is clear to see, and I feel Keanu relax beside me. Despite his protests, he was concerned how his mom would react. But Alex is thrilled for us, and, as expected, she instantly offers to make my wedding gown, and I happily accept. It won't be a chore. I've always loved that woman's designs.

Then we call the rest of Keanu's brothers and my friend Kelly, ensuring everyone knows to keep the news private. We don't want anything leaking to the press in case that bastard finds out where we are. But I also want to enjoy this time with my husband without any media intrusion.

"So, how does it feel to be a married woman?" Keaton asks after we've polished off the delicious wedding cake.

"Pretty damn awesome," I truthfully reply, grinning as I stare at my gorgeous husband. Keanu is deep in conversation with Kent, Keven, and Cheryl, completely oblivious to my ogling.

"I can see that." Keaton clinks his glass against mine. "I'm so happy for both of you. I've always known you were the one for my brother. He's only ever had eyes for you."

"I never even thought to invite Melissa," I blurt, suddenly realizing my faux pas. "I'm so sorry. She could have come. If you—"

"It's fine." Keats cuts in, halting my words. "Honestly. She's at college, and we don't really see much of each other anymore."

"Oh." I'm not sure what to say to that. I don't know Keaton all that well, and I've never met Melissa. All I know of her is from what Keanu has said. "Do you think—"

"No." He shakes his head repeatedly, swallowing a large mouthful of champagne. "We're definitely not heading down the marriage path," he says, confirming he knew what I was going to ask.

"Well, you're still young. I know we're young, but when you know, you know. Waiting wouldn't have made a bit of difference," I confidently exclaim.

"I know exactly what you mean," he cryptically replies.

We stay at the restaurant for hours, laughing, eating, and drinking, and I'm definitely a little tipsy as we make our way back to the villa. But the alcohol takes the edge off my nerves, which are growing in intensity the closer we get to the house.

Tonight is the night I lose my virginity and consummate my marriage.

I'm excited and nervous in equal measures.

"Did you do this?" I ask, gasping as I open our bedroom door. Copious lit candles rim the perimeter of the room, and with the line of rose petals leading from the door to the bed and scattered over the bed covers, it's the most romantic setting. Another bottle of champagne rests in an ice bucket, alongside two flutes and a bowl of chocolate strawberries, by the bed.

Keanu reels me into his arms. "You like?"

"I love it and you." I hug him tightly, and I never want to let go. "I love you so much, K." I look up at him, and I know my eyes are eager, my cheeks flushed. "Thank you for today. It was the most incredible day of my life."

"Mine too, wife." He lifts me up, and I wrap my legs around his waist. He carries me to the bed, gently placing me down on it.

I clear my throat. "Would it be okay if I got changed in the bathroom?"

He sits beside me, cupping my cheek. "Of course. Whatever you need." He leans in, kissing me softly. "Are you still okay with this?"

I nod. "Yes. I'm just a little nervous."

"Me too," he admits, stroking his thumbs along my cheeks. "But I'm going to take good care of you, Selena. You're in safe hands."

"I always know that." I kiss him again before standing. "I'll be back in a few."

I dart into the bathroom, closing the door behind me, reaching for the bag I stashed in here earlier. I remove my dress and hang it up on the back of the door. I shimmy my panties down my legs and slip off my sandals. Then, I pull the sexy lace nightie on, staring at my glowing face in the mirror.

I inspect my hand, loving the new additions to my ring finger.

I'm married.

To the man of my dreams.

Life doesn't get much better than this.

I smile at myself in the mirror, feeling more content and more *me* than I have in a long time. And that's all thanks to the amazing man patiently waiting outside to make love to me.

I quickly remove my makeup, clean my teeth, and take care of business. I spray some perfume on my neck and my wrists, and I give myself one final pep talk. I'm scared, but I know Keanu will make this good for me. And if I'm not enjoying it, I know he'll stop if I ask.

But I'm determined to relax and enjoy his touch, because this is the part where my life truly begins.

And I'm going to embrace it fully.

Chapter Twenty-Eight
Keanu

My jaw slackens when my wife walks out of the bathroom in this sexy, white lace number that clings to her delicate curves, leaving little to the imagination. Her rosy pink nipples are taut, poking through the flimsy material, causing blood to rush straight to my dick. She leans against the wall, her cheeks flushed, looking nervous as hell.

"Wow. You look so beautiful and so sexy." I stand. "I love you, Mrs. Kennedy."

"I love you too," she says, giggling. "And I love hearing that. I can't wait to change my name."

I know lots of women like to keep their own name, and I wouldn't have held it against Selena if she did, but I was overjoyed when she told me she had every intention of changing her name as soon as possible. I grab the small glass of champagne I poured for her, walking toward her. She's consumed a couple glasses over the course of the night, and while I think the alcohol will help her to relax, I want her to be fully cognizant and aware of everything we do. I don't want to make love to my wife for the first time if she's drunk. "Let's toast," I say, handing her the flute while I pick up mine.

"To us," she says, pushing off the wall and chinking her glass against mine.

"To eternal love," I add, taking a sip as I clasp her hand and pull her over to the bed.

We sit cross-legged on the bed, facing one another. Her in her sexy nightgown. Me in only my boxers. Sipping our champagne, our knees touching, feeding each other strawberries, as we gaze into one another's eyes. When we're finished, I set our glasses down and gently haul her into my lap. "I love you, Selena. Thank you for agreeing to share your life with me."

"No one has ever made me as happy as you do, K." She drags her fingers through my hair. "No one has ever loved me as fully as you do." She presses an open-mouthed kiss just under my jawline, and I shiver all over. "No one has ever worshiped the ground I walk on like you do." She runs her fingers along my face. "I am going to spend the rest of my days honoring and loving you, starting with right now."

With shaking hands, she pushes the straps of her nightie off her shoulders. The straps slide down her arms, pulling the top of her nightie down, exposing her bare chest to me.

I caress her tits, one at a time, gently kneading her soft flesh. Her nipples are like bullets against my palms, and I flick at them with my fingers in the way I know she loves. She throws her head back, moaning as she wiggles on my lap, her face drenched with desire. My cock jerks behind my boxers, eager as ever, as I lift her off me, placing her flat on her back in the center of the bed.

With slow, careful movements, I slide the nightie down the rest of the way, kissing every inch of her skin as I pull it off, leaving her totally naked, laid out before me with her hair fanning around her head, like a beautiful Aphrodite in the flesh. I yank my boxers down, kicking them away as I crawl back onto the bed, spreading her legs wide and kneeling between the apex of her thighs. "You are so beautiful, Selena."

Her face relaxes, and the wanton look she sends my way has my cock bobbing against my stomach.

"Make love to me, Keanu. I need to feel you inside me."

"Soon, baby. Let me get you ready first." I take my time warming her up. Licking, kissing, and sucking every inch of soft, creamy skin. I tease her pussy with my tongue and my fingers, and when I suck hard on her clit, she falls apart underneath me, moaning as she fists the covers, her hips bucking wildly as she rides out her climax.

I can't wait any longer, so I climb over her body, keeping myself propped up by my elbows as I kiss the shit out of her. When we break for air, I examine her face closely, looking for any signs of discomfort. But all I see is love and desire staring back at me.

I angle my hips, lining my cock up at her entrance. "You feel me, baby?" I ask, nudging her opening, and she nods, threading her fingers through my hair. "Can I make love to you?"

A calmness washes over her. "Please, husband. I want every part of you."

Very slowly, I push inside her. Keeping my eyes pinned to hers as I dust kisses all over her face. Fuck. She's so tight, and I don't think I'll last long. "Are you okay?" I ask as I inch in farther, groaning as little tremors zip up my spine.

"I'm okay," she reassures me, moving her hands to my back, tracing a line up and down my spine.

I kiss her lips softly as I edge in again, pushing in farther until I'm fully seated inside her.

Selena knows this is the first time I've ever gone bareback as we discussed contraception last week.

She's on the pill, and we're both clean, so we agreed there would be nothing between us tonight. It's only fitting that the one and only person I'm ever inside of with no barrier is my beautiful wife. "You feel so good, baby." I nip at her earlobe, pressing a slew of drugging kisses along her jawline, trailing my nose along the elegant column of her neck, inhaling everything about her.

"You can move, babe," she says, her hands roaming my back. "I need you to move."

I pivot my hips, moving in and out of her in slow, long strokes.

Heavenly shockwaves ricochet all over my body, and I've never felt anything even close to this before.

I make love to her slowly and carefully, watching her all the time, checking in a few times to make sure she's okay.

Her legs wrap around my waist and her hands move to my ass as she pulls me closer. Our lips meet in a melting pot of desire, and it takes effort to keep from thrusting too hard. When she angles her hips, lifting up slightly, I hiss between my teeth as I feel my climax start to build. I draw one tender nipple into my mouth, sucking and lapping at the hard peak as I rock my hips with a little more urgency.

Selena emits all these breathy little moans that enhance my arousal, and I'm close to the edge. Seeing the pleasure and joy on her face almost undoes me.

I'm not going to lie.

I was so scared this wouldn't work.

That she wouldn't be able to relax and enjoy it, and I'm so fucking happy she's happy. That her eyes brim with emotion, her cheeks are flushed from sex, her lips swollen from my kisses, her body arching and writhing as I make love to her.

This is everything I've dreamed of and more.

Some might say I'm crazy for marrying my first girlfriend, my only girlfriend, especially when I'm only turning twenty next week, but I know my own mind. My heart. And Selena has always been it for me.

I haven't ever been this content, and I know this is only the start of something amazing.

Moving my hand between our bodies, I toy with her clit, and a primal groan rips from her lips. "Oh my God, Keanu." Tears glisten in her eyes as she stares at me. "This feels so unbelievably good."

"Love you so much," I say before my lips claim hers again.

"I'm so close," she cries out when our lips part.

"Me too. I want to come with you," I add, rubbing her clit with firmer strokes.

Releasing Keanu

She screams as an orgasm consumes her, thrashing around underneath me, her skin flushed, her eyes alive. My balls tighten, and fiery tingles shoot up my spine, and then, I'm coming too, spilling deep, my inner beast silently beating its chest as my seed lodges inside her.

When we're both sated, I roll onto my side, taking her with me, keeping my cock inside her. "You doing okay, Mrs. Kennedy?" I ask, pushing damp strands of hair off her brow.

"Keanu," she chokes out with tears tumbling down her cheeks. "That was everything I've always imagined it to be."

"That was incredible, Sel," I agree. "And everything I'd hoped for and more. It only confirms what I've always known. We were made to fit together, baby."

She plasters my face in kisses before sealing her lips to mine. Her salty, sweet taste is like heaven on my lips, and I know I'll never get enough of her. I hug her to my chest, savoring the feel of her body against mine, skin to skin, and we drift off to sleep, locked in our embrace.

My twentieth birthday arrives, and it's the second year in a row when the three of us haven't celebrated together. Last year, Kent and I went partying, and I got wasted. Keats was at Berkeley, so it was the first time we were separated on our birthday. I guess it's unrealistic to expect we can continue to do stuff together.

It's a shame the guys couldn't stick around after the wedding, but they have lives back in the US. Plus, any prolonged absence may have drawn interest. While I know Kev went to a lot of trouble ensuring Keats and Kent got here without being traced, we can't be too careful.

So, I find myself without my triplets on my birthday again this year. This time, I spend it with Selena and my brother and his fiancée.

Sel wakes me up by jumping on the bed and shoving a heavy gift wrapped in shiny red paper at me. "Do you like it?" She tugs on the corner of her nail, her face creased with worry as I examine the pile of books she got me. They are all related to setting up your own business. She even registered a bunch of domain names for me, and I love that she remembers the conversation we had about setting up my own designer brand and the tentative names I had in mind.

I haul her into my lap. "I love it." I press a kiss to her lips. "I love how much you support me following my dreams."

"You support mine," she replies. "And I want to see you scale those heady heights I know you'll climb."

"With you by my side, it feels like I can achieve anything."

Her features soften as she wraps her arms around me. "I know the feeling," she murmurs before dropping her mouth to mine.

And that's the last talking we do for a while.

That evening, Selena cooks a French-inspired feast, preparing all of Sandrine's old family recipes, and we eat like kings. The wine is flowing, conversation is lively, and it is hands down one of my best ever birthdays. Especially when my wife gives me a special birthday gift that night in bed.

Slinking out of the bathroom in another new nightie, she looks fucking sensational in a tiny black and red number she wore for all of four seconds before I pulled it off her. Watching my wife ride my cock is out of this world, and the obvious enjoyment she derives from taking control and giving me pleasure almost has me shooting my load prematurely.

Life is good, and I don't want to leave this island, but it's my parents' marriage renewal ceremony next week, so we're going back to Massachusetts for a few days.

Dad is busy with celebratory preparations, so he sends Michael, his standby pilot, to collect us. We sleep for most of the flight, and when we set down in Boston, it's the middle of the night, and unfortunately, we're now all wide-awake.

We spend the night at the cabin on the grounds of my parents' property. Cheryl and Keven stay there too, along with three of the bodyguards. The other three—the ones who drew the short straws—are guarding the grounds. Dad also has extra security on hand for the event tomorrow, so we're safe and protected here, but I'm still uneasy, and I can sense Sel is too.

It was relatively easy to forget the danger of the situation in Santorini. But now we're back home, it's like a slap in the face.

Sinead and Colin come over early the next morning to brief us. Kev kept us updated the whole time we were away, but it's good to sit down face to face with his team.

Lawrence is still under close FBI surveillance, and the team is working nonstop to try to find something to pin on him, but so far, nothing has turned up. Which means we'll definitely be returning to Greece. Something I'm not in any way unhappy about. Neither is my wife.

After the agents leave, we walk to the main house to join the rest of the family for breakfast.

"Prepare yourself," I warn Selena again as we near the back of the house. "My family is crazy and loud, and they're going to want to smother you with love. I apologize in advance."

"There is nothing to apologize for, K." Selena squeezes my hand as we walk in the back door and I lead her through the house toward the open-plan kitchen. "They're my family now, and I don't want anyone to tread on eggshells around me anymore."

"I hope you're still saying that after today," I joke, wrapping my arms around her as we enter mayhem.

"Uncle Kaynu!!! Uncle Keven!!" Hewson shrieks as he spots us, storming across the kitchen on his short, stubby legs. He can't say my name properly yet, but it's cute when he calls me Kaynu. I crouch down, and he throws himself at me, his chubby arms snaking around my neck. "Where's my pwesent?" he asks, looking all around.

"What present?!" I tease, standing with him in my arms.

He spins around in my arms, and I barely manage to keep a hold of him. "Uncle Keven. *You* have my pwesent?"

Kev pretends to look all around him, frowning and scratching his chin. "I don't see any present. Do you, Cheryl?"

"Stop it!" Cheryl shakes her finger at both of us. "Stop torturing the little cutie." She slides the box wrapped in blue paper to Selena, nudging her forward.

"Who are you?" Hewson asks, noticing Selena for the first time.

"This is Selena," I say.

"Auntie Selena!" Hewson wriggles in my arms, catching me off guard, and I nearly drop the little monster. "Do *you* have my pwesent?" he asks in a hopeful tone.

"Oh, boy," Lana says, coming to our aid. "His manners seem to have done a disappearing act."

My brother Kalvin comes up behind his wife, wrapping his arms around her growing baby bump. My sister-in-law is five months pregnant with their second child, and she's due to give birth a couple months after Eva, my other sister-in-law.

Very soon, this house is going to be overrun with kids.

Images of Selena pregnant with my child surfaces in my mind, and I can't wait for that day. But I want to enjoy my wife first. And I want to put all this stuff with Lawrence behind us before we even consider a discussion about kids.

"Hey, little dude," Kal says, snapping me out of my futuristic thoughts. "Don't you have something to say to Uncle Keanu and Auntie Selena?"

His little brow puckers, and then, his eyes light up. "Gratulations!" he shouts, clapping his hands, and we all laugh. Until he spots the present in Selena's hand and skydives out of my arms. Thankfully, his dad has lightning-fast reflexes and catches the little handful before he splats the ground.

"Holy hell." I shake my head. "Let's hope the next kid gets your genes, Lana," I joke.

Selena decides to put my nephew out of his misery, kneeling in front of him and holding out the present. "This is for you. From all of us." She gestures at me, Cher bear, and Keven. "A little birdie told us you like dinosaurs."

"I do! I do!" He starts simultaneously jumping up and down and ripping at the paper. Kal helps his son, and Hewson's entire face erupts with happiness when he spots the miniature dinosaur set. Options were limited on Santorini, but thankfully, we found something that worked.

"What do you say, Hewson?" Lana prompts.

"Thank you!" Hewson singsongs, briefly lifting his head up to shoot us a toothy grin.

"Congratulations, guys," Kal says, straightening up. "We're delighted for you."

"That video you sent was so beautiful," Lana says with tears swimming in her eyes. "It looked so romantic."

"It was," Selena says, leaning into me. I tuck her into my side, kissing the top of her head. "It was everything I imagined for my wedding day and more."

"That's a winner," Kyler says, grinning at Hewson as he approaches with his arm around Faye. Hewson has a dinosaur in each hand, and he's walking them across the tile floor, blabbering away in different voices as he makes them "talk" to one another.

"C'mere little brother." Ky releases his wife to grab me into a strong hug. "Congrats, man. I'm so happy for you. Married life is fucking awesome."

"Thanks, bro." I struggle to speak over the messy ball of emotion that's just materialized at the back of my throat.

Faye is hugging Selena, whispering in her ear. And then, everyone else is on top of us, offering best wishes and pulling us into hugs.

Selena looks happy if overwhelmed.

When I finally pry her out of my mom's arms, I take her hand leading her into the dining room where breakfast has been set up. I press my mouth to her ear. "Thinking about divorcing me yet?" I tease, waggling my brows.

"Never." She nudges me playfully in the ribs. "You're stuck with me now."

Chapter Twenty-Nine
Selena

The ceremony was beautiful, and there was barely a dry eye in the house. Keanu was in the front row, alongside his brothers, all looking so handsome in their tuxes. Mom sat with me, alongside the other wives and girlfriends, in the row behind.

Now, we're sitting at one of two large round tables at the top of the marquee that's been erected on the grounds. We've just finished a delicious five-course meal, and the band has started. The dance floor is already crowded, so Mom can't object when my husband drags her up to dance.

"It's wonderful to see Keanu so happy," Eva says, smiling at me as she sips on her water.

Eva is Kaden's wife, and Kaden is Keanu's eldest brother. They eloped two years ago and got married in secret. Then, Alex planned their lavish Boston wedding which took place last year.

"I hate that I hurt him so much he was miserable, but we needed that time apart," I admit.

"I can only imagine," she says, compassion flooding her eyes.

All of Keanu's family knows about my past. I asked him to tell them because I don't want to keep secrets from my new family. But I wasn't up to a big family meeting either even though it *is* getting easier to talk about.

She clasps my hand. "I'm so sorry for everything that happened to you. I never knew my ex-husband was involved in sex trafficking until much later, and it made me ill to think about it. Cheryl was the same when she discovered her ex-fiancé was knee-deep in that world. At least, both those bastards got what they deserved," she adds, her nostrils flaring. "And those bastards who hurt you will pay the same price." She squeezes my hand more firmly. "Our husbands will accept nothing less."

"I hope it's sooner rather than later," I say. "Because I want to move forward with my life, and that's the only cloud that can cast a shadow over our plans."

"Trust Keven. Trust the guys. They'll nail those monsters to the wall."

A little whimper leaves baby Milly's lips, and we both look at Eva and Kaden's daughter squirming in her stroller. She's asleep, worn out from all the excitement of today.

"She's such a little beauty," I tell Eva, smiling at the gorgeous little baby as she pulls her thumb into her mouth, sucking greedily.

"I can't believe she's nine months old already. That she's crawling and she'll be walking soon. It's happened in the blink of an eye." She rocks the stroller back and forth with one hand while her other hand rests atop her large baby bump.

"I can't believe you'll be raising two little ones *and* building a new business." I sip my champagne before adding, "You're an inspiration, Eva."

Her features soften, and she lets go of the stroller to give me an awkward hug. It's hard to embrace with her pregnant belly between us. "Thank you, sweetie. That's so kind of you to say." She eases back. "What do you plan to do after you finish college? Keanu says you're studying psychology. Do you want to work as a psychologist?"

I nod. "Yes."

"That's a lot of study," Eva says.

And she's not wrong. After I graduate, it will take me at least four years of further study before I'm qualified to practice. "I know, but I'm in this for the long haul. I want to help other victims of sexual abuse. My therapist, Denise, has been a very important part of my recovery and my life, and I want to do for others what she's done for me."

"That's amazing, Selena. And I think you'll make a wonderful therapist."

I clasp my hands in my lap, and I can't believe I'm going to tell Eva this. Keanu, Denise, and my mom are the only other people I've ever mentioned this to.

But I like Eva a lot.

She's easy to talk to, and she emits a mothering vibe I can't help but be drawn to.

"I want to set up a sanctuary. A place where victims can come to heal away from the pressures of the outside world." My cheeks inflame as Eva gives me her full attention. "I want to offer a variety of therapies and supplementary holistic treatments and a bunch of other stuff." I've thought about this in-depth, and I have detailed plans, but I'm sure she doesn't want me boring her about all this stuff.

She stares at me for a few moments with an awed expression on her face. "I think you're wrong, Selena," she says, startling me. "I think it's you who is the inspiration."

"I can't believe your family bought us a boat!" I exclaim a couple hours later after the Kennedys surprised us with an over-the-top wedding gift.

"Don't be fooled, babe," Keanu says, as we sway to a slow number on the dance floor. "It's as much for their benefit as it is ours."

"Even still. I can't wrap my head around it."

He kisses me. "Get used to it, wife. When I come into my full inheritance next year, we're going to be mega rich. You won't ever want for anything."

"You know me," I say, shrugging. "I don't need much."

"That's one of the things I love most about you," he says. "But it's nice to not have to worry about it."

"Keanu!" Keven bursts through the front entrance of the marquee, his cheeks red, looking like he's run all the way from the main house to here.

Bile floods my mouth as he races toward us, and Keanu grabs hold of my hand, leading me off the dance floor. We meet halfway to the door. "What's going on?" Keanu asks.

"You need to come back to the house. There's a breaking story on CNN you need to see."

Keanu and I share a look as we follow Keven back to the house. The rest of Keanu's family follows us, and when we congregate in the living room, where Eva, Kaden, and Cheryl are already lounging on couches, everyone piles into the room, dropping into seats. Keanu pulls me down on one of the leather recliners, positioning me on his lap. His arms automatically go around me, and everyone quiets down as Keven raises the volume on the TV.

A reporter is standing outside an apartment building in downtown Boston with a serious expression on her face. In the background are several law enforcement cars and trucks, including vehicles with the FBI logo on them. A van from the M.E's office pulls up, followed by a blacked-out SUV, and other reporters surge on the new arrival.

"According to our sources," the reporter says into her microphone, "the alarm was raised an hour ago when a neighbor reported hearing gunshots coming from the penthouse suite Mr. Lawrence has been renting since he moved to the city."

Keanu clasps my hands, rubbing his thumb across my skin in soothing circles. My breath falters as I wait for the reporter to continue.

"Police arrived shortly on the scene, quickly followed by local agents from the FBI." She taps her ear, her eyes widening as she listens to whatever is being said. Then she refocuses on the camera. "We have just received confirmation that Clive Lawrence, the Oscar-winning director, has been shot and killed. We have no details at this time, but we'll share more information as we receive it."

Keven mutes the TV but leaves it on. The headline flashes repeatedly across the screen.

OSCAR WINNING DIRECTOR FOUND DEAD AT HIS PENTHOUSE HOME.

"Hell yeah!" Kent shouts jumping up and rushing toward me. He yanks me out of Keanu's lap, lifting me and swinging me around. "The monster is dead. Now, it's truly time to celebrate."

"Put my wife down," Keanu says, getting up and taking me from Kent's exuberant arms. "What's going on?" he asks, pinning that question on his FBI brother, as he pulls me into his chest.

"I'm going in," Keven says. "I'll find out more. Until I have official confirmation, don't go anywhere and make sure the security detail has eyes on you and Selena at all times."

"Go," Paul says, approaching Keven. "We've got this."

"I want hourly check-ins," Keven says.

"You got it."

"I'll call you later," Keven says to Keanu, placing his hand on my shoulder and squeezing it gently.

"Thanks, Kev." Keanu clamps his hand on Keven's shoulder. "We owe you so much."

Keven leaves the room, and Keanu tips my head back with his finger. "You okay, babe?"

"I'm a bit...shell-shocked," I admit. "What do you think happened?"

"He was a pedophile, and I'm betting he had plenty of enemies, so who knows," he says, bending down to kiss my mouth. "Try to put it out of your mind. Keven will find out the truth, and then, we can deal."

SSA Clement calls us into his office the following day to give us the good news in person. Clive Lawrence is dead in an apparent suicide. The motive is unclear, but CSI technicians and FBI agents are crawling all over his home, and another few teams have been sent to examine the other five properties he has in the US and two homes overseas. The SSA is hopeful they will find some damning evidence they can use to haul some of his known associates in.

But the main point is I'm safe. The threat is over, and we can start living our lives.

The FBI pulls their protection from me, and Keanu cuts the private security detail back to two men. I don't argue with him. The truth is, it will take me a while to stop looking over my shoulder, and it gives me peace of mind knowing Paul and Ray are shadowing me whenever I leave the condo.

We don't return to Greece, and Keanu sends someone to pack and ship the things we left behind. I'm sad not to return to the little island we both grew to love, but I'm glad to be back at home. Resuming normal life.

Over the next couple weeks, I start my EMDR therapy. We'd had to postpone it when we left for Greece because the hypnosis therapist explained I'd need to attend sessions two to three times a week for five to six weeks. I've had four sessions so far, and it's going unbelievably well. I'm almost kicking myself that I didn't explore this years ago except I've chosen to not live with regrets anymore.

I spoke to Keanu, and we gave permission to Keven to sit in on the sessions after my first one, because I unlocked lots of memories, and this new intel is proving invaluable to the FBI. They have some strong, fresh leads for the first time in years, and Keven says they are close to cracking Allen's sex-trafficking-ring wide-open.

Unfortunately, someone has been leaking stuff to the media, and it's come out about Lawrence's disgusting past. His show has been canceled amid all the controversy, which shows no sign of dying down.

Lots of stories are doing the rounds.

Including how it connects to me.

Which is why I'm currently locked in what is proving to be our first argument as a married couple.

"Let them speculate," Keanu says, slamming his mug down on the countertop.

"That will only mean more intrusion," I protest, reaching across the counter to take his hand. "Those reporters camped outside here will mushroom in the coming days. They're not going away unless I make them. Telling my side of the story removes the speculation. Removes the power from them and puts me firmly in the driver's seat."

"Let's put an offer in on that house we saw yesterday," Keanu says, slanting determined eyes at me.

"We already agreed it wasn't the right house for us."

We've been house hunting since we returned, both of us eager to start married life in our own place. Even though I've grown close to Kent and I *will* miss him.

"It has high walls, a gated entrance, long driveway, and it's in an enclosed estate, which means it offers us protection from the vultures outside. We can buy it now, and when all this dies down, we'll sell it and find our dream home."

I let go of his hand to massage my throbbing temples. "I know you only want to protect me and that you don't want the population at large to know what I've gone through, but this is my life, Keanu." I slap a hand over my chest. "My story to tell. And I'm not ashamed anymore. I didn't do anything wrong. I'm in a good place in my life. A place where I can talk about this and I won't fall apart."

I stand and go around to him, placing my hands on his shoulders. "My story will get the vultures off our back, because once I reveal the truth, there is no more story to uncover. But that's not why I want to do it." I peer into his big, beautiful, blue eyes. "I want to help others. I want other young girls to be aware of the dangers. To be more vigilant. And I want to help other survivors. I want to show them you can come through it. That life isn't over because someone chooses to violate your body and obliterate your spirit. That there are places and people and supports out there to help."

I exhale heavily after my little speech, hoping he understands.

Slowly, he nods. "Okay." He cups my face. "Are you sure you've given it enough thought? That you're not making a rash decision?"

"I'm sure. And I've spoken to Denise about it."

"Will she be attending with you?"

"Yes, and I'd really like you and Mom there too."

He presses a kiss to my forehead. "That goes without saying, baby. Of course, I'll be there." He threads his fingers through mine. "We're in this together forever."

The interview with 60 *Minutes* is set up for next week, and now, my face is splashed all over more billboards as they build up hype for the talk. The news about my marriage to Keanu has also been disclosed, and the level of interest right now is off the charts.

Unfortunately, that means I can't attend classes for the foreseeable future, so I'm back to watching videos online. But it's a small price to pay, because the potential rewards of this interview vastly outweigh any temporary inconvenience to my life.

I cannot complain because it's heightening awareness of sex trafficking, victims of child sex abuse in general, and it's helping to remove the stigma, which can only be a good thing. The Me Too movement has helped remove the fear of discussing sensitive subjects openly, in public forums, helping pave the way for other atrocities to come to light. The more we talk about these injustices, these acts of violence toward others, the more people will become vigilant and more outspoken in demanding the authorities do something concrete to catch these bastards and provide necessary funding to provide aid to victims.

Part of the contract Dan Evans, our family lawyer, negotiated with the producers of 60 *Minutes* was the inclusion of a donation line so viewers can contribute during the interview should they want to. The proceeds raised will be split equally between my mom's charity and Polaris. Polaris is a nonprofit organization that operates the National Human Trafficking Resource Center, hosts the national hotline on human trafficking, and engages community members in local and national grassroots efforts.

The fee I'm receiving is going toward setting up my sanctuary.

While our house hunting hasn't delivered any results yet, my crazy husband found a couple of large plots for sale in the Massachusetts area, and just yesterday, we put down a deposit on a fifty-six-acre site in New Marlborough. We've decided to focus our house hunting on places halfway between Wellesley and New Marlborough, so we're only a little over an hour away from my future place of work and my in-laws.

My life has changed so much, I think, as I lean against the front of the car, in the small parking garage at the back of the condo, waiting for Paul and Ray to take the grocery bags from the trunk.

Although we are staying in Wellesley for Christmas, along with Mom because Alex considers her family now too, we are hosting a little pre-Christmas party here on Saturday night for Keanu's brothers and their partners, and Kelly and Todd are coming too.

I'm actually looking forward to it.

The old me would never have attended this party, let alone thrown it, and it just highlights how far I've progressed.

I never imagined things could be this good, even a year ago, and I'll never take what I have for granted.

Two loud pops startle me from the rosy cloud in my head, and my heart rate pitches to coronary-inducing territory at the two accompanying thuds.

"Paul? Ray?" I call out, pushing off the hood and peering anxiously at the elevated trunk door.

My knees wobble as the figure rounds the back of the car, and I clutch on to the SUV to keep myself upright.

"Hello, bitch," Freddie says, his dark eyes glaring at me as he points a gun at my head. "Surprised to see me?"

I slide my hand around to the back pocket of my jeans, reaching for my cell.

"I wouldn't bother," he says. "No one can save you now."

Adrenaline courses through my veins, joined by anger that has simmered under the surface for years.

I'm not a victim.

I'm a survivor, and I won't cower to this bastard again.

My spine stiffens, and I tip my chin up, letting go of the car and standing upright before him. "You mean no one can save you, because if you think my husband or the FBI will let you take me again, you are sorely mistaken."

"Such lofty words for a timid little bitch." His eyes rake up and down my body, and nausea twists in my gut. "And you hold no interest for me anymore." He puts his face all up in mine, and my natural instinct is to rear back, but I hold my ground even though I'm shaking like an earthquake on the inside and my sweater is stuck to my back like a second layer of skin. "I like my pussy young and virginal, and you're too old and too used up," he sneers.

The second he presses the muzzle of his gun to my brow, I swing into action, lifting my leg and kneeing him hard in the balls. "Fuu-uck!" he roars, bending over and automatically dropping his arm.

I waste no time, because this might be my only opportunity, darting around him and the dead bodies of my two bodyguards, pushing my limbs faster than I've ever pushed them as I race across the parking garage toward the door.

I don't look back.

I can't.

I've just reached the entrance when a loud pop rings out, the noise ricocheting off the walls, seeming louder. I crash to the floor, slamming face-first into the hard ground, and that's the last thing I register before I black out.

Chapter Thirty
Keanu

Kent pulls up to the curb at the hospital, brakes screeching, drawing the attention of the people loitering outside. "Go! I'll park," he says, but I'm already halfway out of the SUV.

Kev's X5 is parked haphazardly outside the entrance, and a tow truck is in the process of removing it. A trail of blood leads from the car toward the front doors of the hospital, and the most intense pain slices through me, almost rendering me immobile.

But my desire to get to my wife overrides every other emotion, and I push past people as I rush through the entrance, racing up to the hospital desk. "I need to find my wife!" I shout, ignoring the couple already talking with the receptionist.

"Keanu." A hand lands on my back, and I whip around.

"Come with me," Keven says. "I know where she is."

He's covered in blood. *Selena's* blood. There's so much of it! Tears leak from my eyes. "Is she?"

Keven grips my shoulders firmly. "She's alive, Keanu. They took her straight into surgery."

"How bad is it, Kev?"

He takes hold of my arm. "Let's get up to the waiting room, and I'll fill you in there," he says, looking over his shoulder, reminding me we are not alone and there are prying eyes and ears everywhere. I curse the fact we're so well-known in Boston. That there are several eyeballs glued to us. Some taking pictures they'll no doubt post on social media. I give it a half hour before the vultures show up.

I let Keven drag me away, and we've just stepped into the elevator when Kent comes running along the corridor. Kev holds the elevator for him, and Kent jumps inside. His face is a mask of horror as he rakes his gaze over our older brother. "Jesus Christ." He drags his hands through his hair.

"Selena's in surgery," Keven says, because I'm incapable of saying the words.

"What the fuck happened?" Kent asks, his horror giving way to anger.

"Not here," Kev snaps, glancing at the three men and one woman sharing the elevator with us.

Kev leads us to a large waiting room in the private section of the hospital. "This feels like déjà vu," Kent says when we step inside.

Unfortunately, we've been in this hospital, in this room, far too many times in recent years.

The room is vacant because it's a private waiting area. One Mom usually reserves whenever there's a need. "Mom knows?" I ask in a monotone voice.

"Yes. She's en route with Dad. And I called the others and Sandrine too. They are all on the way."

"Have you spoken to any of the doctors?" I ask, spinning around and heading for the door we just came in.

"Yes." Kev grabs me back. "They can't tell us anything yet. The nurse said to stay here and someone will come and talk to us as soon as they have some information."

I pace the floor, yanking fistfuls of my hair. "Who did this, Kev? And how did it happen?"

He takes hold of me, forcing me into a chair. "It was Freddie, Keanu."

All the color leaches from my face, and my fists clench into balls at my side.

"We'd been planning a big operation, and today was D-day," he continues. "We discovered a ton of evidence in Lawrence's vacation home in Hawaii, and we were making several arrests, simultaneously, in different places across the States. Local FBI in Ohio were supposed to be keeping tabs on Freddie Holsworth in the run up to the op. We thought they were," he says, his voice clipped. "Otherwise, I would've put you and Selena on alert, but I didn't say anything as I thought we had it covered. And I didn't want to worry either of you unnecessarily. But when they invaded his apartment today, it was clear he hadn't been there for some time. That he'd run. Someone must have tipped him off."

His jaw clenches. "We were on the way back to the office when we got that news. I was trying to figure out where Freddie might run to because he had to know there was no way he could escape, and Selena popped into my head." His bloodshot eyes peer into mine. "I just got a terrible feeling, so I turned my car around instantly and headed for your place. I called Paul and Ray, but the calls didn't connect because there's no signal in the garage." He sighs heavily. "I would've called you, but I was close to your place, and I didn't want to worry you if my gut was wrong. I got to your condo five minutes later. Parked out front and ran around the back when I heard a shot go off." Raw emotion radiates from his eyes. "I'm so sorry, Keanu. I was too fucking late. Selena was... She was lying on the ground in a pool of blood." He scrubs a hand down his face. "Paul and Ray are both dead."

"Jesus." Selena will be devastated to hear that.

"I know. They were good men. They didn't deserve that."

"Please tell me you got that fucker?" Kent says, wrapping his arm around my shoulder. I'm so cold. Frozen all over.

"I nailed that fucking bastard," Kev says. "I pumped every round in my gun into that motherfucker. He's not getting back up again. I'll probably be suspended, but I couldn't give two fucks."

I grab onto my brother's arm. "Thank you," I croak. "My wife would be dead right now if it wasn't for you."

"I'm sorry I didn't figure it out sooner," he whispers.

"No, brother. You have nothing to be sorry for." I hug him tight.

"She's going to be okay, Keanu. She's a survivor, and she loves you too much to leave you."

"Kev is right," Kent says. "She's strong as fuck, and she'll pull through."

"Darling!" Mom barrels through the door, and I spy Dad in the background talking to a man in a charcoal-gray suit.

"Mom!" I almost collapse as I fall into my mother's arms.

"It's okay, sweetheart. We're here for you and Selena."

"I can't lose her, Mom," I choke. "I will die without her."

"I know, darling, but Selena is a fighter, and I just know she's going to survive this."

The rest of the family arrives except for Lana, Kalvin, and Keaton, who are all waiting to board planes, and soon, the room is full of people and noise, and it helps to distract my mind.

Sandrine is as distraught as me when she arrives, and we hold one another, doing our best to support each other, but it's hard. Because I'm going fucking crazy here. Selena has been in surgery for three hours, and no one has told us a thing so far.

I hop up. "I need some fucking answers," I say, storming toward the door just as a tall man with gray hair enters the room. He's wearing a white coat, and he has a clipboard in his hand. "I'm looking for Selena Kennedy's husband," he says.

I step in front of him, and Sandrine joins me. "That's me. And this is Selena's mom. Is she okay?"

He extends his hand, and I shake it on autopilot. Then he shakes Sandrine's hand. "I'm Doctor Fleming. I was a part of the surgical team who operated on your wife. Selena has lost a lot of blood, Mr. Kennedy, and she took a bullet to the shoulder. Thankfully, the bullet missed her major artery and the bone. It hit her muscle, and there was a little nerve damage, but we've repaired it. We gave her a blood transfusion during surgery, and she's stable now. We'll keep her in ICU overnight, and then, she'll be moved to a private room for a few days, but she can go home after that. I see no reason why she won't make a full recovery."

"She's going to be okay?" I stammer.

"She's going to be just fine." He pats my arm, his brow creasing a little. "I hope this isn't inappropriate, but did this have anything to do with her planned interview?"

"The man who shot her was one of the men who abducted her as a child," Sandrine says.

"And my best guess is he wanted to silence Selena," Keven says, coming up on my other side. "He knew that the FBI had a warrant for his arrest and he was going to be tried for his crimes. I suspect he wanted to remove a key witness in the hope he might get off without her testimony."

"My God." The doctor shakes his head. "That's horrific. As if Selena hasn't suffered enough." He shakes my hand again. "Your wife is an incredibly brave woman, Mr. Kennedy, and she has the admiration of every professional in this hospital. We hope, at some point, she is able to proceed with her televised interview, because her message is a powerful one."

"I know my wife, and trust me, that interview will take place."

A short while later, I'm allowed to see her. She's lying in bed, dressed in a pale blue hospital gown with her hair pulled back in a ponytail. Bruises and cuts cover her beautiful face, but she looks peaceful as she sleeps. She's hooked up to a monitor, and a drip feeds saline and medication into her arm.

I sit down on the chair by her bed, taking her hand in mine, relieved when it's warm to the touch. I keep a hold of her hand as I wait for her to wake up.

Gentle fingers threading through my hair is the first thing I register when I wake up.

"Hey, baby."

Her soft voice is like music to my ears, and I bolt upright, brushing sleep out of my eyes. "You're awake."

"I am." She smiles.

"How are you feeling? Do you need anything? Can I get you water? Or you need more medication?"

She giggles, and my heart soars at the sound. "Relax, there, babe. I'm fine. The nurse already topped off my medication and helped me sip water while you played Sleeping Beauty on my lap."

"Well, that's embarrassing," I mumble, lacing my fingers in hers.

"It was adorable and the best sight to wake up to," she reassures me.

I lean in and kiss her, holding her face as our lips brush. Then, I rest my forehead gently against hers. "I thought I lost you baby, and it was the most painful few hours of my life."

"I told you you're stuck with me," she says, caressing my cheek. "I'm going nowhere."

"I love you, Sel." I kiss her again.

"I love you, too. Forever and ever, Keanu."

Epilogue
Selen

Six Months Later

We pull up to the entrance, and Keanu punches in the code. My eyes ghost over the newly erected sign as the gates open and we drive through.

Moonlight: Support. Survive. Thrive

"You know, you get this dreamy look in your eyes every time we pass that sign," my husband teases. Keanu was the one who came up with the name for the sanctuary. It turns out my name is of Greek origin, and it means moon.

"I still can't believe this is happening," I admit. "That we're building a sanctuary like I've always wanted to do." I swivel in the passenger seat, the leather squelching. "It feels so incredible to be doing something good, and I wish I could click my fingers and all the work is done and it's opening day."

He grabs my hand, bringing it to his lips. "One day at a time, babe, and with everyone helping, that will become reality much quicker than you think." He presses a kiss to my knuckles, and his touch sends the usual shivers skating all over my body.

Another thing I never thought I'd have is a regular, healthy sex life. There are still things I can't attempt in bed, and Keanu is always careful to be loving and gentle, but it's way more than I ever expected. I love making love to my husband, and my hands never stray far from some part of his body.

My EMDR therapy proved to be a huge turning point in my recovery. It's helped lessen my PTSD symptoms and triggers, and it unlocked hidden trauma I'd buried deep. Confronting and dealing with those memories has been freeing, and it has transformed my life.

I will never forget what happened to me. But it doesn't control me anymore. It doesn't hold me back. And when I'm having a bad day, my husband's arms are around me, comforting me and reminding me of how far I've traveled.

The love and support of his family has helped enormously too. "Have I told you how much I love your family?" I croon, knowing I'm probably driving him insane with how often I'm saying it recently. But it's true. Not only have they welcomed me into the family with open arms, accepting me, flaws and all, but they are all actively involved in this project in a way I never expected.

"If I wasn't so secure in your love, I might think you married me for my family."

I reach over the console, kissing his cheek. "It was a package deal, babe." I grin, and while I'm teasing, it's still true.

I love my new family, and I'm glad we decided to buy a house in Wellesley in the end. It will take a good few years before the sanctuary is ready to be opened to the public, so it made sense to buy a place close to the fam. We still stay in the condo during the week, because it's handier for college, but we stay at our new house from Friday to Monday, and I love our little slice of heaven. We're planning on building apartments for all the family at the sanctuary so everyone will have their own space should they want to stay over any time.

Kalvin and Lana have just moved back to Wellesley now they have graduated UF. Lana gave birth to baby Hayley in early March, and Hewson turned four last month. Kal has secured a job with this trendy new architectural firm in town, and we've just agreed to terms with them. Kal is going to work with us on the project, and his firm will oversee the design and construction.

Alex and Brad's mom are going to plan out the interior design. Keven is working with Morgan Security to ensure the sanctuary is safe and well protected, and he's going to set up all the IT infrastructure. Cheryl is setting up a photography studio, and she's going to teach a class one day a week. Rachel is going to teach a class on fashion design once a month, agreeing to jet in from New York, and she and Faye are going to also provide hair and makeup lessons. The men are all involved in the nine-hole golf course we are building on this massive site, and they are working on the layout of the state-of-the art gymnasium too.

When we are ready to start hiring, Faye is going to act as HR manager, helping us to recruit the most appropriate healthcare professionals in the business. And when we are operational, Kyler, Kent, and Keaton have offered to help with the running of the business and the finances.

Eva, Brad, and Kaden are helping us build our website and finalize our business plan and marketing strategy.

Eva and Kaden added to their family when their son Matthew entered the world a couple weeks after Christmas. They have their hands full, but they were still insistent on helping because that's just the kind of selfless people they are.

I know we won't have everyone's time forever, because they all have their own goals and ambitions, and some of them have families, but it means so much to both of us that everyone is enthusiastic about the project and willing to help out in any way they can.

I think, for Cheryl and Eva, it's especially important, because they were both previously involved with men who sex trafficked girls behind their backs.

James and Alex are our biggest donors and put up a whopping fifty percent of the setup costs. The rest of the family is contributing too, and we've also set up a donation hotline, which has a steady flow of funds coming in. Having important connections helps. We plan to apply for state funding once we are ready to open our doors, and we are hoping some of the new laws being proposed at the moment will be in place by the time we are fully functional.

My interview with 60 *Minutes* sparked international debate, and it thrust a spotlight over the huge problem that is global sex trafficking. Politicians are coming under enormous pressure to do more to stop it and to provide support for victims. Only time will tell if it's had any meaningful impact.

"Which paper is this reporter with?" Keanu asks as we travel the rough driveway toward the worker trailers that were erected last week.

"She's not with a paper," I reply, bouncing around the place as Keanu navigates the bumpy driveway.

First thing on my list is to get a proper driveway built.

"She works with Polaris. That charity I told you about. They are excited for this project, and there are lots of ways we can work together for the greater good." Mom is also in talks with them to bring her parent support group charity under their umbrella. "They want to do a big online piece about the sanctuary, so I said I'd meet her here to review the plans and show her the site." I grab on to the sides of my seat as we go over a particularly bumpy patch. "Hopefully, it won't take too long. I don't want to be late for our dinner date with Kelly and Todd."

"We've got plenty of time," my husband says, swinging the car around the last bend. "Kal's already here." He jerks his head at his brother's blacked-out Lincoln Navigator.

"Yeah, he said he would be here at four."

Keanu puts the SUV in park, and we climb out, entering the main trailer.

"Sup, asshole." Kal offers his brother his usual greeting, and they do the whole man hug thing.

"Hey, Selena." Kal gives me a warm hug, steering me around to the long table. He points at the long white roll of paper with the extensive drawing. "I finally finished the first plan, and I've been dying for you to get here so I could run through it."

"Hold that thought," Keanu says, looking up at the camera in the corner of the room. "Our reporter has just arrived, and she needs to hear this too."

We shoot the shit for a few minutes as we wait for Elena to arrive. After introductions and a quick explanation, Kal starts talking us through the design for the build. "The main border of the property will be fenced on all sides with high-tech security monitoring covering the entire perimeter."

"We will also have round the clock security guards and security alarms on all the buildings," I add. Elena nods, smiling for Kal to go on.

"The main facility will be in this building," Kal continues, pointing at a giant building composed of glass, wood, and exposed stone. "This will house the therapy rooms, treatment rooms, recreational spaces, music room, drama room, art room, other training rooms, a couple of eating areas, the medical compound, etcetera."

"We're employing a full-time nurse and doctor, as well as trauma-informed psychologists, specialty therapists, and nutritionists, and we plan to provide complementary holistic treatments like acupuncture, reiki, and so on," I say.

He moves his finger to the other structure on the left-hand side. "This will be the school building, and over here," he says, pointing at a large designated area out in front of the school, "will be the sports arena."

"We will have facilities for basketball, football, hockey, golf, volleyball," Keanu says, ticking them off his fingers. "And we are building a gymnasium. We plan to hire instructors to teach classes like yoga and dance."

"And we're building a pool," I jump in.

"That will be here," Kal adds, pointing to another part of the drawing.

"Wow. This is something else." Elena's eyes pop wide, and Keanu, Kal, and I share an excited look.

"That's not all," I add. "We are building student cabins too. We were going to go for dorm buildings, but I want residents to make this their home. To stay here for as long as they need to. And I wanted to give them someplace comfortable to unwind if they've had a bad day."

"The accommodations will be housed over here," Kal says, moving his finger to the very far left of the paper. "Each large cabin will house six different units, all equipped with a bedroom, bathroom, living room, kitchen-slash-dining room, and a small study."

"They will also have gardens," I confirm.

"We wanted the residential area to be separated from the main buildings," Keanu explains, "so the clients can leave it behind every day and have a quiet place to relax. We'll be running buses at regular hours to and from the main buildings, and we will have loaner cars and golf carts available too."

"We'll also provide bicycles for anyone who wants to bike it," I supply.

"Will you be teaching any modeling classes?" Elena's gaze flits between me and Keanu.

"No. Some of our family will be teaching dress design and providing makeup and hair lessons, but we have no plans to do anything else."

Keanu slides his arm around my waist. "Modeling is in our past. This is our future."

Keanu officially retired from modeling at the end of last year, and I have one more campaign to finish for Miranda Fanning, and then, I'm done. I'm not renewing my contract when it expires in August, because I don't have time anymore, and it feels like the right moment to put that part of my life behind me. We are crazy busy with this project and college, and while I will always remember my modeling days fondly, I'm honestly not sad to be saying goodbye. Neither of us is.

In the aftermath of the shooting and the subsequent arrests of several men involved in sex trafficking, including Hudson and Senator Allen, the level of attention directed my way was too much.

The FBI discovered a partial print belonging to Freddie in Clive Lawrence's penthouse and has ruled the director's death a murder. They think Freddie was tipped off about the FBI surveillance and he panicked. Fled Ohio and came looking for Lawrence. Afraid Clive would spill his guts to save his own ass, he took him out before he could speak one word. And then he went into hiding until he decided it was time to silence me too.

I owe my life to Keven. If he hadn't shown up when he did, I think Freddie would have finished the job. Thankfully, my brother-in-law was exonerated after an FBI internal investigation into Freddie's death.

A shudder passes over me, and I'm not sorry I've taken a step back. Stepping out of the limelight meant the media grew bored of me, and I've reclaimed a semblance of normalcy.

I will have to prepare myself for the trial when the scrutiny will become intense again. But that's still a couple months away, and with the support of my husband, my family, and my therapists, I'll get through it.

It's good to finally see justice prevail.

"What's that place over there?" Elena asks, drawing me out of my mind. She points to a cluster of buildings off to the other side of the drawing.

I place my hand on my husband's chest. "That is where Keanu is building his business empire."

He looks at me in amusement. "I'm setting up my own label when I graduate," he tells Elena. "And it made sense to segregate part of this site to build my premises. I don't want to be far from Selena, and I was keen to set up outside the city, so two birds, one stone."

"It's completely separate," I reassure her. "They will have their own entrance and own facilities.

"You have thought of everything, and it's incredibly inspirational."

"Thank you." I wrap my arm around Keanu's stomach. "It's been a labor of love for all the family, and we had many great minds working on this plan with us."

"Well, I think it's a wonderful project, and I think my boss is going to be extremely happy when I update her. If you are still interested in exploring cross support and cross-promotional initiatives, Polaris will be too."

"We're definitely interested," I say.

"Great." She smiles. "I think I have enough for the article with what you have shown me here today and the information you emailed to me. I'll write it up and send it to you to approve before we publish it."

"That's perfect. Thank you for coming out to see it."

"Pleasure's all mine, Selena." She shakes all our hands, and Keanu walks her back to her car.

"Thank you so much for bringing our vision to life," I tell my brother-in-law, giving him a big hug as he rolls up the drawing.

"Thanks for giving me such an awesome first project. And my boss is going gaga over this project. It's the type of exposure that will launch an already growing firm into the stratosphere, so it's a win-win."

"You leaving?" Keanu asks, lounging against the open doorway.

"Yep. Need to get home to my babies." He flashes us a grin.

"How's the wild child?" Keanu asks as we lock up.

"As wild as ever," Kal replies. "But, man, you should see him with Hayley. He is so gentle with his little sister. We were worried he might get jealous, but he adores her."

"Hard not to," I admit, holding Keanu's hand. "She's a little angel."

"Oh, oh." Kal nudges Keanu in the ribs. "Sounds like someone wants a baby."

I laugh. "I love kids, and I can't wait to have them, but this project and Keanu's new business are our babies right now. We won't be having kids for a while yet."

"We're taking bets on who'll be next," Kal admits when we reach our cars.

Keanu rolls his eyes. "Why am I not surprised."

"Our money was on you two, but we may need to reconsider," Kal says, rubbing his chin, looking thoughtful.

"Now that Kev and Cheryl have set a date for a Christmas wedding and Rach and Brad are engaged, maybe I should put my money on them."

"Rach and Brad are having a long engagement," I remind him. "And while I think Faye and Kyler are the ones who crave kids the most, they are heading to Australia soon, so if it was me, I'd put money on Cheryl and Kev."

Keanu messes up my hair. "Hey, don't encourage that shit." He grins at his brother. "And you haven't mentioned Keats and Melissa."

"I think they are on the outs again," Kal says, opening the door to his car.

"Your mom texted me last night, and she said she was coming to the party on Saturday." Alex is throwing a family get-together to give Kyler and Faye a send-off.

"Huh." Kal frowns. "Maybe, I misunderstood him."

A wicked glint appears in Keanu's eye, and I know he's about to stir shit. "If I was a betting man, which we all know I'm not, I'd put money on Kent. With the way he's racking up notches on his bedpost, it's only a matter of time before he knocks someone up."

"Don't say that," I groan. "Alex would throw a hissy fit."

"Especially if it was Whitney!" Keanu says.

"Thought that shit ended last year." Kal frowns.

Keanu remains tight-lipped, but he's said enough. I pinch his butt in warning, but, thankfully, Kal doesn't pry. We wave goodbye to him and get in our car. "I thought you weren't going to tell anyone what we saw the night of our wedding," I say as I buckle my seat belt.

"Technically, I didn't say anything." My husband arches his brows as he puts the car in gear.

We had a small wedding ceremony at Easter at Keanu's parents' house. Just family and a few close friends. I really didn't want a huge big affair in an expensive hotel, and thankfully, Alex agreed, not making a big deal out of it. That night, after everyone had gone to bed, we were making our way to the cabin where we were staying for the night, and we stumbled across Kent and Whitney having sex outside on one of the loungers. They didn't spot us, so we said nothing, minding our own business.

"Did you ever talk to Kent about it?"

He nods. "Yeah. He said it was a one-off for old times' sake."

"But you don't believe him?"

"He's been spending a lot of weekends in New York. I suspect he's meeting up with her."

"I sense you disapprove."

"I don't dislike Whitney. It's actually the opposite. I think she's misunderstood and troubled, and maybe, that's why her and Kent are drawn to one another. I just worry about him, and it's complicated with her being Faye's sister. But if she's the one he wants, I'll support him all the way." He smiles over at me as we exit through the gate. "Love doesn't always come in a neat little package." He lifts my hands to his lips, kissing my knuckles. "We both know that. And I would never stand in the way of true love."

"And that is one of the million reasons why I love you." I stretch across the console, pressing a kiss to the corner of his mouth. "I love you, K. Thank you for showing me the real meaning of true love."

Adoring Keaton is the next book in the series. Available now and free to read in Kindle Unlimited.

Support Contact Details

To request help or to report suspected human trafficking, please call the National Human Trafficking Hotline, operated by Polaris, at 1-888-373-7888

If you need to talk to someone regarding sexual assault, please call the National Sexual Assault Hotline in the US at 800-656-4673

If you need to talk to someone regarding any mental health illness, please call the National Alliance on Mental Illness in the US at 1-800-950-NAMI (6264) or email info@nami.org

If you require support dealing with PTSD, please contact PTSD United: http://www.ptsdunited.org/contact/

The Child Help National Child Abuse Hotline in the US is available 24/7 at 1-800-4224453
https://www.childhelp.org/hotline/

Keaton

Moving to California was supposed to be my fresh start. A clean slate. An opportunity to drop the façade, escape the lies, find a focus, and just be myself.

But I should have realized it wouldn't be easy, especially when my last name is Kennedy.

I'm not ready to be a gay icon or some celebrity role model. I still haven't admitted the truth to my family or the girl I professed to love, so there's no way I want the public to know I'm into dudes.

Falling for my hot, *straight*, football-player roomie wasn't part of the game plan.

Neither was backing myself into a corner because I trusted the wrong guy.

Now everything is on the line, and it's time to stop pretending.

Austen

From the time I was a little kid, all I wanted is to play football in college and play in the NFL.

As wide receiver for the Golden Bears, I am on track to achieve my goals, but it comes at a heavy price.

Denying who I am—for the sake of my career—goes against everything I believe.

I should never have listened to my high school coach, because all the lies are suffocating me.

Until Keaton Kennedy enters my life, turning it upside down.

Now, there is even more reason to tell the truth, because I'm falling for the famous one and I want the entire world to know.

Available now in ebook, paperback, and audiobook.

pain. Until Jared rocks up to the art gallery where I work, with his fiancée in tow, and I'm drowning again.

Seeing him brings everything to the surface, so I flee. Placing distance between us again, I'm determined to put him behind me once and for all.

Then he reappears at my door, begging me for another chance.

I know I should turn him away.

Try telling that to my heart.

This angsty, new adult romance is a FREE full-length ebook, exclusively available to newsletter subscribers.

Type this link into your browser to claim your free copy:

https://bit.ly/TITMHFBB

OR

Scan this code to claim your free copy:

Acknowledgments

Massive thanks to Jennifer Gibson and her colleagues in the Family Health Center Americana/STS for their help and guidance with mental health illness, dealing with PTSD, and for sharing invaluable insights on EMDR therapy. Selena's background is harrowing, and I wanted to ensure I gave it the appropriate treatment because human trafficking is a serious global issue and one we should all be concerned about.

In no particular order, I would like to thank the following people who contributed to this release: Kelly Hartigan, Ciara Turley, Robin Harper, Shannon Passmore, Daisy Zorman, Sarah Ferguson, Jennifer Gibson, my review team, and all the bloggers/booktokers/bookstagrammers who help to spread the word about this book and the series.

Thank YOU for reading this book, for loving my Kennedy boys, and for everything you do to enable me to continue writing full-time. I appreciate each and every one of you.

Lastly, thanks to my husband and my two sons for believing in me and supporting me in my career.

About the Author

Siobhan Davis™ is a *USA Today, Wall Street Journal,* and Amazon Top 5 bestselling romance author. **Siobhan** writes emotionally intense stories with swoon-worthy romance, complex characters, and tons of unexpected plot twists and turns that will have you flipping the pages beyond bedtime! She has sold over 2 million books, and her titles are translated into several languages.

Prior to becoming a full-time writer, Siobhan forged a successful corporate career in human resource management.

She lives in the Garden County of Ireland with her husband and two sons.

You can connect with Siobhan in the following ways:

Website: www.siobhandavis.com
Facebook: AuthorSiobhanDavis
Instagram: @siobhandavisauthor
Tiktok: @siobhandavisauthor
Email: siobhan@siobhandavis.com

Books By Siobhan Davis

NEW ADULT ROMANCE
The One I Want Duet
Kennedy Boys Series
Rydeville Elite Series
All of Me Series
Forever Love Duet

NEW ADULT ROMANCE STAND-ALONES
Inseparable
Incognito
Still Falling for You
Holding on to Forever
Always Meant to Be
Tell It to My Heart

REVERSE HAREM
Sainthood Series
Dirty Crazy Bad Duet
Surviving Amber Springs (stand-alone)
Alinthia Series ^

DARK MAFIA ROMANCE
Mazzone Mafia Series
Vengeance of a Mafia Queen (stand-alone)
*The Accardi Twins**
*Taking What's Mine**

YA SCI-FI & PARANORMAL ROMANCE
Saven Series
True Calling Series ^

---

*Coming 2024
^Currently unpublished but will be republished in due course.

www.siobhandavis.com